MW00906932

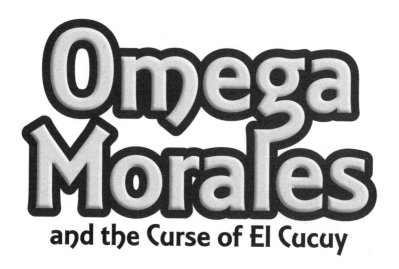

Omega Morales

and the Curse of El Cucuy

LAEKAN ZEA KEMP

ILLUSTRATED BY VANESSA MORALES

LITTLE, BROWN AND COMPANY

New York Boston

This book is a work of fiction. Names, characters, places, and incidents are the product of the author's imagination or are used fictitiously. Any resemblance to actual events, locales, or persons, living or dead, is coincidental.

Copyright © 2023 by Laekan Zea Kemp
Illustrations copyright © 2023 by Vanessa Morales

Cover art copyright © 2023 by Vanessa Morales. Cover design by Gabrielle Chang.
Cover copyright © 2023 by Hachette Book Group, Inc.
Interior design by Neil Swaab.

Hachette Book Group supports the right to free expression and the value of copyright. The purpose of copyright is to encourage writers and artists to produce the creative works that enrich our culture.

The scanning, uploading, and distribution of this book without permission is a theft of the author's intellectual property. If you would like permission to use material from the book (other than for review purposes), please contact permissions@hbgusa.com. Thank you for your support of the author's rights.

Little, Brown and Company
Hachette Book Group
1290 Avenue of the Americas, New York, NY 10104
Visit us at LBYR.com

First Edition: October 2023

Little, Brown and Company is a division of Hachette Book Group, Inc. The Little, Brown name and logo are trademarks of Hachette Book Group, Inc.

The publisher is not responsible for websites (or their content) that are not owned by the publisher.

Little, Brown and Company books may be purchased in bulk for business, educational, or promotional use. For information, please contact your local bookseller or the Hachette Book Group Special Markets Department at special.markets@hbgusa.com.

Library of Congress Cataloging-in-Publication Data
Names: Kemp, Laekan Zea, author. | Morales, Vanessa, illustrator.
Title: Omega Morales and the curse of El Cucuy /
Laekan Zea Kemp ; illustrated by Vanessa Morales.
Description: First edition. | New York : Little, Brown and Company, 2023. | Series: Omega Morales | Audience: Ages 8–12. | Summary: Omega will have to learn to trust her powers once again as she comes face-to-face with the Mexican legend El Cucuy.
Identifiers: LCCN 2023005547 | ISBN 9780316508872
(hardcover) | ISBN 9780316509077 (ebook)
Subjects: CYAC: Emotions—Fiction. | Witches—Fiction. | Magic—Fiction. | Missing children—Fiction. | Blessing and cursing—Fiction. | Supernatural—Fiction. | Hispanic Americans—Fiction. | LCGFT: Paranormal fiction. | Novels.
Classification: LCC PZ7.1.K463 Om 2022 | DDC [Fic]—dc23
LC record available at https://lccn.loc.gov/2023005547

ISBNs: 978-0-316-50887-2 (hardcover), 978-0-316-50907-7 (ebook)

Printed in the United States of America

LSC-C

Printing 1, 2023

IN REMEMBRANCE OF

Makenna Lee Elrod

Layla Salazar

Maranda Mathis

Nevaeh Bravo

Jose Manuel Flores Jr.

Xavier Lopez

Tess Marie Mata

Rojelio Torres

Eliahna "Ellie" Amyah Garcia

Eliahna A. Torres

Annabell Guadalupe Rodriguez

Jackie Cazares

Uziyah Garcia

Jayce Carmelo Luevanos

Maite Yuleana Rodriguez

Jailah Nicole Silguero

Irma Garcia

Eva Mireles

Amerie Jo Garza

Alexandria "Lexi" Aniyah Rubio

Alithia Ramirez

CHAPTER 1

THE MOON IS WHISPERING TO ME AGAIN.

At first, I don't look. Instead, I pull the blankets over my head, squeezing my eyes shut while I pretend to sleep. Even though I've barely slept for days. When the moon's whispers grow louder, I know tonight won't be any different.

Omega.

I slowly roll over to find it staring at me from the other side of my bedroom window. Glowing and golden. Like the face of someone I used to know.

I wonder if it's calling to me more loudly now that I set my cousin Luna free. She says it sings to me because I'm special. Because I can tap into the emotions of supernatural beings in a way that other empaths can't. Maybe the moon is drawn to me for the same reason.

"I knew all that Halloween candy would keep you up." The statue of La Virgen on my nightstand tsks, reminding me why religious keepsakes with the ability to speak are one of the most annoying things about being an empath. Because even when Abuela or Father Torres isn't around to make sure I'm following the rules, La Virgen is always there to chime in when I'm doing something wrong.

Maybe I should move her to the attic with the rest of cousin Kitty's (her previous owner's) stuff. But then who would argue with Aunt Teresa's antique lamp when it makes a snide comment about something that is one hundred percent not its business?

"You should have stuck to the sugar-free kind," La Virgen goes on.

I'd rather eat rocks, I want to tell her. Instead, I say, "If I could sleep, I would," and then I rub my legs together until my pajamas create static sparks under the blankets.

The truth is, I've had enough late nights to last a lifetime. The night of the botched séance, sneaking out to Aiden's tree house, Marisol's disastrous quince. I am very much looking forward to a break from things that go bump in the night just so I can finally go to bed at a decent hour.

La Virgen smiles. "Heroes, especially, need their rest, Omega."

I feel my face warm, not sure if the title fits. Ever since

my empathic abilities first started to reveal themselves, I've been struggling to control them. So even if it feels nice to finally not be the person screwing everything up, is it true? Am I really some kind of hero?

"The girl was simply in the wrong place at the wrong time," the lamp says, unamused, "and it's a miracle she made it out alive. But that's what this family gets for meddling with things that shouldn't be meddled with."

"And what do you call it every time you chime in without being asked?" La Virgen says. "All you do is meddle. And Omega saved Luna's life. That's a fact."

"The whole town too," the Selena poster on the wall above my bed adds in her singsong voice.

I remember grabbing the rope Father Torres was using to tie Luna down and suddenly we were all connected. But not just me and the crowd, me and their memories—each one I brought to the surface like a drop of rain, dampening the flames of their anger.

And then came the real miracle—my powers worked on Luna too, making her human again.

"She saved a bunch of ungrateful humans who have probably already found something new to hate." The lampshade swings its tassels, annoyed. "You could be taking over the world and instead you waste your magic on these boring bags of flesh."

"In case you haven't noticed, I'm also one of those boring bags of flesh," I shoot back, reminding it that I'm half-human.

The lamp harrumphs. "You still believe that?"

I chew on my lip, thinking about all the times my powers didn't work. All the times I thought I was broken. In some ways I feel like I still don't know the answer to the lamp's question. Or maybe I'm not ready, the idea that I could be something different—something *more* than just an empath—setting a small fire in my belly.

Omega.

I turn to the moon again, another fire I don't know how to put out. But instead of burying myself in the blankets, hiding and trying to ignore its pull, I slip out from under them, slowly making my way to the window.

"It's awfully big tonight, isn't it?" Selena says, her face washed in light.

"Omega, where are you going?" La Virgen hisses.

I move slowly like I'm sneaking up on one of our chickens that's escaped the coop. "Just to look..."

As I step into the moonlight pouring through the glass, it feels...magical. But also dangerous. Like getting too close to a hot flame I know I shouldn't touch.

I press a hand to the cold glass instead. Watching the moon as it watches me. Feeling its pull snake around my arms and legs, trying to lure me outside.

"Omega...?"

I look back at La Virgen, her face scrunched with worry.
"What's wrong?" I ask.

Selena gasps. "Your hands."

I glance down and see the faint stripes. Wide and slightly
curved. Like flowing water. As if someone's painted on me
with my godmother Luisa's watercolors.

I jump back from the window, the lines disappearing as
soon as I step into the shadows. And then I just stare at my
reflection in my vanity mirror, breathing hard as I wait for
the strange shapes to reappear.

"Just a trick of the light," La Virgen says, giving me a tense smile. "That's all it was."

"Whatever happened to 'thou shalt not lie'?" the lamp shoots back. "Clearly, the girl is cursed."

Cursed.

That's how I used to feel about my empathic abilities always going haywire. Even now the word feels like sandpaper against my skin, and any pride or wonder I was feeling earlier at the thought of being someone's hero quickly evaporates.

Suddenly, I'm warm, like someone's breathing down the back of my neck. I turn toward the moon again, the light it gives off so bright I practically have to squint. Still reaching for me. Whispering in that strange but soothing voice.

"Please," I whisper back. "Just leave me alone."

Because I know the lines on my skin weren't just a trick of the light. Because if I was *just* special, if this connection to the moon and the darkness around it was *just* a gift, it wouldn't come with a cost. With the risk of turning into a monster.

So, no, I'm no hero.

Because as long as there's this darkness inside me—this magic switch that can be flipped without my control, turning me into a monster just like La Lechuza—it'll never actually be true. No matter what I do. No matter what people think of me. I'll always be holding in this secret.

With my back to the moon, electricity races up my spine. Tiny sparks like the ones ignited by my flannel pajamas. Just then, a shadow passes by my bedroom window, eclipsing Selena's face as the warm glow blinks out like a light.

I spin. "What was that?"

"I'm not sure," Selena says, squinting. "It was too fast. I didn't get a good look."

"Maybe your abuelo's sleepwalking," the lamp offers.

But Abuelo hasn't had one of his prophetic dreams since Luna showed up. In fact, he's been sleeping harder than ever, his snores muffled on the other side of my bedroom wall.

"The cows at Mr. Alan's place could have gotten loose again," La Virgen says.

A cloud slides past the moon and I take the opportunity to peer out. Señora Avila's house is still empty, the for-sale sign blowing in the wind. Nothing passing between the trees. No animals wandering off into the nearby field.

"Maybe some ghosts have decided to cross over early for Día de Muertos," the lamp says. "It wouldn't be the first time one of them has broken the rules."

By the salt in her voice, I know she's talking about Clau and the fact that she has absolutely zero interest in crossing over to the other side.

"Speaking of Clau," La Virgen says, "maybe she went out for a midnight walk?"

"Ghosts don't walk," the lamp says. "They glide."

Selena furrows her brow. "I'd say it's more of a hover."

"It doesn't matter," the lamp says. "Ever since they put up the ofrenda, she's been in the attic like she is every time she gets in one of her moods. Which means my money's on the cow."

The lamp is right. Clau started acting strange as soon as we swapped out the Halloween decorations for the special altar we make every year for Día de Muertos. I haven't seen her since she left me to clean the empty candy wrappers and glitter residue from our costumes all by myself. I thought she was just avoiding doing chores. But that was hours ago.

I stare up at the ceiling, listening for the whistle of a light breeze or even a faint sniffle. But it's quiet.

"Or maybe she's hiding," the lamp goes on. "Who knows what the other ghosts will do to her once they find out she's been refusing to cross over. And tomorrow there will be a whole procession of them."

Tomorrow marks the beginning of Día de Muertos—which is actually a two-day celebration, not just one—and Mami and Abuela have been driving to every farm, nursery, and flower shop across South Texas, picking up bushels of bright orange marigolds and fluffy white chrysanthemums to add to the baskets full of flowers we picked from Abuela's garden.

My fingers are sore from tying them into crowns and bouquets, but Mami always makes a killing at the parade and then again at the cemetery when people need flowers for their loved ones' graves, which means it's all hands on deck.

Even Clau was helping out by counting how many crates had been filled. She seemed like she was having fun, turning it into a game like she does everything else. But Clau only ever disappears when she wants to be alone and if she wants to be alone that must mean...

"She's not afraid," I finally say. "She's sad."

I ease open my bedroom door and spot the light of a single candle at the end of the hallway. When I reach the living room, I see Clau sitting within the golden glow. She's kneeling in front of our ofrenda.

"I thought you were sleeping," Clau says, not taking her eyes off the flickering veladora.

"Tried to." I reach for one of the marigolds forming the arch over the altar, rubbing the smooth petals between my fingers.

"My family didn't celebrate Día de Muertos in Venezuela." Clau turns to me. "How does it work again?"

I sit next to her. "There are three levels: Heaven, Earth, and Purgatory. Some people do just two. Some people get all fancy with it and do seven. But it's just a symbol. Like the other objects on the altar. Salt to keep our ancestors pure on their journey, water in case they're thirsty, the scent of flowers to help guide them home."

Clau stares at a dark blue bow tie that belonged to my tío Arthur before leaning closer to a tube of lipstick that belonged to my bisabuela Ynez.

"Is that why you put out their old things? So they know which house is the right one?"

"Sort of. I guess they're all just like tiny ghost magnets and the better your ofrenda, the better your chances are of having visitors."

"With that bare face?" The tube of lipstick rattles on the table. "You're not ready for visitors. Back in my day a young lady knew how to present herself. Hair and makeup done. You wouldn't catch me dead without my signature red lip."

First of all, you are *dead*, I want to say. Instead, Clau and I just roll our eyes.

"Don't listen to her, niñas," Tío Arthur's bow tie shoots back. "Looks mean nothing without talent."

Clau perks up. "Oh, I've got loads of that."

I think back to Clau's infamous hijacking of the school talent show a few months ago and then her solo dance routine while the DJ at Marisol's quince was still trying to set up his equipment. Clau's definitely got moves. Just none people can actually see.

"Pues, ¡a ver!" Tío Arthur's bow tie eggs her on. "Acting? Singing? Dancing? What's your specialty?"

Clau winks at me. "I'm a triple threat."

She snaps a finger and one of Abuelo's old records starts to play. Samba. Clau's favorite. She wiggles her hips while I crawl over to the volume button to turn down the music.

"You'll wake up Mami!" I hiss, trying to sound serious even though I can't help but laugh.

The next song starts, and Tío Arthur's bow tie is suddenly belting the words. He used to travel with his band all over the Southwest—Texas, New Mexico, California. They even played a few shows across the border, back when the government wasn't so strict about people coming and going.

Every time he stopped by Noche Buena to visit Mami and Tía Tita, he'd bring them a souvenir from some far-off place. A deck of cards with a different luchador on each one, a jewelry box with a flamenco dancer inside. The objects sit right next to his bow tie on the ofrenda and as it begins to sing, their voices join in like he has his own backup singers.

Clau claps, enjoying the show.

"Who's skinning a cat over there?" the lamp from my bedroom calls out, voice gruff.

"Excuse me?" Tío Arthur's bow tie snaps back. "Wait. Is that the *trash* of Teresa Morales I hear? I guess someone took pity on you and found you a new bulb. Though it's obviously still not the brightest of the bunch."

The lamp cackles. "Why don't you come over here and say that to my face?"

Clau shrugs. "Uh, because you don't have one?"

"At least I don't spend most of the year tucked away in some shoebox," the lamp adds, "being eaten alive by moths!"

This doesn't just offend Tío Arthur's bow tie. Suddenly every object on the ofrenda is up in arms.

The flamenco dancer screams about being a sacred object.

The luchadores challenge the lamp to a fight.

The tube of lipstick starts calling the lamp ugly.

Then even more shouting from the ballet slippers that belonged to Papi's little sister, Ana, who died of meningitis; from the pocketknife that used to belong to Abuelo's best friend, Julio, who fell off a horse; and from the paintbrushes that used to belong to my second cousin Mariana, who died in her sleep at the age of a hundred and two.

"What's all this yelling?" Abuela flicks on the light, her hair rumpled. "It's almost morning, Omega. ¿Qué está pasando? You all are so loud you're going to wake the dead!"

Clau raises an eyebrow. "Isn't that sort of the point?"

Abuela sighs as she marches over to the record player and shuts off the music. "The *point* is to celebrate the lives of those we've lost and to remind us that the journey from this world to the next is one we will all take someday."

All except Clau. She looks away and I wonder if she's thinking the same thing. That she should be one of those ghosts, on her way to an altar with her favorite foods and her favorite things, a photo of her smiling face sitting at the very top, surrounded by bright orange cempasúchiles and multicolored papel picado.

But she's not. She's here.

Because she's not like other ghosts.

That's what Luna said when she admitted to being the one who brought Clau here in the first place after finding her family's car turned over in the middle of a terrible storm. Because she's...*special.*

Except Luna and the other adults aren't quite sure *how* yet. So even though there's a part of me that wants to tell Clau that it's not her fault she feels drawn to this side of the veil, I know that still won't answer her questions about her parents and her little sister, Candela. So I don't say anything, listening instead to Abuela as she goes on and on about the Aztec, and the Toltec, and the Maya, and the Nahua.

"...and then all those souls traveled through the nine levels of Chicunamictlán—the Land of the Dead—before arriving at their final resting place."

"Mictlān," I say proudly, remembering the story.

"So it's like a video game," Clau says.

I nod. "And each level is harder than the last. That's why people started creating altars. To deliver supplies to their loved ones who were trying to reach Mictlān."

Clau grows quiet. "You don't..." She looks up. "You don't

think that's where my parents are, do you?" She sits up suddenly. "I didn't make them an altar. What if they don't have any supplies?"

Abuela gently shushes her. "Cálmate, cálmate. The story of Chicunamictlán is only one of many. There are countless versions of heaven and hell and whatever lies between the two." She takes Clau by the hand. "But what I know in here"—she presses their clasped hands to her chest—"is that your parents are somewhere safe and that they are surrounded by love. Which is why Día de Muertos is not a time for mourning or sadness. It's a time for joy and laughter…"

"And *lots* of food," I add.

"And dancing." Abuela holds on to Clau's hand as she twirls her in a circle.

Clau laughs. "So it's a party."

Abuela grins. "Exactly. The biggest party of the year!"

Clau spins. "I love parties!" But in the middle of her next dance move, she pauses, her face growing still. She meets my eyes, then Abuela's. "Do you think my parents will be at the party?" Her lip trembles. "Do you think I'm going to see them again?"

Abuela's quiet, glancing at the ofrenda, at all the objects backlit by flickering candlelight. Ghost magnets, I'd told Clau. But we don't have any for her parents. And if there's nothing calling them to this side of the veil, they might not be able to cross.

"You don't think they're coming…" Clau's face falls.

Abuela reaches for her again. "I'm not sure if they can."

Clau floats over to the altar, gazing down at the objects, all of them just as silent. Then she turns to us, face scrunched with tears. "But I'm here. Isn't that enough?"

"Of course it is." I wrap my arms around her. "Of course you're enough, Clau."

But as I hold her, I feel her wrestling with yet another question I can't answer. What if it's not just *this* Día de Muertos that Clau's parents can't cross over? What if, as long as Clau refuses to cross over herself, she'll never see her parents again? Ever.

And if that happens, if she's earthbound without them for all eternity, will *we* be enough?

"Now, that's plenty of stories for one night." Abuela pinches my cheek. "Omega, you should get some sleep. We've got a busy day tomorrow!"

I groan. "Flower Duty. I know."

"Dulces sueños." Abuela flicks off the light before heading back to bed.

"Hey," Clau says, "I thought you weren't supposed to eat the bread that's on the altar."

"You're not. It's an offering." I kneel next to her, examining the pan de muerto on the second tier of the ofrenda.

"Well," she says, "it looks like someone got hungry."

She's right. A big bite's been taken out of the side.

Suddenly, the hairs on my arms stand up. The same electricity I felt earlier.

"Who would—?" I go to pick up the bread, my fingers touching something cold and wet. I drop the pan and between the bite marks, slimy and squirming...are *worms*.

Clau gags. "Oh my God!"

I crawl away, rubbing my hands on my pajama pants.

"How did those get in there?"

I shake my head and then my whole body's shaking. Like I can still feel them squirming, crawling all over me.

"Deep breaths," Clau says. "Just breathe, Omega."

I inhale but the feeling makes my head swim. Something terrible and taunting. *Mischievous.*

Clau swirls around me. "Are you all right?"

"No," I say, still trying to shake off the feeling.

No. No. No.

Because I can sense it, deep down, that bite was taken by a stranger, which means there's another mysterious visitor in Noche Buena. One Abuelo's prophetic dreams didn't see coming.

CHAPTER 2

I SIT ON THE GRASS WHILE MAMI WAVES a hand at Papi, guiding his truck into our designated parking spot. We're right next to the parade's starting line, which means the dancing skeletons in their giant top hats and Las Catrinas in their big fluffy dresses will toss us the best candy from their elaborate floats.

Usually, I'd already be salivating at the thought of sucking on a sour Lucas Chamoy or a Sparkle Cherry Laffy Taffy but my stomach is still in knots from finding those worms in the pan de muerto this morning.

"You need to eat something, Omega." Abuela tosses me a barbacoa taco wrapped in wax paper.

As my cousins Carlitos and Chale approach, she tosses them some too.

"The weirdest, grossest thing happened." Clau circles Carlitos, wrapping him in a cold frost until he's shivering.

He sidesteps out of her path, peeling back the wax paper on his taco. "If it's going to make me lose my appetite, I don't wanna know."

Clau hovers right in front of his face. Then she says, "Worms! They crawled out of the bread for the dead."

Carlitos chokes, coughing into his hand.

"Oops!" Clau fans him with her hand. "I didn't think he was actually going to get sick."

Carlitos's eyes water and I think he's going to puke. But then I look closer and I realize that it's not shock on his face...it's fear.

The same sickly sweet fear I felt this morning.

I lower my voice. "It looked like..."

"Like someone took a big bite out of it?" Carlitos finishes.

"Wait." I get to my feet. "How did you know?"

"We found the same thing on our altar this morning. We thought Chale had snuck a bite when he wasn't supposed to. Then maybe it went bad. Attracted worms."

"Old food attracts flies," Clau says. "Not worms. Unless maybe it was you who attracted the worms." She ruffles his hair and he jumps.

"Stop that!"

"What do you think it was?" I ask.

"I don't know. But something...not good." He shakes his head. "The feeling it left behind. It was like sinking to the very bottom of..."

"Of everything," I add.

He nods. "Something sad. But also ugly." He sighs. "When Mom found it, she burned it; said it was the only way to kill the eggs if there were any."

"Abuela burned the one at our house too. Told me not to worry."

"Yeah," Carlitos huffs. "Never believing that again. *Don't worry. There's no such thing as La Lechuza. It's just a story.*"

"They also said they were sorry and wouldn't lie to us again."

"Unless that was a lie too," Clau says.

Mami calls from the bed of the truck. "I hear a lot of chitchat over there. If you're finished eating, we need some help setting up."

"We're coming," I call back before scarfing down the rest of my taco.

We help Mami and Tía Tita set up the awning over the truck bed before hanging some baskets over the sides to show off the fresh bouquets. I stop to wipe the sweat from my brow before looking out at the other vendors setting up tables—Mr. Huerta and his shaved ice cart, Señora Ximena and her elotes, Barbie Garcia and her gorditas.

Families lounge in plastic chairs by the side of the road, sipping on ice-cold Jarritos in every color of the rainbow or stuffing their faces with chicharrones covered in lime juice and hot sauce. Fanning themselves with straw hats and paper plates or whatever else they can get their hands on.

Even though it's November first it's still unbearably hot out. We'll get a few weeks of winter if we're lucky but for now late summer still lingers, the leaves on the trees changing color only to match the blazing sun.

"Omega..." Mami wags a finger at me.

I meet her by the passenger-side door where she cracks the top off an ice-cold water bottle before handing it to me.

"There will be a big crowd here today." She looks me up and down. "Lots of energy. Lots of emotions."

"I know."

She presses the back of her hand to my forehead like she's checking for a fever. Instead, I know she's reading me for any signs of distress.

"I'm fine," I say, even though the parade hasn't started yet.

"Sí, pero last year we found you facedown in your cotton candy."

"At least I found a soft place to land."

She smiles, unamused. Then she says, "You *feel* different," and it's not a question.

I go still, sensing the same easy calm she had. Usually, I'm

20

a magnet in public spaces, using up all my energy to swat away people's emotions. Even the positive ones can leave me feeling overwhelmed and exhausted. But for some reason I'm not buzzing.

"Maybe it means I'm getting stronger," I say.

She squeezes my shoulder and I feel her hope like sunlight breaking through clouds. I feel her relief like the biggest, deepest exhale. Until worry creeps in, like a bug burrowing up through sand.

"That doesn't mean we shouldn't still be careful," she says.

"I know. And I will be."

"Good. Because there's a back seat with your name on it if you need to take a breather, okay?"

"Thanks, Mami."

"We're here! We're here!"

Mami and I both turn at the sound of footsteps. The wind catches the lip of my godmother Luisa's giant sunhat and it almost blows right off her head. Her hands are full—her giant bag of paints thrown over one shoulder while she clutches a small black puppy in the other.

"Sorry we're late." My other godmother (and also our school librarian), Soona, drags a cooler behind her. "I had a few things to wrap up at the library."

Clau floats right through her, squealing as she gets a closer look at the puppy in Luisa's arms. "What's his name? Can I pet him? How old is he? When did you get him?"

Luisa laughs, rubbing the bridge of his nose. "His name is Goyo. Yes, you can pet him. He's about six weeks old. And we found him wandering around outside the school a few nights ago."

Carlitos and I approach, each scratching behind the puppy's ears while he lets out a big yawn.

"I wanna see!" Chale tugs on Carlitos's waistband like he's trying to climb him.

Carlitos tries to hold him back. "Wait your turn, Chale!"

"I can't believe Soona finally let you get a dog," I say, knowing how team cat Soona is. They have like seven of them.

Soona gives Luisa a sad smile, something wordless passing between them. Their melancholy floating in the air like the spritz of an old bottle of perfume.

"Does this mean you've stopped trying?" Mami asks quietly.

Luisa gives Mami the same sad smile Soona gave her. "For now."

"Stopped trying what?" I ask.

"To have a baby," Soona says.

Luisa gently pinches my cheek before ruffling Carlitos's hair. "Your mommies are lucky to have you. And maybe someday it'll happen for us too. But we can grow our family in other ways." She gives Goyo a kiss on the head. "Starting with this little guy."

"Wait," Clau says, nose wrinkled. "Why doesn't he have any hair?"

"It's the breed. Xolo are usually hairless."

"And wrinkly," Soona adds. "They're also known to help guide souls to and from the underworld."

"Wait, is that why he's here?" Clau asks. "To help the ghosts find their way?"

Luisa cradles him while he nips at her long feathery earrings. "I'm not sure he's ready for that."

"But meeting a ghost or two today will still be great practice," Soona says.

The puppy yawns again, distracted one second and snoozing the next. Luisa uses her jacket to build him a little bed in the back of the truck before unloading her paint supplies.

Before Soona and Luisa met, Luisa traveled the world painting anything and everything that would hold still. But whether she was painting in the heart of the jungle or in the middle of the ocean or under a million stars, as soon as the paint would dry, she would give each piece away without even signing her name. *Because gifts are meant to be shared*, she always says. And Luisa does have a gift, which is why her line for face painting always stretches the entire length of the parade route.

But since we're her godchildren, we get first dibs.

"Me! Me! Me!" Chale flails his arms, screaming at the top of his lungs.

Carlitos plugs his ears. "Geez, he's *so* annoying!"

"You were the same way," Tía Tita says, trying to quiet Chale down.

"No way. He's like a tiny wrecking ball."

Chale sticks his tongue out at Carlitos, blowing him raspberries.

"Yuck!" Carlitos throws up his hands. "See?"

Tía Tita just laughs.

After Luisa finishes setting up her painting station, she reaches for a brush, reading our minds as Carlitos and I try to elbow each other out of the way.

"I'm older!" Carlitos says.

I shove him back. "I'm a better muse!"

"You know," Luisa says, a sly smile on her face, "I think I'll let…Chale go first this year."

"Chale?" Carlitos groans. "But he can't even sit still."

She shrugs. "Babies first."

Chale wriggles and laughs every time Luisa brushes his face with the cold paint. And yet, somehow she's still able to shade in his skeleton eyes and teeth perfectly. She draws a spiderweb peeking out from his hairline, the design on his chin reaching up like dark tree roots. When she's finished,

Chale jumps down from the chair and starts growling at the passersby.

"Skeletons don't growl," Carlitos corrects him.

Chale turns on him next, opening his mouth wide before biting down on Carlitos's arm.

"Ow!" Carlitos yelps before running around to the other side of the truck, Chale chasing after him.

While they're distracted, I hop on the stool in front of Luisa.

"So, what'll it be?" she asks. "A mermaid calavera? What about something cheetah-inspired?"

"Oh," Clau butts in, "what about a glitter unicorn skeleton?"

"What's with you and glitter?" Carlitos asks, huffing and puffing as he returns from being chased down by Chale. "It took hours to get that stuff out of my hair after changing out of the Halloween costumes that were all *your* idea."

Chale moves on to growling at customers until Tía Tita finally notices and drags him out of sight.

"Glitter makes everything better," Clau argues. "*You* could use some."

"Well, you could use a whole truckful," Carlitos shoots back.

Clau furrows her brow. "Too bad there's not enough on this whole planet for you."

Carlitos crosses his arms. "Well, too bad there's not enough in this whole solar system for you."

"The whole galaxy!"

"The whole universe!"

"¡Ya!" Luisa grabs a handful of glitter and blows it in both their faces. "There's enough glitter for everyone, okay?" She turns to me, still waiting for my answer as Carlitos coughs and sneezes.

I stare at the vibrant colors in her paint tray, my eyes moving between the cool turquoise and the electric yellow and the various shades of purples and pinks in between. But I'm not sure what to choose. I'm not sure who I want to *be*.

Luisa senses my hesitation. "You know, our ancestors believed that death is not the end, but a rebirth. A chance to become someone new. That's what the face painting is about too. A chance to be your most fearless self. The version of you that isn't afraid of anything. Not even death."

"So it's about how the face paint makes me feel," I say. "Not how it looks?"

She nods. "Exactly."

I glance down at Luisa's paints again, the smear of ruby red catching my eye. "I want to feel brave. And strong." I think about my hands gripping those ropes that were tied around Luna. I think about the moon so big it burns. Then I meet Luisa's eyes. "Like a fire you can't put out."

She smiles and then winks. "You got it."

The paint is cool against my skin and I feel her tracing the teeth and filling in the deep black eye sockets. She covers my nose next before drawing a giant red rose right on my forehead, the green leaves dotted with bright gold jewels that she also uses in the orange flower petals around each one of my eyes.

And with each stroke, I feel my own temperature rising. The colors and symbols stoking the flames inside me until I finally open my eyes and it's like the world is on fire. Everything so bright like it's the first day of spring instead of the first day of November.

I race to the side mirror on Papi's truck, and I look like a character from a fairy tale. A beautiful princess. An ancient goddess. But mostly I feel proud to be a Morales *and* a Caamal, to still be connected to something so old and powerful.

"I think it's missing something." Mami comes up behind me and places a crown of red roses and bright yellow sunflowers on my head.

My roots, tying me back to the earth. To the soil where my ancestors first stepped foot. To the ground where they are now buried.

Papi plants a big kiss on the top of my head. "You look beautiful, mija."

And brave, I think. Not like last night when I was begging the moon to leave me alone or when Clau and I found the worms in the pan de muerto. And all because of Luisa's gift for making things beautiful, because of the calavera's gift for making things new.

You have gifts too, a voice calls from between my ribs. And I want to trust it. But then I remember what's beneath the layers of paint, hiding deep beneath my skin. The truth the moon revealed. That sometimes gifts are mistaken for curses and there's danger in not knowing the difference.

I stand back and watch as Luisa takes up her paintbrush like a magic wand, transforming face after face—moons and stars for Belén because of her obsession with aliens, azaleas and hibiscus for Marisol because of her obsession with pink, and red rocks and cactus flowers for Señora Delarosa because of all the time she spends scouring the desert for ingredients for her potions shop.

Luisa paints the past and the people we've lost—the future and the fate that awaits us all—and as each sugar skull leaves her stool, it's like watching the veil between this world and the next suddenly disappear. Noche Buena filled with the ghosts we'll all become someday.

"Do you ever think about what it feels like?" Carlitos asks.

I smile at the next person in Luisa's line before taking their ten-dollar bill and stuffing it in the lockbox.

"Dying?" I say.

He nods and I've never seen him so serious.

I look down at my hands and almost say, *No. I worry about something much worse.*

"Do you think she might tell us?" Carlitos asks.

I watch Clau from across the street as she swims back and forth among the crowd, nosily peering into people's plastic cups and salivating over their churros and tortas and sausage on a stick. Observing from a distance the same way she did on Halloween. The same way she does every holiday, every trip into town, every day we go to school. And I wonder what hurts more. The moment she left her body or all these tiny movements that remind her she doesn't have one anymore.

"I wonder if she even remembers…," Carlitos goes on.

When Abuela first discovered Clau in the attic, Clau

didn't even realize she was dead. For the first week, we weren't allowed to mention it. Not until Abuela had helped her ease into the transition. But it definitely took some convincing, especially since we could all see her. Which meant that not only did Abuela have to prove to Clau that she was dead, she also had to prove that we were empaths with the ability to see ghosts. Which also meant convincing her that magic was real.

"I just want to know if it hurts," Carlitos says.

"I'm sure if you get hit by a truck, it hurts."

"Yeah." Carlitos quirks his mouth. "You're probably right. Or like when Don Luis took that bullet for his long-lost daughter on *Amor Eterno*."

"Also not a great way to go. But at least he was sacrificing himself for someone he loved."

"Uh-uh"—Carlitos shakes his head—"no offense but I will not be shielding anyone from bullets or trucks or trains or anything else that might send me on a four-year journey to Mictlān."

"What? Not even for Chale?"

"Especially not for Chale."

"Some big brother you are," I say before taking money from the next person in Luisa's line.

"You know he drew a green mustache on my poster of José Hernández?"

"But José Hernández already has a mustache."

"Exactly! It was mean *and* redundant! He also keeps putting my Wolverine figurine in the toaster. It's a collectible! Or at least it was."

I shrug. "He's just doing what little kids do."

"Spoken like someone who doesn't have a younger sibling."

"I have you," I say. "That's pretty annoying."

As if on cue, the crowd on the sidewalk parts, and Chale comes at us like a rocket, slamming into Carlitos from behind. I shut the lockbox before the cash goes flying but Carlitos isn't as lucky, falling out of his chair.

"You!" Carlitos catches Chale by the wrist.

But Chale's not empty-handed. Gripped in his tiny fist is one of Luisa's paint tubes. Flamingo pink.

Carlitos's eyes widen. "Oh no you don't."

Chale snickers. Then he squeezes, paint splattering all over Carlitos's shirt.

Carlitos screams. "Napkins! ¡Toallas! Help!"

"You'll just smear it," I warn him.

Chale wriggles free from Carlitos's grasp.

Carlitos grabs for him again. "Get back here!" But there's paint on his hands too, Chale slipping right through his fingers.

Chale takes off running, Carlitos chasing after him again.

"I'm missing a paint tube," Luisa calls out. "Anyone seen it?"

I kick the empty paint tube out of sight and shake my head.

"Flower crowns!" Tía Tita calls from the truck bed. "Get your flower crowns here!"

The crowd in front of Papi's truck gets even bigger, people whistling and waving bills, trying to get a crown before they all sell out.

Marisol's mom buys her the biggest crown we have—an explosion of electric-blue cobalt dreams and giant Casa Blanca lilies and lavender camellias.

As they pin it to her head, Marisol never taking her eyes off her reflection in the window of Papi's truck, I think about Carlitos's question again. And then I think about the moment those flowers were plucked from the ground, how they're withering even though we can't see it. How soon they'll be dry and limp and *dead*.

I've helped Abuela bury the stems, our hands smoothing the soil and leaving behind a prayer for seeds. Not like when we buried Bisabuela Ynez. The only thing we said then was goodbye. Knowing, if we were lucky, her soul would bloom once a year during Día de Muertos. But also knowing that nothing is guaranteed, that the days to come would be painful, that grief never goes away.

I search for Clau among the crowd again. She senses me looking and finally shimmies back over to us, dancing to the music playing from Papi's truck. She flicks her wrist, turning up the volume, and Abuela just sighs, crossing her arms. I guess she gets a pass because of the parade. And because everyone in line is suddenly bobbing their heads too.

"When is this thing supposed to start?" Clau swoops down, ruffling the cash in my hand as I stuff it into the lockbox. "We've been waiting forever!"

Abuela motions down the road where the floats are lining up, flags and streamers fluttering in the wind.

"At the beating of the drum," Abuela says, turning back to us. "And until then we—"

A cold wind rushes past, Clau flying as fast as she can straight for the giant drum attached to the first float. Then they collide, Clau striking the hide and sending out a deep thrum, the vibrations passing over the crowd as everyone turns to look.

Then there are cheers, people raising their cups and whistling between their teeth and gritoing at the tops of their lungs.

Abuela shakes her head. Then she laughs, throwing up her hands. "You heard her. Let's get this party started!

CHAPTER 3

THE CROWD PARTS LIKE A WAVE, PEOPLE drifting toward the sidewalk to make room for the rainbow of colors moving in our direction. A Calavera in a feathered headdress strikes the drum, leading the procession. Behind him, Las Catrinas—female skeletons in long, frilly dresses—twirl pink and lavender parasols to the sound of the Noche Buena high school mariachi band.

I stand on my chair, trying to get a better look.

"Are they tossing the candy yet?" Carlitos stands on his tiptoes.

"There won't be any candy this year," Belén says to us over her shoulder.

We both snap in her direction. "What?"

Belén slumps down into her plastic lawn chair and even

though it's her day off from her cashier job at Allsup's she still smells like their fried burritos. I try to hide my drooling.

"Yeah," she says, "I heard Mr. Montgomery and Mrs. Statham have joined forces and launched a war on sugar. Now that the neighborhood watch group and the PTA are basically the same, they're not selling it at the basketball games this year either."

Which is something Carlitos and I might have known if we ever actually attended basketball games. We tried to. Once. But then the visiting team scored a last-second shot right before the buzzer and the collective boos had me seeing black. I had to be wheeled out on a ball cart.

"Did you just say *no candy?*" Clau reappears in a rage.

Carlitos and I share a look that says, *I guess she's back to pretending to be one of the living.*

"Figures Mr. Montgomery is behind this." Carlitos kicks at the curb.

Aiden's dad is still president of the neighborhood watch group, who have been watching us *extra* closely ever since one of our blood relatives turned out to be a witch with the power to turn herself into an owl.

Soona and Luisa had some special cookies delivered to one of the neighborhood watch group's meetings in order to erase their memories of that day. But you can't erase suspicion. Or fear. And that's the problem with Mr. Montgomery.

He's afraid of so much (especially us) and it makes him angry...which makes him dangerous.

"Yeah," I add. "I heard he was power-tripping at Vidal's Car Wash the other day because he said the music was too loud."

"I'm surprised he's not here using his *presidential powers* to try to shut down the parade too," Carlitos says.

Clau shades her eyes, staring off down the road. "Looks like he is."

I stand on my chair again and spot Mr. Montgomery. "He's standing next to someone in a big black cowboy hat."

"New sheriff," Belén says. "He came into the store yesterday. Didn't say much. Didn't buy anything either. Just looked around the store and left."

"Let me see." Carlitos grabs my shoulders and hoists himself up into the chair.

"Uh, excuse me!"

Carlitos sucks his teeth, glaring at Mr. Montgomery and the new sheriff. "Of course he's buddying up to the cops. He patrols these streets like he already is one."

"Well, we don't have candy or a good view," I say. "Maybe we should find somewhere else to stand."

"Like where?" Carlitos asks.

Clau grins. "I think I have an idea."

We follow Clau to the old radio station across the street just as every other kid gets the same idea. The station used to play everything from old corridos to Chicane rock music to cumbias. Now they mostly use it to commentate student sporting events and tell everyone within a hundred-mile radius how much we stink.

Marisol and her sisters are already there, along with Joon Lee and Naomi Davis, all of them waiting their turn to climb up the roof ladder.

Joon takes a step and almost loses his footing, the soda in his hand wobbling. Naomi holds her elote in her teeth as she grabs the railing with both hands. Carlitos and I follow behind, dodging falling Skittles as they spill out of Marisol's little sister Nena's pockets.

One pelts Carlitos right in the eye. "Yick! I think that one was wet!"

"Hurry up!" I shove him. "I don't want to miss the folk-lórico dancers."

The roof of the radio station is like a dystopian jungle gym, metal structures jutting up at random angles. We hop over thick bolts and cables, racing for the roof's ledge where kids sit, dangling their legs over the side as a Catrin and Catrina dance on stilts. El Catrin twirls La Catrina before dramatically dipping her.

"It's so romantic," Clau squeals.

"It's satire," Carlitos spits back. "The artist created them as a way of making fun of the people in Mexico who started eating and drinking and dancing like the Europeans."

"They're also meant to remind us that whether you're rich or poor, from Mexico or Europe, death comes for us all someday," I add.

Clau wrinkles her nose. "What a buzzkill!" She wedges herself between us and I flinch at her ice-cold skin. "Oh, look, look! The dancers you wanted to see are coming!"

I lean forward, watching as the folklórico dancers raise their skirts, fanning them out as they spin in elegant circles. The men approach in their black steel heel boots and big sombreros, hands behind their backs as they dance in sync with the women. They move in and out of each other's orbit, gazing into each other's eyes.

"Are they kissing?" Clau asks, motioning to the way the male dancers are tilting their heads just inches from the women's bright red lips.

"It's just pretend," I say, even though the sight of it still makes my stomach feel all sparkly.

"Speaking of kissing"—Clau nudges me—"where's *Aiden?*"

She blows me cold phantom kisses and I swat at her.

"Stop that! He probably wasn't allowed to come," I say, gesturing to where Mr. Montgomery is still standing with the new sheriff.

"Or maybe he thinks it's evil just like his dad does," Carlitos says.

"He does not," I shoot back.

Aiden isn't afraid of me. Not even after his sister Abby tried to turn him against me. Not even after I told him the truth—that I'm an empath. Carlitos thinks he still might—turn on us, that is. But for some reason...I'm not afraid of Aiden either.

I'm not afraid of him judging me or betraying me. And if Abby, after all those months of torturing me, of hating me because I wouldn't help her connect with her mother on the other side, can change her mind about magic, can change her mind about *me*, then maybe Mr. Montgomery can too. Maybe Aiden could show him how.

"What about Halloween?" I say. "We all had so much fun together."

"Halloween is about pretend magic," Carlitos says.

"He knows I saved Luna. He knows what we can do."

"And he thinks it's cool, right? But they're not special effects, Omega. Our life isn't some kind of movie with a guaranteed happy ending."

"Of course it's not. What are you talking about?" I say.

I watch Carlitos's face change, his brow wrinkled with worry. He lowers his voice. "I'm talking about how Luna became a Lechuza in the first place. How...if you're not careful, you could turn into a Lechuza too." He meets my eyes. "Then what would Aiden think?"

His words are a punch in the gut. I look down at my hands again, feeling exposed. Like he saw. Like he *knows*.

I grip my jean shorts, palms sweaty. "How did—?"

Carlitos is quiet for a long moment and then he says, "Abuela."

I exhale. "She told you?"

"More like warned me. And now I'm warning you." He nods back to where Mr. Montgomery stands glaring at the crowd. "That kind of hate? It could be in Aiden's blood just like La Lechuza is in ours."

Ours. He thinks it's something we share....

I follow Carlitos's eyes, watching Mr. Montgomery as he watches us. As he shifts from foot to foot, impatient. Like he's waiting for something. I wait too, for a sign that he and Aiden aren't the same...even though all I see is their same light brown hair, the same line of freckles across the bridge of their nose. But just because you look like someone, just because you love someone, doesn't mean your hearts are the same.

"Over here!"

Someone bumps into me from behind.

"Make sure you get the dancers in the background." Next to me, Marisol strikes a pose, smiling wide. "Did you get it?" She snatches the phone from her sister Yesenia. "It's blurry!"

Up ahead, engines rev, igniting a whooping from the crowd. Candy-colored muscle cars snake down the road as a heavy bass blares from the open windows. A fiery red drop-top bounces up and down while the lime-green car next to it rocks from side to side, dancing to the music just like the comparsas in orange skirts and glittering mariposa wings.

But it's like the colors are dull, the music suddenly too loud in my ears. Because all I can think about is what Carlitos said. What he *knows*. What if it's only a matter of time before he finds out the rest? That the warning Abuela gave him might already be too late.

I look down at my arms again, imagining them sprouting feathers. And I realize that Aiden's not the only one who might reject me. From the look on his face, the tone in his voice, it feels like Carlitos already has. Which means I can't tell him the truth.

"Their wings are just like mine, sissy!" Marisol's little sister Nena waves at the comparsas as they pass by, her voice breaking me out of my fog.

"Be careful." Yesenia pulls her back from the ledge.

41

The dancers swing giant baskets full of orange marigolds, carefully scattering their petals on the ground behind them, leaving a trail that the ghosts of our loved ones will be able to follow all the way to the cemetery.

Nena twirls, using her hands to flap her light blue wings like they're real. Luisa matched the colors perfectly when she gave her a fairy-inspired calavera.

Suddenly, Nena stops spinning, transfixed by the giant alebrije slithering up the road. The snakelike body is being held up by stilts, its scales shifting colors in the sunlight. Next up is a winged armadillo, its armor speckled blue like the ocean. It ambles forward, making way for a dark green cougar with the purple tail of a dragon.

The man maneuvering the stilts tilts the cougar's head in our direction, and Nena screams before burying her face in Marisol's dress.

"Nena, you're going to get your face paint all over me!"

Nena harrumphs before hiking up her skirt and climbing back down the ladder.

"You know what? Take your own pictures," Yesenia says before chasing after Nena.

"Yesenia, wait!" Marisol stuffs her phone in her purse before racing after them both.

"Dibs!" Carlitos shouts, sliding over so we can have their spots.

I shove our conversation to the back of my mind and try to get back to enjoying the parade.

Clau and I scoot over just in time to see the escaramuzas on horseback. The eight women are dressed like Adelitas—the women who fought bravely alongside the men in the Mexican-American War—their long dresses draped over their saddles as their horses prance in place. Until the women click their teeth and start leading their horses in a tight circle. They wind back and forth like they're weaving an intricate tapestry, the ribbons on their hats blowing behind them in the wind.

The horses line up again, readying themselves for the next part of the routine. But before they can break, the horse at the front of the line begins to whinny, skittering backward, its eyes wide. The horse behind it leaps up, kicking its front legs, nostrils flaring.

"What's going on?" Clau asks.

I scan the crowd, the onlookers backing away from the street. Then out of the corner of my eye, I see that same black cowboy hat moving closer. The sheriff steps into the center of the parade route and then all the horses are retreating, the escaramuzas gripping their reins and patting their necks, trying to get them to calm down.

But they're scared. Even all the way up here on this rooftop...I can feel it.

Abuela senses something too and she whistles for us to climb down from the radio station.

But just as we're about to back away from the roof's edge, I see Yesenia winding through the crowd as she calls out for Nena. Marisol's behind her, huffing and puffing like she's sick of chasing after her little sister who can't seem to sit still.

"Nena! Nena, where are you?"

A few adults nearby start scanning the surrounding buildings before fanning out to help look.

I follow Carlitos down the ladder and when I reach the bottom, something slams into me. I brace against the wall, trying to steady myself, and I realize it's Nena.

"Your sisters are looking all over for you," Carlitos says.

She tries to run off again and I catch her by the hand. "Nena, wait!"

She tries to wriggle free. "You're going to make me lose!"

"Lose what?"

"The game. I'm supposed to be hiding."

"Hiding from who?"

Yesenia rounds the corner of the building, shoulders slumping in relief. "Nena, there you are!"

I let go of Nena's hand and she runs straight into Yesenia's arms.

"Thanks for finding her," Yesenia says, nearly out of breath.

Then she drags her across the street where their mother is waiting, chancla raised.

I'm surprised Abuela hasn't taken off her chancla too. She stands toe to toe with Deputy Medina while he tries to quiet the crowd behind her.

"Everyone, please take a step back."

Every year Deputy Medina gives a safety training at school, telling us to stay off social media, say no to drugs, and stop climbing the water tower and covering it in streamers after the football team finally wins a game. But no one actually takes him seriously, which is why the water tower's been covered in red and blue streamers since homecoming.

"What's all this about?" Abuela asks him.

He tries to usher her off the street. "Señora...if you could just—"

"Looks like the organizers of this little event forgot to get a permit." Mr. Montgomery steps out of the crowd, a sick grin on his face. "Afraid we're going to have to shut it down."

"We?" Abuela's eyes are slits. "What do you mean *we?*"

Deputy Medina gives Mr. Montgomery a look at his use of the word but he doesn't argue his point about the permit.

The crowd boos, raising their voices until Deputy Medina is shaking in his boots. Last year he was sitting in a lawn chair at the end of the parade route, sipping on some lemonade and enjoying a plateful of carnitas tacos. I can tell by the blush on his face that he doesn't want to be doing this. But for some reason, he's not stopping.

"Probably just a simple mistake," Deputy Medina says. "We'll get this sorted. Maybe reschedule for another day...."

"Reschedule Día de Muertos. *Día*," Abuela emphasizes. "I know your parents didn't raise you speaking Spanish, Tony, but I know you know what día means."

"Señora..."

"Don't Señora me!"

At the anger in Abuela's voice, the crowd begins closing in. Belén wags a finger at Deputy Medina. Soona steps to Mr. Montgomery, almost making him stumble back. When I see Mami approaching the new sheriff I hold my breath.

"You want this to be your new home?" she says. "You have to treat people like family. Not like this."

I can barely see his expression beneath the dark bill of his hat. But instead of responding, he simply turns his back on her, on everyone, and walks away. While the horses kick up dust as he passes, still straining against their reins. *Still afraid.*

A shiver races up my spine, something telling me maybe I should be just as afraid. Luckily, the new sheriff is gone as quickly as he came, the crowd starting to make their way to the cemetery where we won't need a permit to gather.

After we help the adults load everything into the truck, the rest of the parade-goers get a police escort all the way there, the cruiser tires crushing the orange marigolds that are supposed to guide our loved ones' ghosts.

Mami, Abuela, Carlitos, and I sit on the lowered tailgate, looking out at the empty street behind us.

"Here." Mami hands me and Carlitos a bunch of marigolds and we follow her lead as she tosses the fresh petals over the old ones.

"Was that really true about the permit?" Carlitos asks. "I mean, the parade's been happening for years. Like, as long as I've been alive."

"Celebrations like this have been going on since the beginning," Abuela says. "Before permits." She spits on the ground. "Before greedy men crossed oceans and stepped foot on this land." She reaches for my hand, then Carlitos's, giving us each a squeeze. "And they'll continue. Long after Mr. Montgomery is gone. Long after the fear he and so many others carry about people who are different dies too."

CHAPTER 4

WE'RE PARKED AT THE EDGE OF THE CEMETERY, every visitor passing right by us on their way to the gates. They're carrying picnic baskets and portable speakers, Tejano music weaving its way between the headstones. Next to each grave people lounge on blankets, clinking glass bottles and unwrapping warm tamales.

Most people place their flower orders on the spot, Carlitos and I pulling the loose stems from the crates in the back of Papi's truck before Mami and Tía Tita quickly tie them into neat bundles.

"So, like, where are the ghosts?" Clau asks, scanning the gravesites.

"They stop by the altars first," Mami says, "to refuel after such a long journey."

Clau crosses her arms. "So they're late."

Mami laughs. "Maybe a few. But time works differently on the other side of the veil. To them it might feel like years have passed, which means that when they arrive, they need time to adjust."

Abuela nods. "And time to absorb human energy."

"Like one of those photos from an old Polaroid camera," Tía Tita adds.

"Oh yeah," Carlitos says. "The one you always use to take our first-day-of-school pictures."

"That's right," she says. "But the picture doesn't show up instantly. You have to wait, the images slowly rising to the surface. Ghosts are the same way."

Mami nods. "But that doesn't mean we can't still feel them."

"What do you mean?" I ask.

Mami faces me toward the wind, the breeze tickling the hairs on my arms. I stand perfectly still, eyes closed, breathing slow as I try to read the sensations around me. Like slowly wading through a pool. And suddenly, there it is. Something warm and lapping against me.

"What do you feel?" Mami asks.

"Love," I say.

Love like a river running right through the cemetery. I open my eyes and there are flashes of light, tiny sparkles swirling around the living.

"Stardust," Abuela whispers in my ear. "De donde empezamos." *From whence we all came.*

They look like fireflies at first, tiny sparks being tossed about in the wind. But the longer I stare, the more I can see the threads. Just barely. A head. A hand. A woman's long hair.

Mami taps me on the nose, regaining my attention. "Now, when you go around hand-selling these marigolds, mention Luisa's still painting faces for ten dollars a person."

I take the basket Mami's holding. "Got it. One dollar for the marigolds. Ten dollars for the face painting."

Abuela snaps her fingers. "And don't forget to smile."

Carlitos gives her a salty grin and she shakes a rag at us both.

"Do you have family here too?" Clau asks as she follows me and Carlitos through the gates.

I nod. "On the other side of the cemetery there's a whole section of our ancestors. Once the flowers are gone we'll head over there for lunch. Papi usually brings his guitar and we sing songs and tell stories. Things to remember them by."

We stop and sell a few marigolds to a woman with a little boy clutching her skirt and a little girl balanced on her hip. The little girl marvels at my face paint.

"My godmother will paint yours just like it," I tell her.

The little girl squeals.

"What about you, Matteo?" the woman asks the little boy. "You want your face painted too?"

He buries his face in her leg, shakes his head.

"Okay, we'll just watch sissy, then." The woman smiles at us. "Thanks for the suggestion."

"No problem."

Next, we approach Ms. Zapata. She greets us as warmly as she does every time I go to see her in the clinic at school. Turns out the last time I was there, I wasn't actually battling the flu. Instead, I was sensing Luna's arrival and Señora Avila's pending transformation.

The same transformation Abuela warned Carlitos about even though she's barely spoken a word about it to me. Luna's the one who told me the truth. But why would Abuela talk to Carlitos about it and not me? Unless Carlitos was lying about her warning him of a curse we don't actually share. Unless…she was actually warning him about me.

"A bouquet of marigolds would be lovely," Ms. Zapata says.

Before I can reach for the flowers, Carlitos snatches them out of the basket, handing them over before offering to take the money too.

"Gracias," she says, waving goodbye as we continue on our way.

As we walk, I can't help but glance at him out of the corner of my eye, wondering if he's looking out at this cemetery full of families who aren't just celebrating but mourning, and imagining that they're land mines. Emotions being tossed in my direction like hand grenades every time we offer someone flowers.

If he's treating me like I'm dangerous now, what would happen if he found out about the strange shapes beneath my skin?

"I'm fine," I say under my breath. "Just like I was fine at the parade."

His cheeks go red but he doesn't say a word.

I stop walking. "You didn't want me to touch her."

He sighs. "I'm just trying to share the load."

"Because you're scared."

He frowns.

"The energy that flowed through me when I saved Luna was ten times stronger than whatever people might be feeling here."

"Yeah," Clau adds, "if Omega was going to turn into a monster, she would have done it already."

"Exactly!" I say and my heart clenches.

Because it's a lie and I know it, the word bitter on my tongue. And yet, beneath the bitterness, it also feels a lot like hope. Hope that the markings mean nothing. That they'll fade over time.

"I guess you're right," Carlitos says.

I start walking again, not wanting to look directly at him. "And the next time you and Abuela decide to talk about me behind my back you can remind her of that too."

"Come on, Omega…." He quickens his pace, trying to keep up. "All she said was to be careful. That there was stuff about La Lechuza that even she doesn't understand."

I lower my voice. "So you're not afraid of me?"

He stops walking. "What? Of course not."

His words strike me like arrows and I taste the same bitterness as before. I sense the same hope. That he's lying about being afraid of me. That he wishes he wasn't.

"Are those for sale?" A woman in a headscarf waves us over, ending our conversation.

"Absolutely," I say, handing her a bouquet before Carlitos can.

"They're gorgeous." Señora Salas calls us over next. "My mother would love them. Let me just look for my purse." Señora Salas rifles through supermarket bags. "Luis, have you seen my wallet? I need a few dollars for the kids." She lifts the flap on a picnic basket and then she screams. At the top of her lungs. And then she falls back, bumping into one of the headstones on the way down.

Her husband, Luis, rushes over. "What is it? What's the matter?"

She points at the picnic basket, her face pale.

Luis looks inside before bringing the back of his hand to his mouth like he might be sick.

"What's going on over here?" Mrs. Murillo at the next plot over rushes to Señora Salas's side.

"Wo-wo—" Señora Salas finally catches her breath and says, "*worms*!"

The basket of flowers I'm holding tumbles to my feet. Carlitos is frozen next to me. Clau hovers over Luis as he dumps out the picnic basket, her wide eyes confirming the worst.

"Oh, let me see!" Señora Salas's grandson tries to run over and look but she drags him back.

"Did I hear you say worms?" Señora Huerta, the school secretary, stands at the edge of the plot, holding her daughter's hand. "We noticed the same thing this morning." She hoists her little girl onto her hip. "It was horrid. I could barely stand to look."

"Where did you two buy your bread from?" Mrs. Murillo asks. "Maybe we should report them to the city health department."

"Store-bought pan de muerto?" Señora Huerta grimaces, even more disgusted than she was before. "I baked them from scratch." She fans herself with a paper plate like she's about to faint.

Luis kicks at one of the pieces of bread. "Well, at least someone got to enjoy them before they went bad."

The bread rolls, revealing a giant bite mark.

"Do you think it was some kind of animal?" Mrs. Murillo asks. "Like a raccoon or something? I've heard they're pretty mischievous. Smart too and with those little hands just like ours." She shivers.

"We live across town from the Salases," Señora Huerta says.

"Not to mention the fact that nothing else on the ofrenda was disturbed," Señora Salas adds.

"We found the same thing on our altar." Mr. Flores, the school bus driver, approaches. "At first we thought it was our son, Daniel. He's teething and has been trying to get at that bread for days."

"We thought it was the dog." Señor Pérez joins the group, shaking his head in confusion. "Now I'm starting to think it must have been some kind of prank. Our daughter's friends."

"I heard it on the news this morning." Soona suddenly appears behind us, a breezy smile on her face. "Just some teenagers trying to go viral."

Señor Pérez snaps his fingers. "I knew it!"

Mrs. Murillo exhales. "Oh, what a relief."

"These kids…" Señora Huerta shakes her head. "They sure are creative."

Señora Salas gets up, dusting off her jeans. "Thank goodness. I was about to call Father Torres to have him come do an exorcism."

Soona laughs and it feels pretend. "No need. I'll call Principal González instead. Tell her a few students might need a stern talking-to."

"Thank you, Soona." Señora Salas pats her on the hand. "And Omega, I'll whistle once I finally find my wallet."

"Okay, Señora." I slowly back away, still feeling strange about what Soona just said. "Thank you."

Soona follows, pulling me and Carlitos off the path. We stand next to a pair of headstones overgrown with weeds. A cold spot in the cemetery without any food or music or family.

I stare down at the names, barely legible, and say, "It wasn't really a prank, was it?"

Soona sighs. "No."

"So you lied?" Clau says.

"It's for their own good."

"Like it was for our own good when you lied about La Lechuza?" Carlitos shoots back.

Soona crosses her arms. "If there's anything we can all learn from Luna's situation, it's that nothing in life is black-and-white. Sometimes we lie to protect the people we love and sometimes we lie to keep our neighbors from running through the streets scared."

"Scared of what?" I ask, suddenly feeling my own knees quake.

Clau shakes too. "Is it...is it a ghost?"

I wonder if she's thinking, *Like me?* I wonder if that makes it scarier.

"It's not a ghost," Soona says.

"Then what is it?" I ask.

"That, we're not sure of yet. But no ghost could be solid enough on this side of the veil to actually take a bite out of something. The best they can do is move things around, maybe leave behind a few scratch marks. But that takes a lot of energy."

"What if it's someone *possessed* by a ghost?" Clau asks. "Then they could take a bite out of anything!"

Soona shakes her head. "It's unlikely. Despite what the movies say it takes an extraordinary power to be able to control one of the living. Only a handful of ghosts have ever mastered it."

"But Romeo and Julieta did it," Clau says, reminding us all of our botched séance in which Abby was accidentally possessed.

Soona glances at me, a dark twinkle in her eye. "Because a very powerful witch made it possible."

"So maybe there's another witch in town," Carlitos says.

Soona's face darkens. "No. This…" She stares off into the trees for a long moment. "*This* is something else."

My stomach drops. "Something evil?"

Soona looks me in my eyes, and then, more serious than I've ever seen her, she says, "You tell me."

"Wh-what?"

"What did you feel when you found the worms?"

"I…"

"Concentrate," she says. "When you interact with the supernatural, you need to be certain."

"Certain of what?" Carlitos asks.

"Certain if something is safe, if it's redeemable, if there's even a single shred of goodness left in it. Or certain that it's wrong. That it means to do you harm." Soona grips us each by the shoulder. "Being able to tell the difference could mean the difference between life and death." She looks from me to Carlitos. "So which is it?"

For a second, I wish the adults were back to keeping secrets. I don't want to be faced with life-or-death situations. I don't want to know that there might be something out there even scarier than La Lechuza.

"It was evil," Carlitos says suddenly. "I'm sure of it." Then he looks to me.

While I just stare back. Because even though the feeling that struck me as soon as I touched those worms was...terrible and terrifying and I never want to feel it again...I'm not sure if that's *all* I felt, if that's *all* there was. But what I do know for certain is that Carlitos's empathic abilities have always been more accurate than mine. So even though the source of the feeling is something supernatural, which is supposed to be my specialty, I can't help but wonder if I could be wrong.

So I agree, "It was evil," pretending to be as sure as he is.

"Well, then, I think that means we should all be a little more careful today," Soona says. "Which means no wandering off. Stick to the path and then it's straight back to your parents."

Carlitos groans. "Ugh, but we just stopped being grounded. Now you're going to ground us again?"

"You either follow the rules or whatever monster took a bite out of the pan de muerto just might take a bite out of you," Soona says. "¿Entienden?"

This time we both groan. "Yes. We understand."

"Good. Now finish selling the rest of these flowers and then let your mothers know I had some work to do."

"Where are you going?" I ask.

Soona looks back at us over her shoulder and says, "El Otro Lado. To follow my own instincts."

"I don't know about you," Carlitos says. "But I'm more than happy to let the adults unravel this mystery, especially since the last time I almost ended up being the one possessed instead of Abby!"

"Speaking of possession," Clau says, "I know Soona said it's unlikely, but if anyone was going to end up possessed, wouldn't it be tonight? Surely some of those ghosts try to overstay their welcome here on Earth."

Carlitos and I exchange a look.

"Yeah, it's a shame how *some* people think the rules just don't apply to them," Carlitos says.

Before Clau can register his sarcasm something jumps out from behind a nearby headstone with a growl. All three of us jump, my heart racing.

Chale snorts, giggling at the terror on our faces.

Carlitos's nostrils flare. "Chale! I swear if you do not cut this out I will—"

That's when Chale pelts him with a clod of dirt before running back to Tía Tita, who is completely oblivious.

"Yeah, you better run!" Carlitos shakes his fist.

"Maybe Chale's onto something with his whole pretending-to-be-a-zombie thing," Clau says.

Carlitos is still seething.

"Might explain the worms," she adds.

"But it doesn't explain anything else," I say.

We approach the next family, two little boys chasing each other with bubble guns while the adults laugh and flip through an old photo album.

"¿Cempasúchiles?" I offer.

"Ay, que linda," one of the women says.

I hand them a bundle in exchange for a five-dollar bill but before we walk away, I turn back to the woman.

"Perdón, Señora, but I was wondering if you noticed anything…*strange* about the pan de muerto on your altar this morning."

Her eyes narrow. She nods. "There were worms." Then

she lowers her voice. "I saw the commotion earlier with Señora Salas. But Soona said it was just some kids?"

"Yeah, I guess it was all just some kind of prank."

"You kids and your games."

"Yup, we're a menace," Carlitos quips.

I stuff the bills in my pocket. "Gracias, Señora."

"Five for five," Carlitos says, taking the basket of flowers from me.

"I can carry it, you know."

"Abuela's giving me looks. Besides, this way you can do all the talking."

"Gee, thanks."

As we wind our way down the path, I *do* talk. To every family at every gravesite. I offer them flowers and pitch Luisa's face painting and then just before turning to go I ask them about the pan de muerto on their altar. Suddenly, we're six for six, and then seven for seven, until we come upon Señor Jimenez where he sits alone in front of his wife's headstone.

"I always use her secret recipe." He smiles, as if savoring the taste. "They come out perfect every time. This year was no different."

"So you didn't notice any bites taken out? No worms?" I ask.

He laughs. "Nope. No evidence of tampering whatsoever."

His eyes soften. "I wish someone had paid me a visit. Left me a sign like that. But no luck."

"I'm sorry, Señor Jimenez."

And I am. Because I can feel his loneliness like a fist around my heart, feel it squeezing every time he remembers that Señora Jimenez is gone.

His smile returns as he looks out at the cemetery, at all the people eating and laughing and *living*. The way the dead still do in that place we cannot see. The way the dead still *are*, their sparkling outlines coming more into focus.

Señor Jimenez sighs. "Today, mija, there is nothing to be sorry about."

I hand him a bouquet of marigolds and he tips his cowboy hat at me. Then he lays them on the grass in front of Señora Jimenez's headstone and begins to hum.

After we've finished interviewing everyone at the cemetery I can't stop staring at the scene stretching out before me—all the people gathered in face paint and flower crowns, singing and dancing and filling their bellies. I look back at each person we spoke to, all the ones who were paid a mysterious visit. And then next to them, the ghosts of their loved ones, pale and glistening like they're held together by some kind of mystical thread.

"What are you thinking?" Carlitos asks.

"That it's not random." I narrow my eyes, trying to figure out how they're all connected.

Carlitos scrunches his brow too. "But why would a zombie visit the Salases *and* the Huertas?"

Clau shrugs. "Maybe he was just hungry?"

I roll my eyes. "It wasn't un zombi. And it's not about the bread." I snap my fingers. "What else do the Salases and the Huertas have in common? Are they related somehow?"

"Like a long-lost cousin or something?" Clau says.

"Or maybe they ate at the same restaurant last night? Or Señora Salas and Señora Huerta are both on the PTA or something?"

Carlitos throws up his hands. "¡Ay chihuahuas! It could be anything. Not to mention that the connection between the Salases and the Huertas would have to be the same connection between all the other families that found worms in their pan de muerto this morning."

"That's it." I meet Carlitos's eyes. *"Families."*

I look back toward Señor Jimenez, alone in front of his wife's headstone. I see her spiderweb outline next to him, catching the sunlight.

"Neither Señor Jimenez or Señora Delgado found worms in their pan de muerto this morning." I find Señora Delgado, her husband's outline just as translucent as the others.

"They're both widows," Carlitos says, pieces clicking into place. Then he shakes his head. "But what about the Aceveses? They're a couple."

"Yeah," Clau says, "the only couple Omega talked to who didn't wake up to a disgusting surprise."

"So maybe the monster just missed their house," Carlitos says.

Clau shakes her head. "They're a family the same way Soona and Luisa are. They didn't have any mysterious visitors either?"

"You're right," Carlitos says. "Soona didn't mention finding anything at their house."

"Maybe the monster isn't targeting families after all," Clau says.

I watch the Aceveses where they sit at the far edge of the cemetery, the plot there still raised, *recent*, and the tiny figure between them makes my heart stop. The child they lost blows them starry kisses while Mrs. Aceves dabs at her eyes with a tissue.

"Do you see her?" I ask.

Carlitos squints. "I didn't know the Aceveses had a little girl."

I look at the dates on the headstone. "She was only four."

Clau lifts a hand. The little girl spots her and waves back.

I meet Clau's eyes. "You're right." I turn to Carlitos next. "Clau's *right*! Whatever *it* is...it's not just targeting homes with families. It's targeting homes with children."

CHAPTER 5

Usually, we would be sitting around Tío Arthur's and Bisabuela Ynez's graves, the rest of our ancestors' plots stretching from left to right, while Abuelo tells us stories about Tío Arthur opening up for Tortilla Factory and Bisabuela Ynez breaking wild horses, Abuela loading up our plates with tamales and alegrías and candied pumpkin. Papi would be tuning his guitar, humming softly until Tío Juan requested a song his father used to sing, and then everyone would join in.

But instead, the adults are fanned out across the cemetery, smiling and making polite conversation while sneaking in as many questions as possible about the worm-filled bread each family found on their altar this morning, while still maintaining Soona's cover story that it was in fact teenage vandals trying to make a viral video.

Considering time doesn't exist in Soona's magical library in el Otro Lado, it's a little strange that she's not back yet. But maybe this mystery is more complicated than it seems.

"I'm hungry," Carlitos groans.

"Abuela told us to wait." I hop up on the tailgate of Papi's truck, swinging my legs. My stomach's growling too.

"At least they actually took you seriously this time," Clau says.

Clau's right. When I mentioned that our mystery monster might be targeting homes with kids, instead of telling me there was nothing to worry about like they did with La Lechuza, the adults actually *listened*. And then they panicked.

I hear rustling and turn to see Goyo sniffing around the foil-wrapped tamales.

Carlitos scoops him up. "I feel your pain." Goyo licks him frantically, Carlitos laughing. "Stop! It tickles!"

Then Goyo does stop. He stiffens, pointy ears perked up. He stares at the woods over Carlitos's shoulder and then he starts to growl.

"What's wrong, Goyo?" I scratch behind his ears again but he doesn't stop, the sound long and low and...*scared*.

Suddenly, Goyo yips and then Carlitos screams.

"He's peeing on me!" He holds Goyo at arm's length.

"Probably because you scared him!" Clau says.

"Me? How did I scare him?"

"Your face."

"My face? Your face!"

"Give him to me," I snap.

I lower Goyo to the grass and let him finish his business. When I scoop him back up, I see Aiden Montgomery, heading straight for us and carrying a bouquet of pink roses.

"What is *he* doing here?" Carlitos hisses.

Clau snickers. "Maybe he's here to ask Omega on a second date."

"Shh…" I swat at them both.

Aiden raises a hand as he approaches. Then his face lights up when he sees the puppy in my arms. "Oh cool. You got a dog?"

"He's my godmothers'."

Aiden sets the flowers down next to Carlitos before reaching for Goyo with both hands. Goyo sneezes right in his face.

"Sorry, little buddy," Aiden says. "Do you have allergies too?"

Carlitos wrinkles his nose. "Allergic to jer—"

I step between them before Carlitos can finish that sentence. I know he's just angry about Mr. Montgomery ruining the parade. I remember his words—*That kind of hate? It could be in Aiden's blood just like La Lechuza is in ours*—and I understand why he feels the need to put his guard up.

But watching Goyo slobber all over Aiden while he laughs, while he glances at me, brown eyes crinkled in a smile, I couldn't wall myself off if I tried.

Goyo licks Aiden's ear and Aiden laughs. "Thanks for the bath, buddy."

"His name's Goyo," Carlitos corrects him. "And maybe you need a bath because you sti—"

"So, Aiden, are you hungry?" I jump in. "Do you want some food? My abuela made a ton. Here, I'll make you a plate."

"I thought we had to wait!" Carlitos snaps.

"He's a guest," I snap back.

Carlitos throws up his hands. "We're in a public place."

Aiden looks between us before setting Goyo back in his makeshift bed. "Uh, I'm good, actually. But thanks."

"So, what brings you here?" I ask, curious.

"Yeah," Carlitos says, accusatory. "You're not Mexican."

Aiden blushes, reaching for the bouquet of pink roses again. "I just...I think it's cool, I guess." He meets my eyes. "To come here and not be sad. I'd like to learn how to do that."

Carlitos's face falls, no rude comeback for once.

"Come on." I nod to the walking path. "I'll show you."

We enter the gates and suddenly we're surrounded by music. Aiden stares at the other people painted like calaveras, at the colorful flowers pinned in their hair.

"I like your face paint," he says. "It's...really pretty."

"Thanks," I say, grateful that it hides my blushing. "My godmother Luisa can paint yours too. If you want."

"Really?" His eyes light up. "Cool."

We wind down the path, the ghosts starting to fill in, no longer just sparkling outlines. A man in an old-timey suit gives me a wink. A little girl in a beaded buckskin dress chases after a boy in a basketball uniform.

"You know, just because the people here don't seem sad doesn't mean they aren't. Remembering someone who's gone means thinking about who they were and all the things you loved about them. But remembering them also means thinking about all the things they never got to see or do. And that's hard. So it's okay to be sad."

Aiden nods. "Does it make it easier, though? Making an altar and all that. Pretending like they're coming back for a visit."

"It's not pretend," I say.

"I'm sorry." He shakes his head. "I meant, *believing*. Does it make it easier knowing that once a year you'll be connected to them again?"

"I think so. Because it reminds us that goodbyes aren't permanent. That no one's gone forever."

Aiden sniffs, squeezing the roses until I think he might break the stems.

I squeeze his other hand and I feel his excitement and unease—all jumbled together like his heart's trapped in a clunky old dryer set to tumble dry.

Then I ask, "Where is she?"

Aiden walks to the far end of the cemetery where the names on the headstones say things like Johnson and Schneider and Davies. I can feel the moment he spots Mrs. Montgomery's headstone, dread washing over him like a cold wave.

"It's okay," I say.

He nods, leading the way.

When we reach her, he can't take his eyes off his shoes, barely glancing at the words carved in the marble as he rests the roses in the grass.

Then he finally asks, "Can you see her?"

I hesitate, not sure if I should tell him the truth—that she's not here because she wasn't summoned.

Aiden breaks the silence first. "I don't feel her."

My heart aches, his grief hanging over us like a dark storm cloud.

I reach for his hand again, breathing deep as I try to keep the worst of those feelings at bay. "Do you have any old pictures of her?"

"A ton," he says. "In some photo albums under Abby's

72

bed. There's this one of her sitting under a tree, the sun hitting her face. I love looking at that one."

"What about personal stuff? Jewelry she liked to wear. Food she loved."

"Yeah, she had this locket with a family photo inside. She never took it off. Oh and she loved doughnuts. Every year for her birthday she wanted a dozen sprinkle doughnuts instead of a cake and Dad would spend twenty minutes trying to get the candles to stand up without crushing all the icing before he'd just end up holding the lit candles instead."

He smiles to himself and I try to connect the man who tried to turn a dozen sprinkle doughnuts into the perfect birthday cake with the man who doesn't believe the brown people in Noche Buena deserve to have celebrations of our own. But I can't. Maybe because that part of Mr. Montgomery died when Aiden's mom did. Or maybe it's too much work…too painful to try to see the good in someone like that. Someone who would never do the same for us.

But Aiden's different. Despite Carlitos's fears. Aiden is *good*. And I want to help him.

"Do you think you could gather those things by this afternoon?" I ask.

"I could try," Aiden says. "But what for?"

"The altars we make for Día de Muertos aren't just

decoration. The objects on them call the ghosts to this side of the veil."

"So I need to make an altar...."

I nod. "We could try. I could...help."

His eyes glisten. "Thank you."

We both turn at the sound of barking, Goyo running so fast he looks like a jackrabbit hopping between the headstones. Carlitos and Clau are chasing after him, yelling for him to stop.

When he reaches us, he finally does, snarling at the trees at the edge of the cemetery like they've grown legs. But as I stare between the branches, I notice the leaves are shivering. The trees are scared too.

"Matti?" The woman whose daughter was admiring my face paint earlier stands near Papi's truck, hands cupped around her mouth. "Matteo!"

Goyo hops up and down on all fours, barking with all his might.

I search the trees again and then I see him. A little boy barely visible behind the tangle of leaves and branches. Looking up at something big...and dark...and looking right at me.

"Matti, where are you?"

I jump to my feet, just about to wave her over, to call out Matteo's name. And then I can't move.

My throat tightens like it's clenched in someone's fist. And then they squeeze, making me gasp for air. The pressure moves its way down, something heavy pressed against my chest. Holding me still.

I glance to my left and Aiden is frozen too, his eyes drifting closed. Carlitos is just as stiff to my right. Clau circles the three of us, frantically shouting our names.

"Omega, what's wrong? Omega, can you hear me?"

I try to fight it, my heart pounding as a cold sweat drips down my face. *Move. Move, Omega.* But I can't.

I'm so...

so...

...sleepy...

"Matti, I'm going to count to three!"

When I hear Matti's mother's voice, I realize that it's just the three of us who are stuck. Because she doesn't see him, which means she doesn't see that he's not alone.

Laughter trickles out from Matti's hiding place and then the darkness that surrounds him begins to shift. Like it's made of smoke. The dark figure training its red eyes right on my face. Until I feel that same bottom-of-everything feeling I had when touching the pan de muerto this morning. Until I'm sinking into a darkness I've never known.

Suddenly, the grip on my throat tightens. I wheeze, straining for air as my vision goes blurry. I see Matti turn his back. I see him take the monster's hand. I see them walking away.

And then I don't see anything at all.

CHAPTER 6

I wake up to something warm and wet licking my face. When I open my eyes Goyo is standing over me, planting slobbery kisses all over my mouth and nose and behind my ears.

I squeal, "Goyo, stop!" before hiding under the blankets.

But that only gets him more excited, his tiny paws trying to dig me out.

"Omega...?"

At the sound of my name, I peer out of the blankets, and hovering above me are three pale, almost translucent faces, their sparkling bodies flickering in and out like loose light bulbs.

"Maybe she doesn't remember us."

"Of course she remembers us. It's only been four years."

"Which is only three hundred and sixty-five days in human time."

"Exactly."

"But she looks scared."

"Maybe that's because you're hovering too close to her face!"

I match the voices to the objects from the ofrenda, realizing their ghosts must have finally crossed over.

I sit up. "Hi, Tío Arthur. Bisabuela Ynez." I give a wave. "Ana."

Ana squeals. "I knew you'd remember!"

Goyo barks at the sound.

"Ay, there you are!" Abuela scoops him up and he latches onto her glasses chain, yanking hard. "Ouch!" She snaps her fingers and suddenly Goyo goes still.

"We looked for you at the cemetery but everyone had already gone home," Tío Arthur says. "Then we came back here and the adults filled us in. Sounds like it's been a pretty eventful day."

Abuela sets Goyo down on the bed again and he curls up in a ball in my lap. I stroke his fur and am instantly filled with calm.

"Extremely eventful, which is why Omega needs her rest."

"Of course," Bisabuela Ynez says before dragging Ana and Tío Arthur back toward the hallway.

"Feel better, Omega," Ana calls.

Abuela sits at the foot of the bed. "I need to hear what you saw, Omega."

I keep petting Goyo, trying to keep the fear at bay. But it ripples through me again as I say, "A monster."

"The others said Matti wandered off into the trees. That they were frozen and couldn't go after him. They didn't mention a monster."

I remember that first thunderstorm after Luna arrived in Noche Buena—seeing her in the rain on our way home from the doctor's office; seeing her face lit up by the lightning outside my bedroom window. Both times I was the only witness.

"Luna said I'm different from other empaths. That I can control the emotions of magical creatures." I meet Abuela's eyes, searching for secrets. What she said to Carlitos. How she really feels about me. "Is that true?"

Abuela brushes my hair out of my face, her brow furrowed with concern. In her touch, I search for the things I fear most—panic, rejection, disgust. But her guard is up, not letting me read her. Still not telling me the truth.

"We're not sure about that," she finally says, as if she's still wary of Luna's warning, despite the fact that she gave the same warning to Carlitos. But choosing not to believe something doesn't make it not true.

"Abuela, I need to know more about what's happening to me. What I can do." *Because the moon is still whispering to me*, I think. *Because even though Luna is herself again, I'm still scared.*

Abuela squeezes my hand. "I know. We promised you kids no more secrets and we meant it. But this time, the mystery is you. It's going to take some time to unravel." She notices the fear in my eyes and pulls me close. "You're safe, Omega. You're loved. No te preocupes."

I nod, noticing the wall between us finally starting to crack, letting the love filter through until it's wrapping around me like a warm blanket.

"Can you describe it to me?" she asks. "What you saw?"

My throat clenches and I remember the way it held me there, staring. But instead of telling Abuela what I saw, I climb out of bed and grab a pen and notebook from my backpack. I flip to a clean page and then I start to draw, shading in the long shadowy cloak, the wisps of smoke. The beady red eyes.

When I'm done, I carry the drawing over to her, letting her see.

Her eyes widen. "*This* is what you saw?"

I exhale. "That's the thing that took Matti."

She's quiet.

"Is it dangerous, Abuela?"

She folds the sheet of paper. "Soona had her suspicions.

This drawing will help her narrow it down. Until then, yes, we have to assume it's dangerous."

My heart pounds, thinking about Matti. How all I could do was watch. "I tried to help him," I say, remembering the worry in his mother's voice. "I tried to move but I couldn't."

Abuela squeezes my knee. "It's not your fault, Omega. And we're going to get him back. Don't worry." She stands. "In the meantime, your mother and Luisa would like to take you somewhere special."

I raise an eyebrow. "Special?"

"Yes. So special in fact that it took us quite a bit of convincing." She tosses me my shoes. "So we need to hurry before your mother changes her mind."

La pulga is usually bustling in the afternoon, kids racing between the vendor stalls after getting off the school bus down the street, workers in need of an afternoon snack stopping by for bags of watermelon in lime juice and Tajín from Flaco's Fruit Truck, or churros drizzled with honey from Mack Green's Beehive in stall eight, or chili dogs topped with queso and Hot Cheetos from the Aguilars in stall nine.

But the parking lot's mostly empty, people staring down

at their cell phones instead of browsing the tables of ceramics and crates of old records.

"¡Ay Dios!" Señora Cantu, who sells bedazzled cowboy boots, rushes over to us as if she's relieved to see me. "Have you heard?"

"Heard what?" Luisa asks.

"Simon. The Carrillos' boy. He's gone missing too."

"From the cemetery?" Mami asks.

"No. They hadn't made it to the cemetery yet. The boy was playing outside, waiting for the rest of the family to finish loading up the truck with the food. Mrs. Carrillo says she barely took her eyes off him. Swears he was only alone for a second. That was all it took." Then Señora Cantu takes my hand, holding it tight. "You stay with your mother, you hear me? You don't leave her side."

"Yes, Señora."

Señora Cantu throws on a shawl before reaching for the door above her stall. "I'm closing early for the day. I suspect most others will as well."

"Gracias, Señora." Mami nudges me forward. "That means we better hurry."

We pass the inflatable cartoon characters before taking a left at the handmade leather purses and then a right at the airbrushed T-shirts and novelty key chains (there's never one with *Omega* on it). Finally, we reach stall number nineteen where they keep the cobijas—the biggest, softest blankets you've ever seen, each one printed with a giant cat of your choosing. Panthers. Tigers. Lions.

When I turned nine, Tío Juan got me a dark green cobija with a white tiger in the center. It's too hot to use it most of the year, which is why it's currently folded up at the bottom of my closet (also to muffle the purring). But in a few weeks I'll be dragging it all around the house and wearing it like a giant cape to school.

But I don't understand. Why would Mami need convincing to get me another cobija?

"Can I help you find something?" An old woman with a hunched back motions to the cobijas hanging from a turnstile.

"Yes," Mami says. "We're looking for the one with green eyes."

The old woman smiles. "I know just the one." Then she heaves the turnstile, pulling forth a dark red cobija with an alebrije printed on it.

It's a coyote with the dark blue tail of a peacock and giant bunny ears. Its lower half looks like it's covered in scales while its chest is covered in thick gray fur. And its eyes—they're bright green.

But instead of pulling the cobija down from the turnstile, Mami pulls back the corner of the blanket like she's pulling back a curtain, and there on the other side of the fabric is another row of stalls. Another flea market.

The old lady gives me a wink. "You have fun."

I follow Mami and Luisa through the portal, still just as confused as I was when Abuela first mentioned the surprise.

Unlike the flea market we've just left behind, this one *is* bustling—children in line for candy and pan dulce, old women swaying to music as they try on colorful jewelry. There's a stall full of piñatas, the papier-mâché burros braying as we pass by. Clay figurines dance on tabletops while children's toys come to life.

"Will you please tell me what's going on?" I ask.

Only then does Mami speak. "This connection you have with supernatural creatures…we're still trying to understand it. But it's obvious that the energy doesn't just flow one way. They're more sensitive to you and you to them."

"Is this about me passing out at the cemetery?" I ask.

"You need protection, Omega."

My throat goes dry. "From the thing that took Matteo?"

Mami looks to Luisa before turning to gaze out the window of the nearest stall. "And any other monsters that might begin finding their way to Noche Buena."

I shudder. "Wait. You think they're coming here… because of me?"

Mami sighs. "We're not sure yet. But it's possible. And if that's the case, then we need to be prepared."

"That's why we're here?" I glance around again. "What is this place? It feels like el Otro Lado."

"It is el Otro Lado," Luisa says. "Well, specifically the southern region, which is why we needed to enter from la pulga instead of the library."

"What's in the southern region of el Otro Lado?" I ask.

Luisa smiles wide, beckoning me to the same window Mami had been gazing out of earlier. Then she says, "This…"

I peer out and the sky is stuck in a permanent sunset, clouds as big as mountains resting like whipped cream over rolling

green hills. And running through the waist-high grass are creatures of every color of the rainbow. Big and small. Beaked, winged, fanged, clawed. Wild and beautiful. Alebrijes just like the one on the cobija that led us here.

That's when my heart starts to race.

Because suddenly I know why Mami needed so much convincing.

I can't help but squeal, "You're getting me a pet?!"

Mami clamps a hand down over my mouth, shushing me, laughing too. Then she's suddenly serious again, launching into a long speech about maturity and responsibility and how I'm not getting a pet because I deserve one (what with all the recent lying and going behind her back) but because I need protection, which is yet another reason why I need to be more cautious and dependable and—

"Okay, Mami, I get it," I groan.

She looks at me, concerned. "Do you? Because there's a lot at stake if you don't."

And in her eyes I see the same fear that was on Matteo's mother's face. The same fear Señora Cantu had when she told us another child had been taken.

"Mami, I understand. And I promise I will be responsible. I'll prove it," I say. "I'll prove that you can trust me."

She gives me a soft smile. "Okay. Starting now."

"Is that Blanca Caamal I see?" A man in a pair of bright

red cowboy boots with silver rhinestones on the sides saunters over to us.

"I'm married now, primo." Mami sighs, smiling. "You were at the wedding, remember?"

"Excuse me, *Mrs. Morales*. And of course I remember. How could I forget not being asked to be your man of honor?"

Mami wags a finger. "That was between you and Tita and if I recall you two settled it in an arm-wrestling match. She won fair and square."

He laughs. "Uh, there was no fair and the only thing square was that hideous dress you shoved her in."

"Listen, Porfirio," Luisa jumps in. "We're just here to get a companion for Blanca's daughter."

"That's right." Mami shoves me forward. "Po, this is my daughter, Omega. Omega, this is Po."

"Hi," I say. "Are we really cousins?"

He looks me up and down. "*Just* cousins, because not only was I not good enough to be man of honor at your mother's wedding but I also wasn't good enough to be your godfather."

Luisa frowns. "Oh, Po, don't be like that...."

Mami crosses her arms. "Especially when you're the one who suggested yet *another* arm-wrestling match. Again, Soona won fair and square."

He rolls his eyes. "Fine. That's enough rehashing the past, I suppose." He looks at me. "You said you're here for a companion?"

I can't help but squeal again.

He smiles. "Well then, follow me."

Po leads us beneath a sign that says PORFIRIO'S PET SHOP. Inside, well, there is no inside. The entryway opens to a field of green and those same rolling hills I saw from the window. It looks like a safari, alebrijes roaming free while guides wearing cowboy boots and carrying backpacks full of sugar cubes lead families down the walking path.

"What type of companion are we looking for exactly?" Po asks.

"Something with good instincts," Mami says.

"A protector..." Po scratches his chin, thinking.

A pink pony with claws like an eagle trots by, tossing its rainbow-colored mane.

"What about that one?" I plead.

"Ah"—Po nods—"el poni. She's a feisty one."

Po snaps a finger, manifesting a shiny red apple in the palm of his hand. The poni sniffs at it before taking the whole thing in her mouth. Then she nips at Po, asking for more.

Po clicks his teeth, sending the poni on its way. "Still trying to break her biting habit."

"No biting," Mami says.

"Not to mention, the bigger they are, the harder they are to glamour," Luisa adds.

"Glamour?" I ask.

"It means to hide using magic," Luisa says. "We'll need to cast a spell so that anytime it ventures out of the house it's invisible. Well, to everyone but us."

"Exactly," Mami says. "So no show ponies. We need something more discreet, which is why we're doing this the old-fashioned way."

"Are you sure? I know the best breeders in all of el Otro Lado." Po shrugs. "And these days the ancestors are hit or miss."

Mami narrows her eyes at him. "The ancestors never miss."

He throws up his hands. "Fine. But if you end up with a firebreather that burns your whole house down, don't say I didn't warn you."

Po leads us to a big white barn, the floor covered in straw, and nestled in the hay are hundreds of tiny golden eggs.

"Are these alebrijes?" I ask.

"They are." Po motions down the path. "On the right we've got your—"

"I said no sales pitch, Po." Mami comes up behind me, squeezing my shoulders. "She's going to find it on her own."

I look back at her. "But how?"

She presses a hand to my heart. "With this." She faces me toward the rows and rows of eggs again. "Now, remember why we're here."

"For protection," I say, a shiver racing down my spine, "for *me*..."

"That's right. So I want you to imagine what that feels like and then find that same feeling, reflected back at you."

"Like when your papi and Soona take you kids fishing," Luisa adds. "Throw out a line and when you feel a tug, reel it in."

"Reel it in." I nod. "Got it."

I let out a deep breath, focusing on the quiet, and then on why we're here. *Protection.* I chant the word in my mind like when I was trying to keep myself from getting lost in the library. Except this time it's not Clau or La Lechuza I'm searching for, it's a magical alebrije created by my ancestors just for me.

I hear the quiet rustling of the hay as the breeze blows in. I hear pebbles crunching under Po's boots. I hear the beating of my own heart. *Tha-thump tha-thump.*

But no nibbles. Nothing tugging me in one direction or another.

"Trust yourself," Mami whispers.

It's the second time someone's put my empathic abilities

to the test today. The first was when Soona asked me if the monster that slipped into our house in the middle of the night and took a bite out of the pan de muerto was evil or not.

I second-guessed myself then and I'm doing it again now.

Then I remember what Mami said a few moments ago to Po: *The ancestors never miss.*

So even though I'm still learning to trust myself, I know without a doubt that whichever egg I choose will be the right one.

Finally, I take a step, suddenly feeling that tug Luisa talked about. The faintest nudge. And then I'm caught up in some invisible current, my body floating down a river I can't see. Until I stop in front of a golden egg with tiny blue freckles, the specks reminding me of the Little Dipper.

Stardust, Abuela had whispered in my ear at the cemetery. *From whence we all came.*

I kneel down to scoop up the egg, gently holding it in my palms. Inside, something wiggles, the egg almost rolling onto the ground.

"Careful," Mami says, peering over my shoulder. "Before it can protect you, you have to protect it first."

CHAPTER 7

"So now we just...wait?" Clau peers over my shoulder at the egg.

It's gently cradled in a nest I made out of an empty shoebox and some dish towels.

I shrug. "I guess so."

"Hello?" Carlitos taps the shell. "Wake up!"

"Hey!" I swat at him. "You could break it."

"And you have no idea what it's going to look like?" Clau asks.

I stare at the blue specks again—the Little Dipper—and shake my head. "It's a surprise. But Mami says the ancestors never miss."

"What does that mean?" Carlitos asks.

"I think it means that we can trust them. That they know us better than we know ourselves."

"They don't look all that wise." Carlitos motions over his shoulder where the ghosts of our relatives are currently floating around the kitchen table, animatedly telling stories as if we haven't seen them in centuries, even though for us it's only been a single turn around the sun.

"…and then I felt a tug on my swim trunks." The ghost of Tío Arthur tosses his head back, laughing so hard he's wheezing. "And then I'm drifting toward the shore while Tacho is yelling that he's caught the biggest fish in the entire lake." He slaps his knee, guffawing. "So I let him reel me in. Even when I'm right under his nose, he's still convinced. Still yelling and waving, wanting an audience. Then when he reaches for the line with his hand, I reach back, pulling him into the water with me! ¡El chapoteo! He never saw it coming!"

The adults burst into laughter, Papi banging the kitchen table while Tío Juan throws his head back so hard his back cracks.

Carlitos rolls his eyes. "We've heard that story like fifty times. It's not even funny anymore."

Clau snorts, laughing as hard as the adults. "It's *pretty* funny."

"Maybe if you're missing a few brain cells."

"Takes one to know one," Clau shoots back.

"Or maybe that's just what families do when they haven't seen each other in a long time," I say. "Tell old stories that you basically already have memorized just so you can feel what you felt the first time you heard them."

"I guess Tío Arthur's story about getting into that bar fight in El Paso and losing his two front teeth hasn't gotten old." Carlitos laughs. "Remember when he got so into it that he knocked his own bow tie off the ofrenda and then he vanished?"

"Oh yeah," I laugh, "so Abuela put it back but then every time he said something she didn't like she *accidentally* knocked it on the floor again."

Carlitos's eyes water. "She kept cutting him off mid-sentence."

"Wait," Clau says, "so leaving him stuck on the other side was just a joke?" She leaps up. "What about all the people who don't get their objects placed on some ofrenda? Who *can't* cross over?"

Clau's lip quivers and the longer she stares at Tío Arthur the more obvious it becomes that she's thinking about her parents. At the stories they're *not* getting to tell. The laughter they're missing out on. The reunion she doesn't get to have because there's nothing fun about reliving memories alone. Especially sad ones, which for Clau, are mostly all that's left.

"We're sorry, Clau." I scooch closer to her. "We should be more sensitive."

She frowns. "Maybe I'm being *too* sensitive right now." She motions to the ofrenda. "It's just that your abuela said Día de Muertos is a party and today has felt like anything but. The parade got canceled and then some mysterious monster snatched a little boy from the cemetery. You fainted and now we're basically grounded again even though we didn't do anything wrong. And my parents...they're not here. Even though I knew it would be a long shot, I still hoped, you know?"

"Hey"—I reach for her—"who says the party's over?"

"Yeah," Carlitos jumps in, "there's still plenty of food. All we need is some good music."

A small smile creeps onto Clau's face. "Do I get to pick the song?"

I smile back. "You get to DJ the *entire* thing."

She squeals.

A moment later, the disc on Abuelo's old record player begins to turn, igniting the sound of a woman's voice. It's not Clau's usual style—no heavy bass or drums—but she sways, smiling to herself.

"My parents liked this song," she says.

That's when I realize the adults are quiet, listening too.

"They had excellent taste," Abuela calls from the kitchen.

Papi reaches out a hand to Mami before pulling her into an embrace. Then they dance, turning in slow circles around the kitchen table. Tío Juan and Tía Tita join hands next. Abuelo tries to get Abuela to join him on the make-shift dance floor but she's too busy making dinner so he scoops up Chale instead. Soon everyone is swaying and singing along. And without saying a single word, Clau tells us a story about her parents. About who they were. About how they loved.

And even though it's not the same as meeting them, it feels like I know them. Like I know what it must feel like for Clau to be loved by them.

Clau takes Carlitos and me each by the hand, turning us in circles. I laugh while Carlitos tries not to trip over his feet. He blushes when Clau tells him he's a good dancer. Even Goyo jumps onto his hind legs, tongue lolling as he turns in circles too.

Out of the corner of my eye I see Chale break away from Abuelo and then suddenly he's busting through our clasped hands.

"Me next!" he yells, trying to get Carlitos's attention like he has been all day.

Carlitos shoves him. "Dance over there."

Chale throws his body against Carlitos, then me, like he's jumping up and down in a bounce house. But we're not inflatable, Chale's tiny light-up sneakers stomping all over my bare feet.

I wince. "Careful, Chale."

And then Goyo squeals, caught under Chale's heel as he leaps onto the couch.

Carlitos reaches for Goyo, checking his paw, and then he turns to Chale, red-faced, and yells, "What is wrong with you?"

"Mijo." Tía Tita raises an eyebrow at Carlitos, a warning to watch his tone.

Chale clenches his tiny fists and then he runs straight for the ofrenda, knocking the objects off the altar.

Bisabuela Ynez gasps as Tío Arthur disappears. I lunge for her tube of lipstick to keep her from disappearing too.

Carlitos grabs Chale by the arm and Chale draws back his foot, kicking Carlitos in the shin.

"¡Ay Dios!" Tía Tita pulls Chale away.

Tío Juan grabs Tío Arthur's bow tie and places it back on the ofrenda, Tío Arthur reappearing in an icy whoosh.

"Whoa," he says, holding his head like he's dizzy. "What did I miss?"

Nobody answers him. We're all still staring at Carlitos who's staring right at Chale.

Then, in a strained voice that sounds like a stranger's, Carlitos says, "I wish...I wish you were never born!"

At that, Tía Tita stares at him, shaking her head like she can't believe what just came out of his mouth.

Carlitos goes pale like he can't believe it either.

"Well, looks like someone's overdue for a nap," Tío Juan says, breaking the awkward silence.

I wait for Tía Tita to say something next. To threaten Carlitos with her chancla. To ground him on the spot. But she doesn't. Instead, she just looks at him, long and hard. Her lip trembles and she bites down on it. Then she shakes her head and turns to go, dragging Chale behind her. Tío Juan swipes his keys from the kitchen table before following without a word.

The second the door slams closed behind them, it's like my ears readjust to reality, the music filtering back in. But no one feels like dancing anymore.

"I didn't...," Carlitos starts, his cheeks burning red.

"Hey..." Tío Arthur floats over to us. "We all say things we don't mean sometimes."

"Nothing an apology won't fix," Bisabuela Ynez adds.

"You're not wrong though," Ana says, eyeing Papi from across the room. "Brothers can be the absolute worst sometimes."

"Not helping," Tío Arthur says.

Clau flicks her wrist, turning down the music, but just as the trumpets reach a crescendo, the phone rings. Louder than I've ever heard it. Or maybe it just seems that way because of the look on Mami's face. Because of the way Papi wrings his hands, staring at it. Because suddenly we all remember.

Matteo.

Simon.

Clau flicks her wrist again, cutting the music.

Mami takes the phone off the hook, pressing it to her ear. "¿Mande?"

The voices on the other side are muffled. Frantic.

Mami presses a hand to the wall like she can barely hold herself up. "Gracias, señora." She hangs up the phone.

Papi reaches for her. "What is it, Blanca?"

Mami looks at the three of us and even from across the room I feel her fear like a live wire. "Carmen's girl. Pia. She was playing alone in her room. When they went to check on her, she was gone."

My knees quake like the ground is giving way beneath me. The whole world filling with fault lines. Sinkholes ready to swallow me whole.

That's when the sound of an engine pulls my gaze, car doors slamming shut outside. Still on edge, Mami rushes to the door before our visitors have even had a chance to knock.

Behind the screen is Deputy Medina, signature goofy

smile on his face. As if he didn't just shut down our parade this morning. As if there's not a serial kidnapper on the loose. But the more closely I examine him, noticing the way he's tapping his fingers against his shiny black belt, the more I realize that he's nervous.

Then I see why.

Next to him, the new sheriff towers over everyone in his big black boots and big black cowboy hat. He peers at us from beneath the brim, his face pale, his eyes as hard as stone. This close up he's giant. Like a tree that's carved itself into a man.

After a moment he catches me staring. He winks.

"Hi, can I help you?" Mami joins them on the porch.

"Hi there, Mrs. Morales." Deputy Medina blushes. He's always had a crush on Mami.

Mami crosses her arms, unamused.

"Look, uh, I don't know if you've heard but this situation with the missing kids is escalating. We've got an investigation underway, starting with Matteo. We got word that your kids may have been the last to see him. If that's the case, we'd love to ask them a few questions."

Mami's arms are still crossed. She glances back at us, her eyes full of warning. To tell the truth. But not all of it.

Then she pushes open the screen door and says, "Come on in."

Deputy Medina makes his way over to where Carlitos and I are sitting on the couch. When Goyo senses him getting a little too close, he starts to yip and gnash his teeth. Luisa quickly scoops him up and out of the way before Deputy Medina slumps down into Abuelo's recliner.

"Cute dog," he says, that nervous smile still stuck to his face. "Does he bite?"

"Hard," Carlitos says, stone-faced.

Deputy Medina clears his throat. "Listen, kids." He sounds like he's going to launch into another safety training. "We're working really hard to try to find Matteo and the others."

"Simon," Carlitos says.

"And Pia," I add.

"Right." Deputy Medina frowns. "Matteo, Simon, and Pia. Their parents are really worried about them. I'm sure you can imagine. And so, if it's all right with you, we just wanted to stop by to—"

"What did he look like?" the sheriff interrupts, his gravelly voice making the hairs on my arms stand up. It's deep, like the words are forcing their way out through mud.

Even Deputy Medina sits silent.

Carlitos speaks first. "I didn't see anyone with Matteo."

He's telling the truth, like Mami expects us to. But it's not the whole truth. He doesn't mention that we were stuck, unable to move. He doesn't mention that I passed out. That something powerful overwhelmed me.

And I don't either.

When the sheriff's dark gaze falls on me, waiting for me to speak, my throat goes dry.

"You," he says. "You saw something...."

It doesn't sound like a question.

It sounds like *he knows*.

"Excuse me." Mami comes over, standing beside me. "They said they didn't see anything." She turns to Deputy Medina. "If they had, we would have called right away. You know as much as we do."

"Of course." Deputy Medina stands.

And then I hear a faint crack.

I look down at the alebrije egg, still nestled in the bed of old dish towels I made, and I see a long, jagged line across the shell. That's when I remember that the glamour Luisa put on it only works outside the house. My heart leaps into my throat.

"Is that thing about to hatch?" Deputy Medina's eyes light up. "What is it exactly? Doesn't look like a chicken egg. Maybe quail? Or a turtle?"

I nod, slow. "Yeah, uh, a tor, tur—"

"Turkey," Carlitos cuts in.

"Wow." Deputy Medina cocks his head. "I've never seen

a turkey egg before." He pulls out his cell phone. "Can I take a video?"

There's another crack, a small piece of shell falling away. This time I lock eyes with Mami.

"You know what? You two are probably in a hurry." Mami tries waving them toward the door. "The cemetery was packed this morning. Lots of people to interview. So you should probably—"

"Whoa, I think I see the beak!" Deputy Medina's already pressed record.

My heart pounds in my chest.

Suddenly, Clau flexes her fingers, her stare hard on Deputy Medina's phone. The screen flickers and then it goes black.

He presses the glass, groaning. "Dang it. Battery just died."

That's when Mami gives me a small pinch. I jump to my feet, taking her silent instructions and running out back with the shoebox.

Abuelo is waiting, wearing a face mask and holding a catcher's mitt.

The egg splits open.

I hear the front door swing closed, followed

by Deputy Medina's and the new sheriff's footsteps down the porch steps.

The alebrije's head pops through, pink and wrinkly, its eyes still pinched shut.

A car engine starts.

And then the alebrije leaps from the egg and fires like a rocket straight into Abuelo's glove. He tumbles back with a groan and we race over to him.

"Abuelo, are you okay?"

He throws off the mask, letting out a deep belly laugh, and then he holds out the catcher's mitt. In his palm sits the alebrije—part jackalope, part snow leopard—with bright purple eyes and fur so thick it looks like snow.

And giant turquoise wings just like an owl's.

CHAPTER 8

THE ALEBRIJE RAISES ITS TINY HEAD, ANTLERS too heavy and making it wobble. It blinks, taking in our faces, and then it sneezes, rolling back into Abuelo's glove.

Carlitos wrinkles his nose. "You're telling me this puny thing is supposed to protect you?"

The alebrije sits up again, sniffing at the air. Then comes another sneeze.

Carlitos turns to me. "That's the sissiest sneeze I've ever heard."

The alebrije stretches its neck, still sniffing, and then it roars, breathing fire.

We all jump back.

Abuelo laughs. "Every alebrije has at least three out of the four elements."

"So, what are the other two?" Carlitos asks, still keeping his distance.

"Wind, obviously," Clau says, "because of the wings."

I examine the alebrije more closely, searching for gills or webbed feet. Proof her third element is water or maybe earth. But there's nothing I can see. "Maybe the third one's a secret?" I say.

"A secret that will be revealed when you need it most," Abuelo says.

The alebrije begins to purr, rubbing against Abuelo's hand.

He beckons me closer. "Here. Introduce yourself."

I reach out a hand to her, her eyes wide as she takes me in. "Hi, I'm Omega."

She brushes against me and her fur is like butter, even softer than the cobija at the bottom of my closet. She purrs, the gentle vibrations tickling my skin.

"What are you going to name her?" Clau asks.

I look into her purple eyes, sparkling like jewels. "I'm not sure yet."

"What about Snowflake!" Clau offers.

"Snowflake?" Carlitos rolls his eyes. "When was the last time you even saw a snowflake? We live in, like, the hottest place on earth."

"You got any better ideas?" Clau shoots back.

"Tiffany."

Clau and I exchange a look.

"Tiffany?" Clau laughs.

"What?" Carlitos frowns. "It's a nice name. A normal name."

"You mean a boring name," Clau shoots back. "It's an alebrije. Not a substitute teacher. How many Tiffanys do you know with wings and purple eyes?"

While Carlitos and Clau keep arguing, I just keep staring at her. At the way the sunlight glistens against her turquoise metallic wings. At the tiny freckles on the bridge of her snout. Her bright pink paw pads and long floppy ears.

And I just keep thinking—*she's mine*.

She hops up on her hind legs, licking my face, like she knows it too. That whoever I am, we belong to each other now.

"Did you hear me, Omega?" Clau waves a hand in front of my face. "What about Periwinkle? To match her eyes."

"Tiffany's still better."

"Uh..." I shake my head, unsure.

"Maybe you should get to know her first," Abuelo offers, handing me the catcher's mitt.

"Yeah," I say. "I think that's a good idea."

Suddenly, the alebrije tumbles from my grasp but just before she hits the ground, her wings snap open. She lowers slowly, feet grazing the grass, before hopping and stretching her wings, as impressed by them as we are.

"Uh-oh," Carlitos says. "She's on the move."

"Here, girl." I try to lure her back. "This way."

But before I can snatch her by the tail, she bolts, running past the chicken coop and Abuelo's shed.

Straight for the trees, vanishing just like Matteo did.

"Stop!" I race after her. "Come back!"

"I told you she needed a name," Clau says, floating alongside me.

"Can you catch up to her?" I ask.

Clau winks and then she's gone in a flash, her silhouette guiding the rest of us through the shadows. It's already starting to get dark, the sun setting in a purple haze, and I pray we catch the alebrije before night falls.

The ancestors never miss.

I remember what Mami said before I made my choice. That it was fated. That the alebrije and I would be connected by some invisible thread, that I would feel it between us, leading me straight to her.

I slow my breathing, concentrating like Soona and Mami have been teaching me to do, and I try to feel that thread again. To reach for her.

Stop. Come back to me.

Up ahead, Clau slows down. Then the rest of us do too.

But as we step into the small clearing, Abuelo clicking on a flashlight so we can see, I realize the alebrije didn't stop because I told her to. She stopped because she found something.

Tail straight up, snout to the ground, she sniffs at a pile of leaves. Then she paws at them, like she's looking for something. I kneel next to her and she boops me on the nose before pawing at the ground some more. Trying to tell me: *Look. Look here.*

"What is it?" Carlitos asks.

"I don't know."

Abuelo shines the light on the leaves as I sift through them and then I feel something cold. Plastic.

But that's not all I feel. I also feel...*joy*. Sticky and sweet like Abuela's cajeta.

Except there's something strange about it. Like...if I were to bite into that piece of caramel there would be something hard and bitter inside. Something rotten.

Just like the pan de muerto.

"El Pitón," Carlitos says. "He's a superhero character."

I brush off the dirt before turning the small toy snake man over in my hand. Then I squeeze and behind my eyes I see Matteo, a big smile on his face. I see his hands—one holding El Pitón and the other holding on to the shadow figure, tiny fingers clutching tight. Like he can't let go. Like he doesn't want to.

My heart races, the monster's face partially coming into view. But it's hidden in shadow and all I can make out is the smoke billowing from its open mouth, twisting between sharp black teeth. But Matteo isn't afraid. He's giggling, their linked arms swinging. Like he's in some sort of a trance.

But I see the truth and it grips me like a bad dream. Cotton candy and stagnant water. Bubble gum and weevils. I feel them crawling all over me like I'm the sugary thing they're trying to devour.

I try to toss the toy but my grip won't loosen.

Wake up! Snap out of it, Omega!

But I'm trapped. Frozen and staring at Matteo's memories like when I watched him being taken the first time. Unable to move. To even blink.

Omega! Wake up!

Suddenly, I feel the alebrije's warm kisses, her head nuzzling my face and purring loud until it's the only sound I hear. My fingers twitch, barely moving, and then my hand lifts, stroking her soft fur. The more I pet her, the easier it is to breathe, until the vision lets go of me and I can finally move again.

When I open my eyes the first thing I see is Abuelo.

He wraps his arms around me. "You're safe."

"What happened?" Carlitos asks.

"I saw it take Matteo."

"Again?" Clau says.

I nod. "Except I saw everything this time. I saw...that he wasn't scared."

"What do you mean he wasn't scared?"

"I mean he went willingly. He thought they were playing some kind of game."

"A game...?" Carlitos shakes his head. "But what kind of monster likes to play games?"

As we race up the back porch to tell the adults what we found, I see Luisa through the screen, stomping around the room and grabbing her things. We push through the door and I sense her worry like static, the air thick with it.

"I'm going to look for her," Luisa says. "It's been too long."

Abuela tries to calm her. "Luisa, she can take care of herself. You should stay here with us until—"

"Something's *wrong*." Luisa shakes her head, on the verge of tears. "I can *feel* it."

Luisa's not an empath like the rest of us but the look on her face reminds me of Mami's when she's waiting by the phone because Papi's late for dinner, her brow furrowed, her eyes trained on a thought she's too afraid to say out loud. Luisa vibrates with that same sense. Like the strings between her heart and Soona's are growing taut the farther Soona drifts away.

Luisa presses a finger to her temple. "I shouldn't have let her go alone."

"I thought Soona was just going to the library," I say.

Mami takes a step closer. "Luisa…?"

"She did go to the library." Luisa looks down. "And then she called me. She said she had a hunch. That she was going to look one more place."

"What kind of hunch?" Abuela asks.

"Did Soona know…?" I ask, interrupting. "Did she know how the monster likes to play games?"

Luisa meets my eyes. She's breathless.

"That was her hunch," Mami says, "wasn't it?"

Abuela's face hardens. "If Soona knew about the monster playing games, there's only one place she would have gone."

Mami brings a hand to her chin. "And if she stepped through that door alone…"

Luisa's lip trembles. "I have to go to her."

"Is Soona okay?" I feel myself shaking too.

Abuela turns to Luisa then Mami and I can tell she's wrestling with whether or not to tell us the truth. Just like she did with La Lechuza. Because she was scared. I can tell by the way she's twisting the rag in her hand that she's scared now too.

But so am I, and being kept in the dark only makes it worse.

"You promised," I remind her. "You promised no more lies."

"We did." Abuela sighs. "But the truth is...we don't know. If Soona was still in the library, time wouldn't be ticking forward like it has been. She'd be back by now. But if she left the library—"

"You said something about a door," I add. "What kind of door? Where does it lead?"

Mami rests her hands on my shoulders, trying to calm me the same way Abuela was trying to calm Luisa. "Do you remember the turnstile of cobijas at the flea market?"

I nod. "One of them was special. It led us to el Otro Lado."

"That's right," Mami says. "And there are doors like that all over Noche Buena. All over the world, even. Including in Soona's library."

"What does that have to do with the monster?" Carlitos asks.

"Some monsters are more mischievous than others," Abuela says. "They like playing tricks. Games. As if hunting alone is not enough. They have to turn it into some kind of sport. Which means that any books about them in the library will be playing games too. Hiding behind riddles and elaborate traps."

"Is that where you think Soona is?" I swallow and it feels like glass. "Trapped?"

Abuela doesn't answer, probably afraid of telling another lie.

That Soona's okay. That she's safe. Because I can tell by the look on Luisa's face that she's not so sure.

"I'll find her." Luisa squeezes my hand. "That's what I know."

In her touch, I feel her certainty. I try to let it fill me too.

"In the meantime, I need you to do as the adults say and stay here where it's safe," she says. "Can you promise me that?"

Clau, Carlitos, and I nod.

"And one more thing." She hands Goyo to Carlitos, Goyo's tiny legs kicking with excitement. "I need you to look after him while I'm gone, okay?"

"I'll keep him safe," Carlitos says.

Luisa gives Goyo one last scratch behind the ear and then she disappears through the screen door while the rest of us watch, hoping that she's right. That she'll find her.

Before I can ask a million more questions, Abuela claps her hands and says, "Necesitamos una limpia."

After we build a little nest for the alebrije in Mami and Papi's bathtub and she finally dozes off to sleep, we're shoved outside again, along with Papi who's been tasked with picking bright red apples from the tree next to the chicken coop. We stoop next to him, picking chokecherries and catching them in the hem of our shirts. I hear Abuela call for Mami to gather the sage. Abuelo busies himself grabbing vials of holy water. Goyo runs in circles in the grass.

"Shouldn't y'all be gathering, like, soap and bleach and stuff like that?" Clau asks.

"It's not that kind of limpia," I say. "It's to cleanse the house of bad energy and to protect us from any of that bad energy getting inside."

"And how dirty are you getting to need bleach?" Carlitos gags.

"Your breath could use some," Clau shoots back.

"Your feet could use some."

"Your butt!"

"Your face!"

"Your face that looks like your butt!"

"Your butt that looks like your face!"

"Stop it!" I step between them. "We're supposed to be getting rid of negative energy, not creating more."

Clau wrinkles her nose, another mean quip on the edge of her tongue. Instead of hurling it at Carlitos, she asks, "What are the chokecherries for? Do the evil spirits choke on them or something?"

"Abuela used to tell us that eating too many chokecherries could make a person lose their voice. She's been selling them to Señora Delarosa's potions shop for years. But today we just need them for the color."

"Does the color red have special powers?" Clau asks.

"We mark the windows and doors with red crosses."

"Yeah," Carlitos adds, "and it's either chokecherries or our own blood."

"Yikes!" Clau says. "And the monsters don't know the difference?"

I shrug. "I guess not."

"So they're not that bright." Clau taps her chin. "Maybe that's good news, though. If one of them's got ahold of Soona, escaping them should be a breeze, right?"

"If she's even been taken by monsters in the first place," I remind her. "You heard the adults. They're not sure where she is."

And I don't want to think the worst. *Not yet.*

"But it's definitely not somewhere good," Carlitos adds.

"The best thing we can do," Papi calls down to us from his ladder, "is wait and try not to worry. You know the women in this family are nothing to trifle with."

"Yeah." I exhale. "And Soona's the strongest of all."

Papi laughs. "Don't let your mother hear you say that. Or Abuela. Or Luisa for that matter." Papi tosses me a bright shiny apple. "And never forget that you're strong too." He tosses one to Carlitos next. "Both of you."

"If we're so strong," Carlitos says, "then shouldn't we be out there hunting that thing? Not just sealing ourselves inside the house with spells until the monster gets bored and decides to go terrorize the next town?"

Papi climbs down from the ladder. "Strength can look like all kinds of things. It can look like patience. Like planning." He takes a big bite out of one of the apples. "Today, strength means doing what your abuela says. That's how you play your part."

"But it's so boring." Papi's little sister, Ana, suddenly appears, twisting her cold ghost body around each of us before pretending to faint. "Can't you do anything cooler with your powers than mashing up a bunch of berries?"

"Well…" Clau bats her eyelashes. "I can summon Omega's one true love."

My face screams red and I'm just happy Papi can't hear her.

"What are you talking about?" Carlitos says, suspicious.

Clau clears her throat. "In one…two…three…"

Suddenly, there are voices on the other side of the house, the crunch of footsteps on the caliche road. Carlitos and I race for the front porch, the cherries almost spilling out of our shirts.

"Soona?" I yell.

But as we round the corner, it isn't Soona walking up the porch steps. It's Aiden.

I stop short, Ana's cold body slamming into me.

Clau snickers.

Carlitos throws his head back. "Just kill me now."

The screen door pushes open, Mami searching for Soona the same way I was. When she realizes it's just Aiden and Abby, she hurriedly ushers us all inside.

"Did you kids walk all the way here by yourselves?" Mami asks before handing me and Carlitos a bowl to drop our freshly picked cherries into.

Aiden's carrying something too—a cardboard box. Behind him, Abby's holding a box of doughnuts from Dinamo Donas, her cheeks red.

"Dad wouldn't drive us," Aiden says.

"We knew the way," Abby offers.

"But it's not safe. Those other kids are still missing."

Mami runs a hand through her hair. "Does your dad really know you're here?"

Aiden and Abby exchange a look.

Mami sighs. "This is not the time for sneaking out. He's probably worried sick."

"He doesn't know we left," Abby says.

Mami reaches for the phone. "He will when I tell him."

Abby whines. "No, please, Mrs. Morales."

Aiden pleads with her too. "We just want to make Mom an altar." His eyes glisten. "He can't know."

Mami's face softens. She puts the phone down. "Okay."

Abby squeals.

"You've got ten minutes and then I'm telling him where you are. I don't want you two walking home alone." She glances at the box Aiden's holding. "And I won't mention the altar."

CHAPTER 9

SINCE DOWNSTAIRS IS BURSTING WITH GHOSTS WE venture to the attic to set up the altar for Mrs. Montgomery while the adults finish the rest of the limpia.

I imagine Abuela setting the bowl of apples by the door, the skin and meat bruising and turning black when evil is near. Next comes the sage, Abuelo lighting the frayed ends and tossing the smoke into every corner and seam of the house before Mami uses the stepladder to mark the doors and windows with red crosses, sealing off every possible entrance.

The rest of us sit silent a moment, listening to them chant, the sound floating up through the floorboards.

"What does it mean?" Abby whispers.

"It means we're safe," I whisper back.

"Will she still be able to get in?" Aiden asks. "Mom…"

I nod. "The spell they're casting only keeps out evil." I motion to the boxes in front of us that hold our old family photo albums. "We can set up the altar here."

Abby lays a quilt over two of the cardboard boxes. "She made it using our old baby clothes." She grazes the stitching and I wonder how she must be feeling, knowing that her mother might be close. That she might be able to feel her for the first time in so long. "Do you really think this is going to work?" she asks me.

I feel Clau bristle next to me. She's been quiet since we came upstairs and as my arm brushes hers, I feel what's keeping her lips pinched tight. Envy. Sharp like thorns. She's jealous that Aiden and Abby might actually get to connect with their mom again. She's sad that she doesn't know if she'll ever get to experience that.

"I wouldn't sugarcoat it," Clau finally says, nodding to Abby.

That's when I sense what else is there—anger.

Anger that the dead could be closer to the living than to her. Anger that she lost her life and her family too.

I look from the objects on the altar back to Abby. "Even if you don't get the answers you're looking for, it's still important to remember her. To celebrate who she was."

Abby nods before setting out a bouquet of pink daisies. Next to them Aiden gently places their mother's locket, the box of sprinkle doughnuts, and a few photos of her—the one of her in the sun that Aiden mentioned at the cemetery and one of the whole family in ugly Christmas sweaters.

Goyo lunges for the doughnuts immediately and Carlitos snatches him back, holding him tight while he grunts and kicks his little legs.

"Those aren't for you," Carlitos scolds him.

Abby reaches for the family photo on the altar, her eyes crinkled with laughter. "Mom was obsessed with ugly Christmas sweaters."

Aiden snorts. "The uglier the better, she'd say."

"How many years did we win first place at the community center?"

"Five in a row."

Abby shakes her head. "Brian and Caleb were always so embarrassed."

"Watching them squirm up on that stage was the best part."

They stare off into space, smiling at the memory. And then the memory slips from their faces.

"I miss her," Abby says, tears welling up in her eyes.

Aiden reaches for her. "I know. Me too."

Carlitos hands them each a candle. I strike a match and light each one. They place them on the altar. And then we wait.

"Is that it?" Abby asks. "Are we supposed to say anything? Like a spell or something."

"It's not magic," I say. "More like a ritual. But if you want to say a few words about her, you can."

"Then she'll hear us?" Abby asks. "Then she'll come?"

I'm not sure what to tell her. What if Abby and Aiden's mom is in another afterlife? Another dimension far from Mictlān where our ghost magnets won't reach. Abuela said it's just one version of the story. One possibility out of many.

But if I tell Abby that, what if she hates me again? What if Aiden hates me too? But wouldn't a lie be worse? Giving them false hope…

"Mom?" In the quiet, Aiden speaks. "I don't know if you're listening. If you're really here. But…I miss you. Every day. I wish you were home. That everything could be like it was."

Abby squeezes Aiden's hand. "We need you, Mom. We still need you. Dad especially. He's not the same. He's so… angry." Her face falls. "I've been angry too. Even though you taught me to be kind. To be good to people. I forget sometimes. When I'm so sad I can't think straight. When it hurts too much. But I'm trying, Mom. I'm trying so hard."

For a few long moments we just wait, sitting in silence, as the faint sound of Abuela's chanting slips between the slats in the floorboards. Aiden fiddles with his shoelace. Abby pinches her eyes shut like she's praying. Clau stares longingly out the window.

Then a cool breeze blows in, gently twisting between us, gathering strength. The candles on the altar flicker, casting strange shadows on the walls. Then the hairs on my arms stand up like we're swimming in electricity. Sparking warm…and then cold. So cold that I can see my breath, tiny plumes escaping from my lips.

"What's happening?" Abby swivels, searching the darkness.

"It's okay," I say.

Moonlight pours in through the dusty attic window. I hadn't realized before that it's full again tonight, face shining bright like it's waiting for something too. I follow the glow where it pools in the corner, casting a honey film over a single speck of light.

It dances closer and closer before landing like a tiny firefly on Mrs. Montgomery's locket. The light throbs and then it swells, slowly taking shape.

Just like the ghosts at the cemetery, Mrs. Montgomery is nothing more than a sparkling outline. A glistening spiderweb in the shape of long hair and limbs.

Aiden turns to me, noticing the change in temperature. "Is she here?"

Mrs. Montgomery smiles at me, sparkling like she's

made of powdered sugar. But she can't speak, her voice still trapped on the other side of the veil.

And then I feel a nudge from somewhere deep down inside. From that place Mami and Soona have been trying to teach me to listen to. In this moment I hear it loud and clear.

Show them.

So I reach out my hand and Mrs. Montgomery reaches back.

We touch, light exploding from the tips of our fingers, and then she's almost human.

Without a word, I reach out my other hand to Aiden, and the second he grabs hold, he gasps, shaking as he takes in the sight of her.

"H-how…?" Aiden stammers.

"I don't know." My heart races, just as confused. But it's like my empathic abilities have turned me into some sort of looking glass.

Aiden reaches for Abby next, Carlitos taking her other hand so that we form a perfect circle. And suddenly, we are their eyes. Letting them see the person who for so long has only appeared in their dreams.

"Momma?" Abby reaches out to touch her but her hand glides straight through.

"You found me." Mrs. Montgomery's eyes fill with tears. "You *found* me."

And then Aiden and Abby are both talking a mile a minute about how much they miss her and how Brian and Caleb keep getting in trouble at school and how Mr. Montgomery is the new president of the neighborhood watch group and how he's angry all the time and they're scared and they wish she could come back.

"Please. I need you to come back." Abby's shoulders heave, her lungs finally out of air.

"Abby..." Mrs. Montgomery leans in, instinct trying to force her arms around her children. But she can't touch them. She can't hold them in this moment. "Abby, you're my sweet girl. But you're also strong. And you and Aiden, you're even stronger when you're together." Mrs. Montgomery meets his eyes next. "Aiden. My brave boy."

"I don't feel brave," he says. "Dad says I'm too soft. That I'm—"

"Shh..." she soothes him. "Your softness is what makes you brave. Don't let them harden you. Not Daddy or your brothers. Not the world. You keep being the kind person you've always been. That's how you keep me alive." She turns to Abby. "Do you understand? You keep being strong and brave and kind. You keep loving. That way...we never have to say goodbye."

The word *goodbye* sends tears rolling down Abby's cheeks. Aiden wraps his arms around her. She hugs him back.

"You can let them feel you…" Clau's voice is small over my shoulder. "If you concentrate hard enough."

Mrs. Montgomery stares at her.

"If you imagine it hard enough," Clau goes on. "What it would feel like to be whole again. To be able to reach out and hold them."

I didn't realize before that every time Clau comforted me with a hug, every time she became solid enough to touch, it was because she was using every ounce of energy to remind her body what it meant to be human. And not just to keep up her own game of make-believe but to be the friend she knew I needed.

Mrs. Montgomery looks from Clau to Aiden and Abby and I can feel her reaching for them. But she's not quite strong enough. Not without help.

I place a hand on Aiden's shoulder, my pointer finger still pressed to Mrs. Montgomery's palm, and then I close my eyes, reaching deep down in his memories like that night in his tree house when I made him remember her. This time I search for an embrace. The kind of hug that puts your entire world back together. The kind of hug only mothers can give.

I find it on a rainy morning in December. Aiden's wrapped in a dozen blankets, home sick while Mrs. Montgomery rocks him in her lap. There are cookies baking in the oven. Chicken noodle soup on the stove. And she's singing gently in his ear, the melody coaxing his eyes closed as he sniffles and buries his face in her chest.

She holds him tight. Rocking. Singing.

The memory so real that the sound almost makes its way to my own lips.

Instead, it's Mrs. Montgomery who starts to hum, the memory playing behind her eyes just as vividly as it's playing behind mine. Then she opens them, concentrating like Clau told her to, and this time when she reaches for Abby and Aiden, they don't slip right through her fingers. The three of them crash into one another, hugging as tight as they can. Until the glow around Mrs. Montgomery spreads to them too. A miniature sun that spills light into every dark corner of the attic.

They stay like that. Hugging and crying and laughing.

I hear a sniff. Behind me, Clau's crying too.

Because all that's left of her family...is her.

And Candela, I think. Candela who's lost out in the world somewhere. That's when I remember the promise I made to Clau to help her find her sister. A promise I've been breaking every second we haven't been searching for her. Not using every ounce of my energy to be the friend she needs like she's done so many times for me.

"Clau," I whisper, reaching for her. "I'm—"

But she doesn't let me say I'm sorry. She just shakes her

head and then she disappears, evaporating in a cold mist. Not wanting to watch what she doesn't have.

I meet Carlitos's eyes.

He frowns. "I'll go check—" But then he stops.

Outside, tires spit up gravel. Car doors slam shut. Then there's yelling.

We all rush to the window to see Mr. Montgomery and his buddies from the neighborhood watch group fanned out in front of the house. But they're not alone. I also see Matteo's mom. Behind her is Pia's. And next to them both is another couple that must belong to the other missing boy, Simon.

"What's going on?" My breath catches as I scan their angry tear-filled faces.

"We know they're in there!" Mr. Montgomery yells.

Aiden's eyes widen. "What does Dad think he's doing?"

"I will tear this place to the ground! I swear it!"

"I don't know." Abby shudders. "Do you think he means it?"

"I don't think we should wait to find out." Mrs. Montgomery sighs, shaking her head. "He'll listen to you kids. If—"

"He won't," Aiden says.

Glass breaks. A bottle shattered on the ground at Mr. Montgomery's feet.

"You have to try."

"But I don't want to leave you," Abby says.

Mrs. Montgomery brushes away a strand of Abby's hair. "You could never leave me. Do you understand? We belong to each other." She pulls them in for one last hug, her face twisted as she finally lets go. "Now hurry."

Aiden grabs Abby's arm, pulling her back down the stairs. He pauses and then they both look back.

"I'm with you." Mrs. Montgomery's eyes well up with tears. "Everywhere. All the time."

Aiden nods. Abby wipes away tears. And then they race down the stairs and through the screen door.

The rest of us watch through the attic window as Mr. Montgomery snatches Aiden up by the collar of his shirt.

"Let the boy go." Papi comes down the steps next.

"You lured them here, didn't you?" Mr. Montgomery spits. "With whatever poison you put in those candles. You trying to make them demon lovers like you?"

Mami appears, her hands balled into fists. "That's enough of this, Jack."

"Not until you turn over the rest of them," he snaps. "Tell us where you've got them caged up."

Mami steps past Mr. Montgomery, approaching Matteo's mother. "Rita, you know we have nothing to do with this."

Rita stares at the ground. "I know strange things have been happening in this town." She still can't look at Mami as she speaks. "Strange things that always seem to be connected to your family."

"Strange is one thing," Mami says. "We grew up on strange. I know you heard the same corridos I did growing up. It's part of our culture. It's part of this place." She shakes her head. "For heaven's sake, we spent the morning at a parade honoring the dead and lavishing gifts on their ghosts. But you're not here to accuse me of being strange. You're here to accuse me of being a monster."

Rita's lip trembles.

"If that's what you think of us…it's because that's what you think of yourself." She eyes Mr. Montgomery. "What you've let people convince you of. *Actual* strangers. Because you know me, Rita. You know I would never"— Mami shakes—*"could* never…"

"Enough with the waterworks," Mr. Montgomery growls.

I remember that night in the clearing when I journeyed through Mr. Montgomery's memories. There was so much light. So much *love*. But when Soona delivered those enchanted cookies to the neighborhood watch meeting to erase their memories of La Lechuza, it must have erased his change of heart too. Except, somehow, this version of him seems even more full of hate.

He takes a step toward Papi. "Times are changing. People don't want stories and superstitions. They want the truth."

He glances back down the road. "And if you're not going to give it to us, we'll find out another way."

As if on cue, sirens suddenly begin to wail, red and blue lights dancing on the walls of the attic. Two police cars screech to a stop in our front yard, their tires tossing up clouds of dirt.

Carlitos presses a hand to the glass. "It's Deputy Medina and that creepy sheriff again."

Deputy Medina jumps out of his cruiser before rushing to step between Papi and Mr. Montgomery.

"What is all of this?" Abuela says, her voice hoarse.

Deputy Medina exhales, then he holds something out to her. I squint and then my heart stops. "Soona's school badge."

"We found it in the woods," Deputy Medina says.

"Proof!" Mr. Montgomery spits. "She took those kids and if I hadn't shown up here, you all would have taken mine too."

Mrs. Montgomery turns her face away, shame rippling off her like a small flame. "He wasn't always like this. But when I got sick and he couldn't fix it he needed someone to blame. For everything. Then when I died he couldn't stop fighting. So he had to create new monsters." Tears roll down her cheeks. "The anger...it gives him purpose. But he can't see that it's destroying him." She meets my eyes. "I'm sorry for what he's become."

As if he could hear her voice, as if he knew we were watching, the sheriff steps out of the patrol car and looks straight up.

Carlitos and I try to back away from the window but it's like our feet have been glued to the floor. Carlitos tries to open his mouth to speak and then everything slows down like we're all moving through sand.

My head swims, drowsy and on the edge of sleep. Carlitos's eyes widen and suddenly Goyo is limp and snoring in his arms. The three of us frozen just like this morning at the cemetery.

"What's happening?" Mrs. Montgomery swirls around us, concerned.

Ana shoots up through the floorboards, a burst of white. "They didn't finish."

I blink, confused.

"They didn't finish the limpia!" she says.

And then all we can do is listen. To the scrape of chairs across the kitchen floor. The heavy fall of footsteps.

In my head I scream Clau's name. But she doesn't come.

Someone downstairs screams too.

Bisabuela Ynez.

Suddenly, the ghosts are in a frenzy. Glass shatters. Something heavy thuds to the ground.

Clau's voice rises above the noise. "You stay away from them!"

The lights flicker and I sense her anger. Just like the night of Marisol's quinceañera. I hear the TV clicking on and off. The volume turned all the way up. The air teems with electricity. Like when you rub your socks on the carpet and ignite a spark. Except the whole house feels like it's about to ignite.

Clau!

This time I think she's heard me until all the lights go out and Bisabuela Ynez lets out another scream.

Suddenly, Tío Arthur floats up from the floorboards.

My eyes plead, *What's happening?*

"He's arresting them." He shakes his head. "He's arresting them all."

CHAPTER 10

MAMI AND PAPI ARE SHOVED INTO ONE of the patrol cars while Abuela and Abuelo are forced into the other. Their panic strikes like lightning in my chest until I'm on fire with it too.

"Can't they do something?" Ana asks. "Cast a spell?"

Not if they're already in handcuffs, I think, still unable to speak. *And not with everyone watching.*

Car doors slam. Engines rev. And then they're gone.

That's when I smell it.

Sickly. Sweet. Rot.

Like the worms squirming inside the pan de muerto.

Something heavy reaches the first step leading to the attic, floorboards groaning as it climbs higher. I strain against whatever's holding me still but it's no use. I still can't move. I can't *run*.

Clau. Please.

My eyes start to drift closed, a mind-numbing sleepiness trying to drag me under.

No. No. No. Fight it, Omega. You have to fight!

But I'm so tired.

I'm so...

"Concentrate." I hear Clau's voice. "Imagine yourself holding the door. Using all your strength."

Mrs. Montgomery repeats Clau's instructions, showing the other ghosts how to become solid on this side of the veil. I hear Tío Arthur grunting. The sound of Bisabuela Ynez's jewelry jingling. Ana groaning as she gathers her strength too.

The heavy footsteps finally reach the landing.

Then come three loud bangs.

Let. Me. In.

The door opens a crack but the ghosts force it back, pushing as hard as they can.

"*It's...too...strong!*" Tío Arthur grits his teeth.

Bisabuela Ynez presses her back against the door. "I can't hold it much longer!"

None of them are as solid as Mrs. Montgomery was when

I touched her hand. When I forced that memory of the perfect hug beneath her skin. But I can't reach them.

That's when I remember touching Matteo's toy in the forest. How I would have stayed trapped in that vision if it hadn't been for the alebrije.

Except she's locked in Mami and Papi's bathroom.

Help! I need your help!

My thoughts couldn't reach Clau, but the alebrije and I are connected. If I call to her loud enough maybe she'll actually be able to hear me.

Come to me. Please!

There are three more loud bangs. This time harder. *Angrier.*

Like the monster knows we're all alone. Like it was waiting for the adults to be out of the way. Is this how he came for the others? By knocking down doors? Trapping them in a deep sleep before dragging them away?

I shudder, the only movement my body can manage.

Bang. Bang. Bang.

Please. I call to the alebrije one last time. *I need you.*

"It's getting stronger!" Ana squeals, pushing with all her might.

Suddenly, I hear something wriggle through a gap in the floorboards and then the alebrije's wings pop out like the bright purple sails on a ship as she hovers in front of my face.

I sigh with relief. *Yes. Good girl. Over here.*

She comes closer.

I'm stuck. I need you to release me like you did before.

She purrs before landing on my shoulder and curling herself around my neck like a warm scarf. The invisible chains around me loosen a bit. I take a giant deep breath, finally able to control my own lungs. But when I try to move my legs, they still feel like lead.

It's not working. Why isn't it working?

The alebrije hops off my shoulder, hovering at eye level again. She boops me once on the nose and then starts sniffing at the pockets of my jeans.

Tío Arthur slips. "I'm losing it!"

The alebrije lets out a small growl, pawing at my right pocket. When I reach inside, I feel something soft and squishy.

Chokecherries.

I pull them free, mashing them between my fingers until I get at the red guts inside.

"Clau," I call. "I need you to mark a cross above the door."

The door heaves open an inch. She grits her teeth, slamming it closed again.

She looks back at me. "But if I let go…"

"I don't know if we can hold it," Tío Arthur groans.

"We have to try." I reach out my hand, covered in the red paste. "I believe in you, Clau."

Bang! Bang! Bang!

She furrows her brow, and then she leaps, swooping over my hand before racing back to the door. It shudders against the force of the beast on the other side. It heaves open an inch. Then another.

Clau draws the first line.

Light from the stairway spills inside.

Thick black claws wrap themselves around the edge of the door.

Clau finishes the cross.

The door is thrown open, sending the ghosts tumbling back. Carlitos and I topple over too, Goyo yipping as he knocks Mrs. Montgomery's altar to the ground. She vanishes

and I wish we could disappear too. But it's too late. The door is open. We're in its sights.

The monster is a cloud of smoke. A rumbling storm with claws and gnashing teeth, barely visible within the fog swirling around its body. Not like the cloaked figure I saw in the forest with Matteo. That monster was almost human. This one is pure chaos. But the *feeling*...it's the same. Like they're connected somehow.

It throws its head back and growls, the sound reverberating off the walls.

I reach for Carlitos. He reaches back. Our fear bouncing back and forth between us like a giant ping-pong ball.

But when the monster tries to take a step, it stops short. It reaches an arm toward us next but it can't get through.

"It worked!" Clau yells.

I slowly begin to stand, realizing the drowsiness that had come over me earlier is gone too.

Carlitos staggers to his feet. "What is that thing?"

"I don't know." I take a step back.

"Ugly, is what it is," Clau says.

It lets out a wild growl in response, green goo stretching between its rotten teeth. Goyo hops onto one of the cardboard boxes, barking and jumping onto his hind legs.

"Ugh"—Carlitos holds his nose—"and that stench. It's got

worse breath than Chale after a week of refusing to brush his teeth."

Smoke plumes land against the invisible barrier as if the monster is breathing behind a pane of glass.

"No way kids went willingly with this thing," Clau says.

"They didn't," I say. "This isn't the monster I saw with Matteo."

And I can tell by the wild look in its eyes that it's not the game that makes it tick. It's biology. The need to feed or else.

The monster throws itself into the invisible barrier, scratching and clawing at the air.

"We can't stay here," Carlitos says, scooping up Goyo who's still thrashing and barking like he's three times his size. "We don't know how long the limpia will hold, especially without the adults here to reinforce it."

My throat throbs, remembering their faces behind glass. The sirens. The sight of them being dragged away.

"But where do we go?" Clau asks. "The moon's hidden behind clouds with barely enough light to see by. It's getting late."

I watch the clouds slide past, grateful for their cover even if it means we'll be stumbling in the dark all the way to safety. We've dealt with enough monsters for one day. I don't want the moon exposing the strange markings under my skin and making Carlitos and the others suspect I'm one too.

Suddenly, the fog monster lets out another roar, except this time it's given up on the barrier, the floorboards rattling instead.

I lose my footing and the alebrije snatches me up by the shirt, keeping me on my feet.

Ana zigzags across the room. "What's happening?"

"The cracks." Tío Arthur points.

"And we're out of chokecherries!" Clau raises her stained red hands.

The boards shudder beneath our feet and I hear the faint squeak of nails coming loose.

"The window!" Carlitos yells. "It's the only way out!"

We stumble to the glass before pushing it open, the cool night air stealing my breath as I stare down at the ten-foot drop.

My knees quake. "I don't think I can jump."

Clau squeezes her way through first and then she says, "You don't have to."

Clau helps the other ghosts as they try to become solid again. It takes a few tries, Ana struggling to concentrate as the fog monster lets out a grating scream. But finally it works and we use their bodies as a makeshift ladder, scaling the side of the house until we reach the grass. Just then, floorboards snap and go flying, the monster breaking through like a giant grenade.

We take off running, Goyo up ahead, leading the way.

"Where are we going?" Carlitos huffs.

I glance back, the fog rising above the house. Like it's searching for us.

"We have to get out of its line of sight!" Clau yells.

I take a hard left into the trees, Carlitos and Goyo following behind.

Clau swoops down in front of us. "Isn't your house just up ahead, Carlitos?"

He shakes his head, trying to catch his breath. "And lead that thing straight there?" He follows me over the rocky terrain. "No way."

"Where else is there to hide?" Ana asks.

I stop, listening for the sound of fog rustling the leaves, for another hungry growl. It's the wind that passes by instead, tossing the branches blocking our path and revealing the clearing on the other side. It's Oak Park, the school just across the playground. The safety of el Otro Lado just a hundred yards away.

Except it's locked.

The alebrije hops up onto my shoulder again, her small heart pounding hard from our wild sprint.

I reach up and scratch behind her ear and suddenly I

wonder. "Hey…how did you get past that locked bathroom door?"

The alebrije grunts before slithering out her long, forked tongue and flicking it as if she's picking a lock.

Something in my brain clicks too.

I look to Clau and the others. "I think I know where we can go." I nuzzle up against the alebrije again. "And I think I know how we can get inside."

When we reach the doors to the school, we collapse, Carlitos and I gulping down air as we try to catch our breath. We sprinted the rest of the way here, not knowing if the fog monster was still close behind or if other, even worse monsters were lurking in the darkness.

"Are you sure this is going to work?" Carlitos wipes his brow with the hem of his shirt before Goyo snatches it between his teeth, thinking they're playing a game of tug-of-war.

I click my teeth, summoning the alebrije to my shoulder again. "Can you get us inside?" I ask her.

She gives me her signature boop before slithering out her tongue and jamming the forked end into the keyhole. She grunts like she's playing with some kind of toy and then I hear a soft click. I push against the door and it opens.

"Neat trick," Carlitos says, scratching behind the alebrije's ears.

We slip inside, the ghosts trailing behind us. Our footsteps echo off the linoleum floor and the draft from the empty hallway makes the hairs on my arms stand up.

"Sheesh," Carlitos says. "This place is even scarier than it is during the day."

"Maybe it's haunted," Ana says.

He smirks. "Yeah, by you."

Ana scrunches her nose. "Rude."

"Just ignore him," Clau says. "That's what I always do."

Before they can get into another argument, I ask, "Can someone get the lights?"

All four ghosts raise their hands, the fluorescent lights above our heads flickering until bursting with light.

Carlitos lifts his arm. "Ah, my eyes! You want to get us caught?"

I blink against the bright white light. "Yeah, maybe just one of you should get the lights."

Ana harrumphs, lowering her arms. Tío Arthur and Bisabuela Ynez follow suit. Then on Clau's command, she dims the lights so there's just enough to see by but not enough to draw attention.

"So where exactly is this magical library?" Ana asks.

"Inside the regular library but in a section that's off limits to students."

"Except us," Carlitos says.

"And you think Soona will be there?" Tío Arthur asks. "That she'll be able to help you?"

The thought of Soona quickens my steps. "I'm not sure. But even if she's not, there's still the books. That has to be why Soona came here in the first place. To try to find the monster's origin story."

"Why is that important?" Ana asks.

"Because the only way to destroy something," Carlitos says, "is to understand how it was made."

Destroy. My stomach clenches at the word. I didn't have to destroy Luna to stop her. I just had to help her remember who she was. What if this monster is just suffering from a little amnesia too? *But if it has Soona…*

The alebrije nuzzles against my cheek, sensing my unease.

"You okay?" Carlitos asks.

"Yeah," I say. "I'm okay."

"Maybe we'll be able to find the door Luisa mentioned," Clau goes on.

"And then what?" Bisabuela Ynez asks. "If it's the reason Soona went missing, what makes you think stepping through it won't make you disappear too?"

"She's right," Carlitos says. "Maybe we should slow down for a second. Think this through."

I turn to Carlitos. "Remember when we played capture the flag in PE?"

"Yeah, our team lost," he says.

"We lost because the other team had twice as many players." I motion to our ghost family. "If Soona lost whatever game this monster is playing in order to hide the book with its origin story, it's because she was playing alone. But there are six of us."

Carlitos hesitates. "And if we still lose?"

"Then more kids go missing. And without proof that our family isn't responsible, Papi, Mami, Abuelo, and Abuela stay locked up. Maybe forever."

Carlitos nods. "Sounds like we've got a game to play."

He marches toward the library doors but the second I follow, my eye catches the moonlight pouring in through the window and washing across my skin. The clouds have retreated and in the light, my arms are covered in those faint lines again. Instinctually, I try to swipe them away, scratching at them, but they're deep. Almost like a tattoo.

"Hey," Carlitos calls back, "you coming?"

I quickly step out of the moonlight before someone sees, and the strange shapes vanish. "Coming," I call.

CHAPTER 11

"Now, do not, under any circumstances, untie these knots." I tighten the rope around my waist before taking the other end and tying it around Carlitos too.

Our first stop after getting into the library was rifling through the lost and found. We snatched a couple of backpacks. One for Goyo who is seriously overdue for a nap and one for the book. Once we actually find it, that is.

Under Soona's desk, we also happened to find the rope Father Torres used to tie up Luna. Soona must have taken it that night from the clearing, which is perfect since there is absolutely no way I'd be able to chase down four ghosts, Carlitos, one puppy, and an alebrije who thinks it's a puppy through an enchanted library the same way I chased Clau the last time we were here.

"Is a leash really necessary?" Carlitos squirms.

"In case you forgot, the last time Clau and I snuck into el Otro Lado we almost didn't come back out."

And I'm not taking that chance again, which is why I tie ropes around the ghosts too. Here in el Otro Lado, they don't have to work so hard to be corporeal, which means that these ropes won't slip if we happen to need to make a quick escape.

"I feel like a balloon," Ana whines.

Bisabuela Ynez rolls her eyes. "And I feel like a hog."

Tío Arthur tugs his a little tighter. "I think it's kind of neat."

I tie the final rope around the alebrije just as she tries to take flight, before tying the loose end around my wrist. Carlitos and I split up the other loose ends until they *all* look like a bunch of globos.

Clau shrugs. "And if I make myself fuzzy and *accidentally* slip out of this thing…?"

"Then you might accidentally be eaten by one of those fog monsters," I warn her. "Or something much worse."

Clau gulps. "Okay, got it."

Carlitos tugs on the rope tied to Clau, jerking her around. "Hey, this is kind of fun."

She growls. "Yank on me one more time…"

He grins, yanking on her again. She gnashes her teeth, lunging for him.

"Cool it!" I shout. "We don't have time for this. We're on a mission, remember?"

I drag everyone forward as I scan the rows.

"Now, we all have to concentrate on the same question. That way the magic of the library will lead us to the same place."

"And what question is that?" Carlitos asks.

"What monster is terrorizing Noche Buena? It'll also help to think about what we know about it so far."

"He likes to play games," Clau says.

"Good."

Carlitos grimaces. "His breath has got to be lethal, even worse than his fog-monster lackey if it's a breeding ground for worms."

My stomach twists. "He's targeting children."

Everyone grows quiet, remembering Matteo and Pia and Simon. The reason we're here.

"Now chant those thoughts in your mind. Almost like putting yourself in a trance. The library will hear your heart's desire and should lead us straight to the answers."

I face the rows and rows of shelves, watching as they stretch into shadow, and then I wait. For that soft nudge that turns into a fishing hook, dragging me forward. But it's quiet. My heart steadily beating instead of racing into a gallop.

I glance back at the others. "It's not working. Are you sure y'all are concentrating?"

Clau elbows Carlitos.

"Hey!" He bumps her back. "I know how to follow instructions."

"And you, Ana?" Bisabuela Ynez tsks. "Your head was always up in the clouds."

Ana crosses her arms. "What is that supposed to mean?"

"Cálmate," Tío Arthur hushes her. "Maybe we just need to—"

But before he can finish that sentence, I'm jerked into a run.

"Wait up!" Carlitos calls.

We race down row after row, looking like our own parade procession. Finally, my steps slow at a fork, the ghosts slamming into me from behind. On our right is a wall of birdcages, winged books squawking as loose pages fall from their spines like feathers. On the left is a giant clam, shiny white books as iridescent as pearls winking at us from its open mouth.

"Well, which way is it?" Tío Arthur says.

I let my feet decide, following the gentle push to the left. There are more shelves, spiraling like the whorl on a seashell. We pass sleeping sea turtles, books nestled under them like eggs, and jagged tomes as hard as stone. There's a rainbow up ahead, the whorl leading us toward the pot of gold at the end.

Carlitos wobbles. "I'm getting dizzy."

"I think we're almost out."

We reach the end of the rainbow to find books encased in giant lollipops. The Tootsie Roll center that would probably take a thousand licks to get to. Goyo chomps down on a giant gummy bear and Carlitos has to force open his jaws to get him to let go.

"I knew it!" Bisabuela Ynez throws up her hands. "I knew you weren't following Omega's instructions, Ana."

Ana blushes—as much as a ghost can blush. "Why come all the way here if we can't have a bit of fun?"

"You brought us here?" I groan.

"A sweet tooth just like your brother." Bisabuela Ynez shakes her head and I know she's talking about Papi.

My heart clenches at the thought of him in the back of that police car. But I shove the thought away, focusing on the book, knowing it's the key to rescuing us all.

"Great job," Carlitos snaps. "What if we're even farther from this stupid door than we were before?"

As soon as he says "door," we're off again. This time Carlitos is leading the way, something dragging him with such force that his feet almost come off the ground.

"What's happening?" He flails his arms, trying not to fall. "Where's it taking me?"

"Just relax!" I call out from behind, my arms pumping hard as I try to keep up. "Keep thinking about the door."

We turn the corner to a row of phosphorescent mushrooms, books gently nestled beneath their wide caps. Down the next row are thousands of monarch butterflies, wings barely moving as they rest atop books disguised as moss-covered stones.

We pass forests and sand dunes and an ice-covered pond.

We walk through piles of leaves and down a dimly lit road.

Past weeping willows and stained-glass windows and low burning candles that make me feel like we're in outer space. Surrounded by nothing and everything at the same time.

Suddenly, Carlitos stops.

Then he looks up.

We all do.

I've never traveled deep enough into the library to find a door before. This one looks ancient. The wood is charred black like it's been burned and there are seven locks, each one shaped like the letter C.

I reach for the first lock and Carlitos lifts a hand.

"Wait," he says. "What if it's locked for a reason?"

I stare at the strange carvings. Vines and round shapes that remind me of things Abuela has dug up from her garden. Gourds and squash and wart-covered pumpkins. I lean a little closer and smell the damp earth. The sweet scent of rot.

"This is the one," I say.

"What if the locks are meant to keep something inside?" Carlitos asks.

Clau hovers between us. "Or the monster put them there to keep us out."

"We can turn back," Tío Arthur offers. "We can find another way."

But I don't know another way. Without Mami or Abuela. Without Soona. I don't know what's right or what's dangerous. What's helping or only making things worse.

What if I'm just trying to play the hero again even though I don't know the first thing about it? What if I got lucky with Luna and my powers, but my instincts are still just as unreliable as they've always been? So unreliable that I'm about to walk us straight into danger with no plan for getting us out of it.

"Omega...?" Clau's voice is soft.

"I..." I search for the words. *I'm scared. I'm confused.*

But Mami... another voice shouts from deep between my ribs. And then, even though I'm still heavy with doubt, I turn to the others and speak the only words I know to be true: "We don't have time to wait."

At that, they don't argue. No one knows better than a ghost how fleeting time is.

I reach for the strange letter Cs, my hands trembling a little as I begin to turn them. The locks snap into place and slowly take shape, revealing small key holes that the alebrije works to unlock.

Carlitos shudders behind me. "Is that…?"

I take a step back, looking at the shape as a whole.

Clau gasps. "A worm?"

Ana backs away slowly. "I'm with Carlitos. Are we *sure* we want to open that?"

"You holding tight to those ropes?" I ask.

Carlitos winds the rope around his wrist one more time. Clau holds on to hers with both hands. I feel a tug, the other ghosts tightening their grips as well. And then I push open the door.

Inside, it's cold and dark and it takes a moment for my eyes to adjust. But then they do and my stomach twists. Because we're standing in the middle of a child's bedroom. There are glow-in-the-dark stars on the ceiling and a tower of stuffed animals on the bed. And the longer I stand there, the more I get that same sickly sweet feeling.

Like there's something wrong.

Like we're being watched.

"So…" Ana shivers behind me. "Where's this book?"

"It'll be hard to find on purpose," I remind her. "It might even be glamoured behind some sort of riddle."

"Glamoured?" Clau asks.

"Hidden using magic."

"We should split up," Carlitos says. "We'll turn this place upside down if we have to."

"I've got the drawers," I say.

Carlitos nods. "I'll take the closet."

While the ghosts generate a light breeze to ruffle the curtains and bedsheets, I dig through the navy-blue dresser drawers, sifting through socks and art supplies and a small rock collection. From the closet, Carlitos tosses out balls of various shapes and sizes, winter coats, and even more stuffed animals, all of it landing in a heap in the middle of the room.

"Nothing here," he calls.

"Yeah." I get up, dusting off my knees. "Nothing in the dresser."

Clau suddenly pops out of a toy trunk. "I didn't have any luck either."

I scan the room again, waiting for another nudge, some kind of sign. That's when the alebrije starts barking. She paces by the edge of the bed, sniffing the ground.

Goyo gets all riled up too, wriggling free from Carlitos's backpack and joining the alebrije in her search. He catches the bed skirt between his teeth and starts to pull.

"What is it, Goyo?" I kneel and then I stop.

Because they're right. There's still one more place we haven't looked.

Under the bed.

The alebrije lets out a small growl before snapping at the bed skirt, Goyo next to her still trying to rip it free. Fog begins to seep out from beneath the bed like it's breathing, waiting for us to come closer.

I lower myself to the ground, hand outstretched and shaking.

"Omega, wait…" Carlitos lowers himself to his belly too.

"We've got your back," Tío Arthur says, bracing himself.

Bisabuela Ynez's voice quakes. "Just be careful."

I take a deep breath, let it go, and then I lift the bed skirt.

First comes the smell. Like an entire Thanksgiving dinner has been left under there to rot. For a hundred years. Under the hot sun.

"Blech!" Carlitos dry heaves. "I think I'm going to be sick."

I hold my nose, my eyes watering too. I blink back tears and then I see a strange mist, green swirls steaming up from a distant bog. It bubbles, belching up green goo onto muddy banks held together by the gnarled roots of trees.

"It's a portal," I say. "Like the one at the flea market."

Carlitos gags. "To where? The forest of hot garbage farts?"

I hold my nose, venturing a little deeper, until my hands scrape the damp grass. The alebrije wriggles through next to me and then she starts digging. Her tail wags as she drags something out of the mud.

"Find anything yet?" Clau calls.

I grab the book before shimmying back out from under the bed. It's slick and covered in slime. Carlitos follows, his nose still pinched between his fingers as I let the book fall open with a squish in my hands.

Dark purple fog twists around the binding, static sparks leaping from the wet mud-stained pages.

Ana shudders. "What's it say?"

"Any clues?" Tío Arthur asks anxiously.

Clau peers over my shoulder. "Is it going to turn into the monster like the book about La Lechuza?"

In case the ropes tied around our waists weren't enough of a reminder of the thin line between story and reality, Clau's question sends a shiver down my spine. When she and I found the history book with La Lechuza's origin story, La Lechuza herself had appeared to tell it to us. We watched her grow up. We watched her fall in love. And then we watched her lose herself.

Soona saved us just as she tried to attack. But Soona's not here. What if by reading this book we release something even more dangerous? Something we can't put back?

"It looks like an instruction manual," Carlitos says, pointing to the faded ink on the first page.

I exhale, relieved.

Cures, Curses, and Sacred Canciones: Banishing the Cucuy and Other Boogeymen.

I wobble on my feet, suddenly breathless again. "El Cucuy..."

There's a collective gasp.

"Wait..." Carlitos's brow furrows. "You mean...the boogeyman? As in the monster Mom promised would eat me if I wasn't tucked in by bedtime?"

My voice trembles. "The monster Abuela told me would grab my feet and pull me under the bed if I dared to sneak to the kitchen for a midnight snack."

Tío Arthur lets out an uneasy laugh. "My parents scared me so badly with those old stories that I didn't sleep for months. Until my mother told me the key to warding off El Cucuy was singing him a lullaby. I already loved music but those dark nights, singing to the shadows on my walls, was how I learned to fall in love with the sound of my own voice."

"At least you got a career out of it," Carlitos says. "All I got was a year's worth of nightmares."

"But he's *just* a story," Ana says, "right?"

They're the same words I said to Mami when I asked her about La Lechuza.

She's just *a story.*

Right?

But I was wrong. And if La Lechuza is real...if El Cucuy is too...maybe that means there's no such thing as *just a story.*

I slowly thumb through the pages, past drawings of different types of boogeymen. The Butzemann from Germany who brings shiny red apples to well-behaved children and drags the naughty children away in a sack. The ghoulish Hombre del Saco from Spain who's bold enough to kidnap children in broad daylight. In Japan he goes by Namahage and only hunts on New Year's Eve. And in Haiti, they call him Mètminwi, a man who stalks the night on long legs and eats anyone he finds.

The full index of boogeymen around the world goes on for pages with information about their appearance, their hunting style, calling cards, preferred locations and time of day. What they smell like. What they sound like. How many teeth they have.

"He's been called a hundred different names and has worn a hundred different faces," Clau reads over my shoulder. "But they all share the same appetite."

Carlitos gulps. "For children?"

I flip to the next page to an anatomically correct drawing of a heart. It throbs, quietly beating. I flip the page again, a hand with sharp claws gripping the heart, squeezing hard until it's covered in thick vines and puss-filled warts.

"Ugh!" Carlitos gags again.

"Is that what he does to his victims?" Clau asks.

Ana shivers. "Before he eats them?"

"There's a footnote," Tío Arthur points out.

In tiny print I read the words *Grief Eater*.

The next page shows a drawing of an empty bed. Just like the one in front of us. Blankets rumpled. Pillow sunken in where a child's sleeping head should be.

El Cucuy is a dangerous trickster, often shape-shifting into human skin in order to walk among them. El Cucuy may hunt at night, forcing his victims into a deep sleep before snatching them from their beds or he may hunt in plain sight, entrancing his victims with the proposition of playing a game from which they cannot escape.

Stolen children are treated as valuable collectibles by El Cucuy and he is constantly looking to add to his collection. Contrary to popular belief, he does not hunt children for food. What sustains this beast is the sadness left behind when they're gone, his diet mostly consisting of sorrow, anger, confusion, loneliness, and other isolating emotions.

I stare at the heart, completely still. "I don't understand."

"Me neither." Carlitos shakes his head. "He *eats* emotions?"

"Do you remember how scared Matteo's mother was when he first went missing?" Clau asks. "How the people at the cemetery panicked?"

I remember all those pounding hearts. The tears.

"That's what he needs to survive?" My stomach knots. "To see people suffer?"

"Wait," Carlitos says. "Does that mean he's not actually going to hurt Matteo?"

"I guess he doesn't have to." I meet Carlitos's eyes. "He just has to keep him hidden."

"Long enough for his mother to think she's lost him," Tío Arthur adds.

A tear falls from Bisabuela Ynez's eyes. "Long enough for her to grieve."

"La Lechuza got her strength from people's fear," I say. "He gets his strength from their sadness."

Carlitos flips to the next page. "Does it say how to get rid of him?"

"Check the table of contents," Tío Arthur offers.

I flip back to the beginning, searching the list of section and chapter titles.

- Hunting Style
- Diet
- Common Disguises
- Games
- Lullabies

I turn back to Tío Arthur. "You said you sang to El Cucuy to keep him away."

His eyes widen. "I thought it was just something my mother invented to make me feel better."

I flip to the correct page where the section on lullabies should be but the seam is rough. Like something's been torn out.

I trace my hand down the center. "No..." I shake the book, hoping for something to fall out. "No, no, no."

"Maybe Soona has it," Clau says.

I shake my head. "Soona would never rip the pages out of a book. They're too sacred."

"Yeah," Carlitos agrees. "Even ones about horrible monsters." He exhales. "Maybe there's another copy of it in the library somewhere."

"If there is, guaranteed it's missing the section on lullabies too. No, this was done on purpose."

I feel the weight of the book in my palms, the mud slick against my fingers. *Please. Tell me where you are.*

I don't know if I'm speaking to the missing pages or to Soona or even to El Cucuy himself. But it's the book that answers, the pages suddenly fluttering before flipping to a new page.

Everyone gathers behind me, staring down at the chapter title: *Games.*

"You said the answers might be hidden behind some kind of glamour," Tío Arthur reminds me. "What if this is it?"

I gulp down hard, trying to keep from shaking. Then I flip the page.

The lights inside the bedroom flicker but just before they vanish, leaving us in the pitch black, I see the words that make my heart race. *An invitation.*

"What did it say?" Carlitos breathes.

I find his hand in the dark, squeezing hard. Then I say, "*Hide-and-Seek.*"

CHAPTER 12

IT TAKES A MOMENT FOR MY EYES to adjust. When they do, I see the faint glimmer of green fog spilling out from under the bed.

Carlitos gags again. "Where's the door?"

In the dark, I feel the ghosts bumping into one another.

I tighten my grip on the ropes that are tying us all together. When Carlitos takes a step toward the door we first came through, I yank him back.

"Not that one…"

"Omega, we have to get out of here!"

I hear the sirens again. I see Mami's face.

"Omega, let's go," Carlitos pleads.

"Not without the lullaby."

Then I sink down to my knees, reaching under the bed

until I feel the cold mud between my fingers, and start crawling.

I'm covered in green goo by the time I reach the other side, the slime smeared across my shirt and dripping from my hair.

"Help!" Carlitos groans behind me. "I'm stuck!"

I yank on the rope around his waist, trying to pull him out of the mud. The alebrije locks her jaws around his shirt sleeve and starts pulling too. But the harder we pull, the farther he sinks.

"It's like quicksand," Clau says.

"You have to relax," Tío Arthur warns. "The more you squirm, Carlitos, the more you stick."

Carlitos grimaces, trying to hold still as the rest of us try to heave him out.

"On one…" Tío Arthur counts down. "Two…" We pull with all our strength. "Three!"

The muddy bog lets out a loud belch as Carlitos flies onto the bank. Immediately, the alebrije gets to work trying to clean his face while Goyo licks all over his legs.

Carlitos laughs, getting to his feet. "Stop it! It tickles!"

Suddenly, Ana screams.

Bisabuela Ynez blushes, looking away too.

Clau cackles.

That's when Carlitos looks down and realizes that the

muddy bog that just spit him up like school lunch literally ate his shorts.

"Ah!" Carlitos covers himself. "Stop looking at me!"

Clau tumbles in the air, laughing so hard she's literally doing somersaults. "Your shorts...you lost...oh my God... I can't...*I can't!*"

The alebrije grunts, pawing at something on the ground. Goyo gets ahold of the other end, the two tugging the fabric back and forth.

"Oh thank God!" Carlitos falls to his knees before snatching back his mud-filled shorts. "Good girl." He kisses the alebrije on the nose before giving Goyo a scratch next. "Good boy!"

The alebrije boops him back before doing figure eights between my legs until I reach down to reward her with a scratch too.

The pockets on Carlitos's shorts sag, clods of mud plopping to the ground as he turns them inside out.

Clau still hasn't contained herself. "It looks like your pockets are full of poop!"

"It's not poop!" he shouts back.

"Sure smells like it," Clau says.

Carlitos reaches for one of the mud clods and hurls it at Clau. She dodges it and it explodes against a tree.

"He's here!" The tree tosses its branches like it's waking from a deep slumber.

"He's here!" The tree next to it echoes its frantic calls.

Soon all the trees in the forest are whispering a warning to one another, the sound so sharp I have to hold my ears.

"What's happening?" Clau spins, startled.

I press a finger to my lips, trying to concentrate.

"What are they talking about?" Ana groans.

Bisabuela Ynez presses a hand over Ana's mouth, holding her still. All of us staring after the sound as it disappears at the far edge of the forest.

After a beat of silence, I shout, "*Who's* here?"

The branches of the tree next to me whip in my direction. "You speak the language of the forest."

The tree next to it calls out. "She speaks the language of the forest."

"She speaks the language of the forest."

"She speaks the language of the forest."

The same message over and over again until I see trees a hundred yards away waving their branches.

"I can understand you," I say, trying to keep talking so the trees won't start up their whisper network again. "We're here looking for missing pages from a book. We think they can help us banish El Cucuy."

"They're here to banish El Cucuy."

"They're here to banish El Cucuy."

"They're here to banish El Cucuy."

"Do you know where we can find them?" I ask.

The tree points north to where the forest grows dense and the shadows gather like darkened doorways.

"That way."

"That way."

"That way."

"Thank you." I wave, taking off in the direction they pointed.

"The game has already started."

"The game has already started."

"The game has already started."

"Run."

"Run."

"Run."

My knees quake. "Run?"

"Run!"

"Run!"

"Run!"

I skip into a jog, feeling unsteady.

"Maybe this means we're seeking." Carlitos exhales. "That's a relief."

Up ahead, there's a sharp crack, the trees bending and thrashing like something giant is pushing them out of the way. Heading straight for us. Then there's a loud familiar roar.

"What was that?" Clau pulls on her rope as she tries to get a closer look.

Bisabuela Ynez stares straight ahead as she says, "The thing that's seeking us."

I spin around, examining the knots in our ropes.

Carlitos shakes me. "Omega, they told us to run!"

"I know but…" I start untying the rope around my wrist. "I think we should split up."

"What? Why?" Ana asks, frantic.

"Remember what I said about capture the flag? If we stay tied together, we'll be playing as one. That means one chance to get across the forest. One chance to win the game."

"But if we split up, we'll have more chances," Carlitos says.

"Exactly."

He hesitates and then he nods. "Okay. We split up."

We quickly undo the rest of the knots, letting the rope fall to the ground.

The branches of a weeping willow tap me on the shoulder. "If it sees you, you'll be stuck to that spot, unable to move."

"Like at the cemetery," I say. "So it *was* El Cucuy that froze us all in place?"

"Sleep paralysis," the tree says. "And these are just his minions. They place his victims in a deep slumber."

Tío Arthur glares at the distant fog. "And then El Cucuy comes and snatches them from their beds."

My skin crawls, remembering what it felt like to be frozen in place. Helpless.

"But in the attic, only you and Carlitos were affected," Bisabuela Ynez says.

"Same in the cemetery," Clau adds. "I was still able to move, no problem. Maybe that means it only works on humans. Maybe that means we'll win the game."

A cool breeze blows between the willow tree's branches. "Things are different here. In el Otro Lado we are all the same."

Ana motions to the rope on the ground. "We're more solid on this side. Maybe that means we're more vulnerable too."

Suddenly, the roaring moves closer until I can see the monster. Another giant rain cloud, lightning striking like veins across its fog-like body. Just like the one that chased us here.

"Oh no"—Carlitos shudders—"it's back!"

"How did it get in here?" Ana squeaks.

"Do you think it followed us?" Clau asks.

"Maybe…" My knees quake. "Or maybe this is where it escaped from in the first place."

"Remember, the fog will make you drowsy so don't get too close," Bisabuela Ynez says.

The alebrije climbs onto my shoulder, one paw resting on my head as she lets out a low growl of her own.

"Wait!" Carlitos turns in a circle. "Where's Goyo?"

My heart stops as I scan the bog behind us, fearing the worst. That he's been sucked in. That we've lost him. But he's not there. Suddenly, I hear a faint yip, and as I squint, scanning the grass, I see the tip of his tail, ramrod straight. Ready to charge.

"Goyo!" Carlitos yells.

Goyo's ears poke up next but he doesn't seem to hear us calling.

"Goyo, get back here!"

The fog monster, on the other hand, hears us loud and clear. It puffs up its chest, throws back its head, and then lets out a scream so powerful that the trees bend like they're caught in a storm.

They cry out in response, howling and shedding their leaves. But the trees aren't the only ones who are terrified. Goyo retreats too, tail between his legs as he scurries away.

"Where's he going?" Carlitos cups his hands around his mouth. "Goyo! Goyo!"

The fog monster charges forward, straight toward us.

"Run."

"Run."

"Run."

The trees begin to chant again.

Carlitos stands with his mouth open, unable to speak.

Clau cracks her knuckles.

I let out a long deep breath.

Then I yell, "Go!"

We split up, taking off into the trees. Fog swirls as the monster spins in a circle, confused by the sound of so many footsteps, the ghosts rustling the leaves. Its mouth appears like a black hole and out of the darkness comes another scream, this one so loud it almost knocks me off my feet.

I glance up at the alebrije. "Hold on, little one!"

The monster jerks its head in my direction and I throw myself against the trunk of a tree. My heart pounds and I try to slow my breathing.

Quiet. Quiet.

I smell the smoke on the alebrije's breath as she peers around the edge of the tree, ready to breathe fire again. I reach up to scratch behind her ear, trying to quiet her too.

The ground begins to shake and then the tree I'm leaning against is yanked up by the roots, sending me tumbling to the ground. The alebrije latches onto my shirtsleeve, trying to pull me back onto my feet.

"Hey, loser!" Carlitos shouts before hurling a rock at the monster's head. "Over here!"

The monster whips around, staring right at Carlitos. Carlitos stares back and then I watch him stiffen like he's suddenly made of concrete. Nothing moving but his eyes telling me to *run*.

I do, pumping my arms as fast as I can, the alebrije flying close at my side, before the two of us duck behind a tall bush. Up ahead, Ana's huddled behind a moss-covered boulder. Even at a distance I can hear her teeth chattering. The monster hears it too, whipping around like it's caught her scent. It howls, lightning striking the ground and sending up clods of mud. Ana yelps, darting between the trees.

But it's too late. The fog engulfs her until she's trapped

midair. Midscream. Bisabuela Ynez gasps, revealing her hiding spot next. But then I hear a sharp whistle, Tío Arthur luring the monster away with the sound.

Once its back is turned, the alebrije and I make a break for it. I sidestep stones and hop over thick roots as the trees whisper, *This way, keep going, you're almost there.* Bisabuela Ynez zips forward too, she and I glancing over our shoulders every few seconds looking for Tío Arthur.

"I don't see him," she says, frantic.

I press a finger to my lips but the monster lets out a roar and I know it heard her. It charges through the trees, the ground shaking so wildly that I land on my butt next to a muddy puddle. I crawl out of sight, just as the fog reaches Bisabuela Ynez, making her grow still.

I'm sorry, her eyes say.

"Psst!"

I jump at the sound but then I look up and see Clau hiding in the branches of the tree above me.

"This way," she says.

The monster whips its head around, searching for Clau.

She darts out of sight just as the monster yanks the tree out of the ground. It shakes the tree until all the leaves have fallen off before tossing it to the side, growling in annoyance. Then it throws its head back, letting out a howl as its body doubles in size, the storm inside it raging too.

I stumble back, just out of reach of the fog, but Clau isn't as lucky. I see her caught in it, a dark cloud slowly lowering her to the ground as she fights to keep her eyes open. But a few seconds later she's snoring, sprawled out in the grass like she's taking a nap.

I search for Tío Arthur, hoping he's still in the game, but the fog is so thick I can only see a few feet ahead. What if he's trapped in it like the others? What if I'm the only one left?

I follow the alebrije as she bolts for the next cluster of trees and then I finally see the door, a break in the fog forming a path straight to it. I crawl forward, crouched low to the ground, and ducking behind a tree every time I hear a roar. They're getting louder, which means they're getting closer.

"Straight ahead!" Tío Arthur hisses from the shadows, waving me over.

I follow behind as we try to steer clear of the fog but the monster's quickened its pace too, every step making the ground shake. It stomps closer, the forest floor beneath us cracking, and I stumble.

Tío Arthur yanks me up by the arm. "We're almost there!"

There's a loud boom like lightning striking between my ears and I hit the ground again. When I look up, another tree's been ripped from its roots, the leaves falling down over my head.

And there's Tío Arthur, trapped in the fog, trying to scream. But he's stuck, twitching, before growing completely still. But not before finding my eyes.

"*Go*," he says.

I crawl until I feel steady enough to break into a run. The monster lets out another roar. Searching. *For me.*

The alebrije zigzags ahead of me as I race from one tree trunk to the next, throwing stones and pine cones to force the monster to turn the other way. It works and I circle the door, inching closer with every pass, until I finally reach the handle. I grip the cold metal and then I twist, pushing it open.

But before I can make it inside, something heavy grabs hold of my legs. I glance back and see the fog, tendrils twisting like fingers, clutching me tight.

No. No. I'm almost there!

The alebrije lands on my shoulder, spitting fire.

"Stay away from the fog!" I croak. "We have to find the missing lullaby!"

Her ears perk up. She understands me.

Suddenly, her wings snap open, her body wobbling as she tries to take flight.

"The song!" I plead. "We have to get the song!"

The fog slides over me and I claw at the ground, trying to wrench myself free. But it's warm and comforting and I feel myself falling... falling...

No. Don't sleep. Don't...

With my eyes closed, I hear rustling, the alebrije sniffing frantically. Something clatters to the ground. Then something shatters. She races across the room like a mini-tornado, knocking things over, tearing them apart.

There's a thud, something tumbling to the ground, and then I hear the soft tinkle of music. The melody is familiar, like something Mami used to hum to me as I fell asleep in her arms. But it's different too. Strange like something old. Something magic.

I blink, the fog around me loosening its grip. I stretch one arm and then the other. Finally, I'm free enough to turn and see the monster. It sways, almost like it's dancing, and then with a thunderous boom it falls to the ground. Snoring.

I crawl forward, finding the music box where it landed on the floor.

"The lullaby," I breathe, glancing back at the monster, still sound asleep.

The metal cogs inside the music box slowly come to a stop, the music disappearing too. In the silence, the monster stirs, rolling like it's in pain. It huffs, trying to get to its feet again, and I scramble for the hand crank on the box, turning it until the song starts again.

At the sound of the first note, the monster slides back to the ground, snoring even louder than before. But beneath the sound, there's something else—footsteps. Behind the monster's bulbous body, breathing in and out, I see Carlitos, Clau, and the others.

Carlitos's mouth falls open and I press a finger to my lips. Then he tiptoes around the beast, Clau not passing up the opportunity to kick it once in the stomach, as they make their way over to me. Still it doesn't wake.

"How did you do that?" Carlitos asks.

"This." I hold up the music box.

"Very clever," Bisabuela Ynez says, proud.

"It wasn't me," I admit. "It was…" And then I realize the alebrije still doesn't have a name. Because I haven't given one to her yet. "It was Canción."

"You finally named her?" Clau squeals. "I love it!"

"What about the lyrics?" Carlitos asks. "These are just his minions and the best the melody can do is put them to sleep?"

"You're right," Tío Arthur says. "To banish El Cucuy we'll need something much stronger."

"Exactly," Bisabuela Ynez says. "What if for the lullaby to actually work like a spell, the melody's only half of it?"

Suddenly, I hear a sharp snap, the music cutting out and wrapping us in silence.

Carlitos's eyes widen. "What was that?"

I turn the crank, frantic. "I don't know."

"Is it broken?" Clau asks, trying to get a closer look.

I keep turning the crank, over and over, but no sound comes out.

The ground rumbles, the monster slowly heaving itself back onto its feet. It's slightly dazed, rubbing its eyes and sniffing at the air.

Carlitos trembles. "Play it again."

I give the box a shake. "I can't!"

The monster turns, slowly, until it's looking right at us. Then it screams.

"Run!"

"Run!"

"Run!"

We race through the trees, back to the bog, before wedging ourselves through the portal. And then we don't stop running. Not once we've made it through the beaded archway separating the school library from el Otro Lado. Not even when we reach the double doors that open out to the empty clearing. We run through the pitch-black night without thinking. Without looking back.

CHAPTER 13

WE KEEP OUR EYES PEELED FOR ANOTHER fog monster all the way to Carlitos's house, footsteps quickening at every night sound and moving shadow. But we make it there in one piece, the light that's still on in the kitchen sending us bounding up the porch steps.

"They didn't take them!" he shouts. "They're home!" Carlitos throws open the door. "Mom! Dad!"

"¡Ay, Dios mío!" Tía Tita throws her arms around Carlitos, practically smothering him. She reaches for me next, brushing my hair out of my face like she can't believe we're alive. "We raced back to your house, Omega, as soon as we heard." She shakes her head. "The phone was ringing off the hook. Luna was looking for you all too. She looked for you everywhere. We all did."

"I'm sorry, Mom." Carlitos's face is flushed. "Abuela never finished the limpia and a monster got inside the house."

"A monster?" Tío Juan furrows his brow in concern.

"Yeah," Ana says, "and it had big sharp claws and gross jagged teeth and it sort of looked like a giant fart and it sort of smelled like one too and—"

Tía Tita interrupts her. "Was this before or after the police showed up?"

"Sort of at the same time," I say. "But we were able to escape through the attic window."

"We thought about coming here first," Tío Arthur adds. "But we were afraid we'd lead the monster right to you."

"So we went to the library." I hold up the music box. "That's where we found this. Somehow the melody knocks the fog monsters out cold."

"But…" Carlitos's lip trembles. "But we lost Goyo. He got scared and ran off. I tried to call him back." He chokes, crying harder than I've ever seen him. "I called to him. But he couldn't hear me. I couldn't save him."

I remember Goyo, barely visible behind the tall grass. Just a speck compared to the size of the fog monster. Then I remember Luisa's words, how she asked us to take care of him. And suddenly I feel what Carlitos does. The sharp sting of regret. Like we failed her. Like we betrayed them both.

I throw my arms around him, absorbing his sadness, shouldering the weight of it as much as I can.

"It wasn't your fault," Tía Tita says, wrapping her arms around us both. "It was an accident."

"But what if he's hurt?" Carlitos says. "What if he's...?"

He lets the words trail off but I taste them like bile. *What if he's dead? What if it's all our fault?*

"Listen to me," Tía Tita says, "Goyo's been domesticated for a mere few days. His survival instincts will kick in. That's why he ran away in the first place. Because he knows how to survive." She squeezes us tighter. "And so do we. Which means food and rest for the two of you. We'll look for Goyo first thing in the morning."

Carlitos relents, probably because he's exhausted, because the tears have wrung him dry of whatever energy he had left. My body craves sleep too, muscles sore from sprinting for my life.

So when Tía Tita ushers us all inside, insisting we sit at the kitchen table so she can stuff us full of poblano chili and pan de campo, I let her. And in between bites, we tell her and Tío Juan everything—about the magic door in el Otro Lado and the missing pages from the instruction manual and how the music box put the fog monster in a deep sleep so we could escape, except now it's broken and we don't know how to fix it.

Tío Juan immediately reaches for the music box, already tinkering with it.

Meanwhile, Tía Tita just listens, gritting her teeth at every close call. "And you supervised this?" she says to Tío Arthur and Bisabuela Ynez.

"I know you know how stubborn they both are," Bisabuela Ynez says. "You raised them."

"They're safe," Tío Arthur reminds her. Then he turns to us. "And brave."

Carlitos blushes, his face still puffy from crying. "It wasn't really that scary."

Clau snorts. "I mean I was pretty terrified when you flashed us your chonies."

"Excuse me?" Tía Tita says.

Clau reenacts the entire thing while Carlitos stares into his bowl of chili.

"And then it shot him out like a giant loogie and he was covered in mud and green goo and then Ana screamed bloody murder and—"

"We get it!" Carlitos tosses a piece of bread at her and it misses just like the dirt clod.

Tío Juan howls with laughter. "Wait, I want to hear it again!"

Tía Tita sighs. "I think once is enough." Then she turns to

Carlitos. "And who do you think you are? Wasting food like that." She tsks. "What would your abuela say?"

At that, everyone falls silent, even Clau. My body rumbles with another flashback and I wonder when I'll ever be able to get the sound of those sirens out of my head. A hot tear rolls down my cheek and I bite down on my lip to keep from sobbing.

"It was all Mr. Montgomery's fault," Carlitos says. "He thinks our family has something to do with the missing children. So they took them away. Even though they barely have any proof. Even though they're wrong." He shoves his bowl of chili across the table.

"What do you mean *barely* any proof?" Tía Tita asks.

"Soona's school badge." I grip the edge of the kitchen table. "They found it in the forest where Matteo was taken."

Tía Tita sighs. "Speaking of stubborn." She pinches her eyes shut. "I should have known she'd try going after him alone."

"But why?" Carlitos asks.

Tía Tita frowns. "Do you remember how La Lechuza turned out not to be a stranger? For someone who's lived as long as Soona...there's no such thing."

"So she knows him?" I say. "El Cucuy?"

"She *did*. But people change. Monsters too."

I remember Matteo's mother standing next to Mr. Montgomery, Deputy Medina doing his bidding. How we were all neighbors one day and enemies the next.

Anger bubbles up inside me and then I can't hold back the tears anymore. "What's going to happen, Tía?"

And why are people like Mr. Montgomery so much scarier than actual monsters?

Tía Tita takes me in her arms. "It's going to be okay, Omega. We'll get them back. Don't worry."

Tía Tita and Tío Juan keep repeating those words. When Tío Juan fills our bowls with seconds. When Tía Tita runs me a warm bath. Things Mami and Papi would have done if they were here. They hug me and remind me that everything is going to be okay.

And they seem so sure. Until I'm coming out of the bathroom and I hear Tío Juan's voice.

"He's not going to get away with this, Tita. I won't let him." I hear him throwing on his jacket. The sharp hiss of the zipper.

"Stay calm, Juan. This isn't the time to lose our heads."

I peer around the corner, listening.

"Why hold on to reason when a person like Jack can't be reasoned with? And now he's got the new sheriff involved. I'm telling you, Tita, if we don't put a stop to this now, it'll be our door they're knocking down next."

"That's exactly why you can't go barging in there demanding answers. You'll just be giving them an excuse."

"An excuse? You think they actually need an excuse? The excuse is that we exist. That we dare to live and breathe at all."

"Juan…" Tía Tita exhales. "Just…be careful."

He gives her a kiss on the cheek. "Oh, and tell the kids it was just the off plunger that was stuck on that old music box. I fixed it with some tweezers. Maybe playing it will help them sleep."

She cups his face, the two of them exchanging a look that makes my chest ache, and then he heads out to his truck.

That's when Tía Tita notices me peeking out from the hallway.

"It's way past your bedtime, Omega."

I nod. "Sorry, Tía."

I tiptoe back to Carlitos's room but he isn't sleeping either. He's got Abuelo's old chess board open on the bed, he and his poster of astronaut José Hernández in the middle of a tense game.

"Pawn to E4," José says, one eyebrow raised.

"Pawn to E5," Carlitos says.

"This is the most boring game I've ever seen." Clau flops down onto the bed, jostling the chess pieces.

"I second that." Carlitos's poster of NBA player Juan Toscano-Anderson yawns like he's about to fall asleep.

"You beat the Boston Celtics to win the NBA championship," Carlitos shoots back. "Everything is probably boring in comparison."

"Yeah, you're probably right." Juan grins, tossing his basketball in the air before catching it in a spin on the tip of his pointer finger. "It's tough being an elite athlete."

"Excuse me," José says, "but I lived on the International Space Station for two whole weeks. There were mandatory two-hour workouts a day on top of continuing my work as a scientist. I think I know what it takes to be elite."

"Yeah, but have you ever hit the game-winning shot with a concussion and thirty-five stitches in your head?"

"Have you ever used a crowbar and a can of hairspray to save the earth from hostile extraterrestrials?"

"Whoa"—Clau jumps up—"you've seen aliens? As in, aliens are *real*?"

José clears his throat, looking away. "I've said too much."

"Will y'all be quiet?" Carlitos growls. "I'm trying to concentrate."

"Your mom says we should be sleeping," I remind him.

He looks over his shoulder at me. "You really feel like sleeping right now?"

I lie on the bed next to Clau, hugging my knees. My stomach is in knots. What if Mami and Papi are hungry? What if Abuelo and Abuela don't have a comfortable place to sit? What if they're trapped in there with actual criminals? What if they're scared?

The thoughts come so fast I have to squeeze my eyes shut just to steady myself. But they're still so loud. That's when I feel Clau's cool embrace, Canción snuggling up between us as Carlitos looks on, just as scared.

"What if they won't let them out?" My lip quivers and I bite down hard.

"We've defeated monsters before," Clau says.

"Yeah," Carlitos adds. "And La Lechuza had a beak like a broadsword."

I squeeze my knees to my chest. "For some reason this feels different."

Carlitos fiddles with the chess piece he's holding. "I know…"

On the other side of the door, the phone rings, loud and shrill and making the three of us jump. I hear Tía Tita's footsteps, her voice speaking in a low whisper.

"And she's never run off before…Was her bedroom on the first floor or the second…How long did you say?"

I hold my breath.

We all do.

Then she hangs up and I hear her let out a sob that rattles my insides.

"Another one…" Clau breathes.

I wrack my brain, trying to imagine who it could be. Whose family has been torn apart.

Carlitos gets up, checks the lock on the window, and then he flicks off the light, before finally crawling under the blankets like we should have done hours ago.

I curl up at the foot of the bed, too scared to speak my thoughts aloud. I clutch the quilt Tía Tita stitched with magic the same way Mami channels her empathic abilities into candle wax, the way Abuela channels emotions into food. I rub the soft fibers against my skin, waiting for it to swaddle me in calm. For sleep to finally come and rescue me from this nightmare. But it doesn't. Sleep doesn't come and I wonder as I stare out the window into the inky black night if it ever will again.

I'm swimming in darkness. Hanging by an invisible thread in the middle of nothing and nowhere. Just floating. Until my eyes finally adjust and I see a speck of light. It glimmers in the distance and then it splits in two. I blink and there are more bright spots winking at me from far away. Waking up the darkness until there are stars everywhere.

And I realize that I'm not floating at all.

I'm flying.

The wind ripples through my hair, warm and grazing my skin.

I stretch my arms, gathering strength, and that's when I realize...they're wings.

My feathers are the color of honey and speckled with brown and white spots. A constellation to match the stars that feel close enough to touch. I soar higher, reaching for them. But no matter how hard I flap my wings, I can't quite make it.

The wind shifts, forcing me in a new direction. I try to fight it but it's too strong. That's when I look up and see the moon. Scarred and cratered and burning bright. Suddenly, I'm as weightless as the tide, drawing closer and closer until its golden halo is all I see.

"Omega…"

I hear my name on the wind but I don't turn to look. I can't even blink. All I can do is stare. Stare until it burns.

"Omega!"

I feel the sting of something cold. I blink, waking from whatever strange dream I'm in.

"Omega, can you hear me?"

It's Clau, her eyes almost as wide and bright as the moon I was just lost in. She blinks, afraid.

"Omega, I need you to take a step back. Don't look down. Just trust me."

But I do look down. I look down and see my bare feet gripping the shingles on the roof of Carlitos's house as Canción whines and tugs on my pajama pants. And then below that, the hard ground that I almost dove into headfirst.

"Careful, now." Tío Arthur appears behind me.

I lose my balance, arms swinging. Canción bites on the hem of my shirt, tugging me away from the edge.

"That would have been a nasty fall," Bisabuela Ynez says.

Clau eyes me, concerned. "You're dreaming again."

She's right. The last time I sleepwalked, she'd been the one to stop me from crawling out of my own bedroom window. At the time, I thought it was a nightmare, something sinister trying to lure me into the darkness. Instead, it turned out to be more of a premonition. I look up at the stars, wondering what my dreams are trying to tell me now.

"Are you all right?" Tío Arthur asks.

I nod, though I'm still shaken. "I just don't understand how I got up here."

Unless the flying part wasn't just a dream.

I look down at my arms and legs, searching for scratches, for feathers. But there's nothing. Nothing *except*...

"Whoa..." Ana swirls around me.

Clau blows a breeze in my direction, ruffling my shirt sleeve and revealing the faint lines and spots underneath. The same markings from my dream.

"What *is* it?" Clau asks.

I clutch myself, trying to hide.

Ana peeks down my shirt collar. "Is it all over?"

Bisabuela Ynez eyes me, concerned. "What does it mean?"

"I don't know," I say, afraid even to think about the answers to their questions. "Just..." I tug on my shirt, suddenly feeling like my skin is on fire. "Please...don't tell anyone."

"What?" Clau asks. "Why?"

I think back to my conversation with Carlitos at the parade, to the night Abuela told Luna to stay away from me or else. *She's not like you*, she'd said. And there was so much fear in it. Fear that Luna was right about us being connected. Fear that Abuela was already losing me.

"Because Carlitos is afraid it could happen to him too," I finally tell Clau. "Because...Abuela thinks it's wrong."

"But what if your abuela is right?" Ana asks. "What if it *is* wrong?"

"And what if there's a cure?" Bisabuela Ynez says.

My throat aches. Because the dream didn't just make me realize that the transformation Luna warned me about might have already begun. It also made me realize...that I like the way it feels. That maybe a cure is the last thing I need.

No. Fight it, Omega.

I slowly back away from the roof's ledge, trying to shake off the dream.

Fight it.

You have to *fight.*

"Let's get you inside, mijita." Bisabuela Ynez waves me toward the seam between the roof and the garage, motioning for me to step down.

Canción hovers close like she's still afraid I might fall.

"Wait." Clau's voice is sharp. She stares into the darkness.

"What is it?" I ask.

She's quiet for a moment and then: "You don't feel that?"

Ana floats to her side, trying to sense what she does. "Feel what?"

Clau's eyes widen as her whole body shudders. She flickers in and out like a light bulb about to go dim.

I rush to her side. "Clau, what's wrong?"

She lifts a hand, watching herself slowly disappear. "What's happening to me?"

I reach for her but my hand goes straight through.

"Clau!" Tío Arthur tries next but it's too late.

Suddenly an invisible current is pulling Clau up and over the trees.

I step onto the roof of the garage before climbing down the trellis where Tía Tita's growing tomatoes. Then I run, head back as I search the treetops for Clau. The others follow, Tío Arthur scanning the canopy and shouting down for me to make a left.

When we finally catch up to Clau she's floating above a road sign marking the county line. The very edge of town.

I double over, panting. "Clau, what happened?"

She's still flickering, low and slow like the flame on a dying candle.

My chest squeezes. *No, no, no...* "Clau!"

She finally looks up, her eyes wide and bright. She smiles. "She's calling to me." And then she disappears.

For a long time I'm frozen, staring at the empty air, feeling for the cold spot Clau left behind.

"What happened?" My heart pounds. "Where did she go?"

Canción nuzzles my cheek, reminding me to breathe.

I turn to the others, their faces in the same state of shock. "I don't understand."

The tears come again, just as hard as when the sheriff took Mami and Papi away. As when we lost Goyo.

Not again, I plead. *Please.*

"Omega…" Tío Arthur hovers in front of me and gently wipes my tears.

"Is she gone forever?" I ask.

He shakes his head. "No."

"Then where is she? Who took her away?"

He looks down at me, his eyes just as bright as Clau's as he says, "She wasn't taken." He gives me a crooked smile. "She was called."

I wipe my tears, confused. *"Called?"*

"Someone must have made an ofrenda for her after all," Bisabuela Ynez says.

"Candela," I breathe. "But… if I don't have anything that belongs to Clau, how will I be able to call her back? What if she gets lost? What if she can never find us again?"

Tío Arthur frowns, not sure how to answer my questions. Because there are no answers except to find Clau ourselves. *I have to find her.*

Before I can even take a step, the night sky suddenly darkens.

When I look up, the moon is masked. But the clouds are strange. More like fog. An entire wall of it moving in our direction.

"That looks familiar," Tío Arthur says.

The hairs on my arms stand up. "That's because it is."

The roar is piercing and then I see the fog monster from el Otro Lado. It's glowing red eyes are trained right on us.

"It's getting closer," Ana says, backing up a few paces.

The three of them could disappear in a snap, leaving me to outrun the monster alone, but they stay by my side, all of us shaking.

"Back to the house!" Bisabuela Ynez yells.

"No." I shake my head. "Carlitos is still asleep. We can't lead it straight to them."

"Then where?"

Suddenly Canción's ears perk up, listening.

I turn back to the trees, concentrating on the shadows moving in the darkness, and then I hear it too. The tinny sound of bells. *The music box.*

Suddenly, Carlitos appears holding the box with one hand while the other furiously turns the crank. He takes a shaky step toward us and then another, never taking his eyes off the fog monster who is gently beginning to sway. The sound slowly guiding the fog monster to the ground where it curls up into a giant ball.

"That thing snores like a semitruck," Carlitos whispers. "Thankfully that loud roar led me right to you."

"How did you know we were gone?"

"Juan and José started yelling. They said they saw you crawl out the window. Then something strange flew past."

I gulp down sand. *They saw me.*

"Figured it was another one of those fog monsters." He wrinkles his nose at the beast, still snoring. "Guess I was right."

"Yeah, I guess you were." The lie makes my stomach twist. "Anyway...thanks for rescuing us."

"I couldn't let you get eaten by that thing." Carlitos smirks. "Then who would I blame for always getting us into trouble?"

"Excuse me, but you and Clau have equal ownership over the trouble we get into."

"Wait," Carlitos says. "Where *is* Clau?"

The panic takes over again. My mouth hangs open. "She..."

"She's gone," Bisabuela Ynez says.

"She's what?"

Suddenly there's a snap, the crank sticking as the music becomes a garbled mess.

"No!" I reach for it. "Not again!"

Wind whistles between us, the silence sending a cold

shiver down my spine. I tremble, barely able to turn around and look.

I don't have to.

The crunch of gravel makes my knees quake, the fog monster sniffing at the air like it knows we're near. When it lets out another wild growl I know it's spotted us.

Carlitos glances down the empty road.

Then I breathe, "Don't look back."

We take off running, Ana, Tío Arthur, and Bisabuela Ynez acting as our eyes and ears as they shout, "It's coming closer!" and "It's right behind you!"

I feel the fog lapping at my ankles.

I feel my body slowing down.

Just. Keep. Going!

Beneath the sound of our heavy breathing I hear the sharp drone of a car horn. Loud and endless like someone's pressing into it with all their might. I dare to glance back and that's when I see headlights, the car barreling straight for us.

Carlitos and I tumble off the side of the road just as the car screeches to a stop. The door's thrown open, Luna behind the wheel.

"Get in!" she yells.

We scramble into the front seat, Canción curling herself around my neck before Carlitos throws himself into my lap.

We barely get the door closed before Luna slams on the gas. Suddenly, Ana, Tío Arthur, and Bisabuela Ynez pop up in the back seat, the three of them staring out the back window as the fog monster gets tangled in the car exhaust.

Tío Arthur whoops. "You're losing him!"

Luna jerks the wheel, sending us into an empty field. "We've got to get out of its line of sight."

"There!" Bisabuela Ynez points to a cluster of cornstalks.

Luna cuts left, straight for the cornfield, and then it's like those stars I was staring at earlier are falling from the sky, hard corn husks knocking into the car on all sides. We jostle forward, Carlitos's elbow digging into my side. We ram into something hard and Carlitos's head slams into my nose.

"Ow! Get off of me!"

"I can't!"

Just when I think the car is about to fall apart, we're breaking through to the other side, moonlight burning a trail all the way back to Carlitos's house. I keep my arms pinned to my chest, trying to stay out of the light. Carlitos is too busy clutching the dash to notice anyway.

As soon as the car jolts to a stop, he bounds up the porch steps. I scramble for the broken music box before following right behind him.

"We've lost it, for now," Luna calls, making her way up the steps too. "But we shouldn't stay here long."

"I'll wake Mom," Carlitos says, flicking on the hall light.

He tiptoes to Tía Tita and Tío Juan's room, lamplight spilling under the door seam. He gently pushes it open, Tía Tita moaning in her sleep.

"Mom...?" Carlitos whispers.

She doesn't stir, just keeps mumbling between snores.

"It's been a long day," Tío Arthur says.

"Mom...," Carlitos calls, his voice a little louder this time. But she doesn't answer.

Carlitos sits on the edge of the bed and reaches for her hand. "Mom, it's me. Mom, wake up."

"What's wrong with her?" Ana asks, hovering closer.

Carlitos shakes Tía Tita's hand. "Mom, wake up! Mom!"

I crouch next to him. "Tía? It's Omega. Tía, can you hear us?"

Luna tries next. "Tita...?"

Even Canción joins in, barking and pawing at the blankets. But she doesn't answer.

Carlitos tries to shake her awake. "No no no."

But she just rolls, still sleeping.

"The trees in the forest," Tío Arthur suddenly says, "they mentioned sleep paralysis, didn't they?"

"That's what it felt like when the fog finally caught me." Ana shudders, remembering. "It felt like falling asleep."

"Like when I had my tonsils taken out," Carlitos adds.

"I remember trying to rip off the oxygen mask, fighting to keep my eyes open. But eventually the drowsiness dragged me under."

At the word *dragged* my heartbeat ticks up. "You said it must come in handy…" I turn to Tío Arthur.

His eyes widen. "For snatching children from their beds."

We barrel down the hallway, straight for Chale's bedroom. The mobile on his nightstand burns bright, stamping the ceiling with constellations. But his rocket ship bed, the one Papi and Tío Juan built for his second birthday, the one they painted the colors of the Mexican flag…is empty.

In the dark, I step on something hard and plastic. Chale's toy rocket ship. It spits out engine sounds and high-pitched beeps, startling the tower of stuffed animals spilling out of his closet.

They whine and chirp as we approach. "The window… under the bed…the smell was…that horrible smile…took him by the hand."

"Whoa," I plead. "Slow down. One at a time."

Chale's stuffed sloth slowly raises its hand. "The… monster…was…under…the…bed…and…then…it… reached…out—"

I toss the sloth aside. "Okay, someone else. Please."

Chale's stuffed gorilla beats its chest. "The boy went willingly. Like he knew the monster. Like they were friends. It slipped out from under the bed, woke him from his sleep, and then led him out the window and into the night."

"And this monster, what did it look like?" I ask.

"Big. It was a dark shadowy figure."

"But its head." The stuffed seal barks. "It was so strange."

"Strange how?"

"Strange because..." The stuffed flamingo shudders. "It wasn't there."

"Wait, so it was headless?"

"No," the gorilla says. "Not completely." Then it points to the orange basketball that's halfway rolled under Chale's bed.

I frown, confused. "Its head was a basketball?"

"Not a basketball." Luna appears behind me, her face pale. Then she says, "A pumpkin."

I race back to Carlitos's room and rifle through the backpack we snagged from the lost and found. When I find the instruction manual I immediately flip to the section on physical appearance.

There are cucuys of all shapes and sizes. Some with webbed hands and teeth like a piranha. Some with one eye and some with six. There's a half-man half-goat and a demon dog with bear claws and bat wings.

"There..." Luna points to the shadowy figure in the long dark cloak.

Made of wisps of smoke and sharklike teeth. Rows and rows of them behind a jack-o'-lantern face. The mouth and eye holes misshapen like they were carved by a child.

"He's not answering." Carlitos stands in the doorway, the phone in his hand. "Dad's not answering."

He hangs up, dials again. Then the police station. Father Torres. Señora Delarosa. Belén. Even Marisol's parents. We call every adult we know, the phone ringing and ringing and ringing like we're the last three people at the end of the world. Like there's no one coming to save us.

CHAPTER 14

"We'll head to the jailhouse first." Tío Arthur turns to Carlitos. "If your father isn't with the rest of the family, we'll continue the search. I promise we'll keep an eye on them."

"The altars should be up for one more day, which means we should be able to find other ghosts too," Bisabuela Ynez adds. "They might have answers about where to find the children."

Ana offers us a cool embrace. "I'll find you if we have any news."

Tío Arthur and Bisabuela Ynez reach for us too.

"Listen to Luna," Bisabuela Ynez whispers in our ears. "Do as she says."

Carlitos and I both nod, then we watch as Ana, Tío

Arthur, and Bisabuela Ynez blink out one by one, before we head back to the car.

The town of Noche Buena recedes behind us as we head east. Toward the slowly rising sun and the caves that will soon be alive with flapping wings. It doesn't take long for us to reach Gallegos territory. They're magic folk like us and if El Cucuy or the sheriff hasn't gotten to them yet, I know they'll give us a warm place to stay.

Mrs. Gallegos is standing on her front porch as we approach, like she knew we were coming. She probably did. Forecasting is their specialty and each morning and each night as the Mexican free-tailed bats race from those first and last beats of light, they read their formations the same way we read people and objects. The same way mystics read tea leaves and coffee grounds.

The Gallegoses have predicted floods, fires, and meteor showers. They told Mami she was pregnant with me before Abuela even sensed it. So when Mrs. Gallegos embraces us with open arms, I know we were meant to come here. I know they're going to help us.

"You're safe now." She wraps each of us in a thick sarape.

I tug mine over my shoulders. "Thank you."

Carlitos sniffles next to me, still in shock. "It's going to be empty." He bites his lip. "When Dad finally comes home. He's going to wonder where we are."

"I'll call him again," Luna offers. "I'll keep calling until we reach him."

But it's been hours since Tío Juan left to confront Mr. Montgomery. Which can only mean...either they've taken him too or he's fallen into a deep sleep the same way Tía Tita has.

Luna takes Carlitos in her arms, gently shushing him while he tries to cry as quietly as possible. I lay a hand on him and I feel his worry like a desert. Endless. Hopeless. I squeeze him tighter and we trudge through it together.

"We're going to find them," I promise even though it feels like we're all alone and Mami and Papi aren't here and Clau's gone and our whole world is ripping apart at the seams. "We're going to get them back," I say because there is no not putting this back together, no future without them at all.

"Finding lost things is the bats' specialty, you know." Mr. Gallegos brings us each a cup of yerba maté and the cinnamon tickles my nose. "Sometimes the goats get loose, wander off," he says. "The bats lead us straight to them."

"Really?" Carlitos asks. "You think they can help us find my little brother, Chale?"

"You listen to me," Mrs. Gallegos says, staring deep into Carlitos's eyes. "We will search every inch of this land. We will not stop."

Carlitos nods.

I hear the click of a flashlight. The screen door slams behind us. The rest of the Gallegos family is slipping on their cowboy boots and zipping up their jackets. Around each of their necks is a small brass compass but instead of just North, South, East, and West, there are other symbols and letters I don't recognize.

"How do the compasses work?" Carlitos asks.

"Same as normal ones. Except Earth's magnetic field isn't the only force they measure."

"El Otro Lado…" I breathe.

"Los Otros *Lados*," Mrs. Gallegos corrects me.

"There are others?" I ask.

"Other worlds. Other dimensions, even."

"And Chale could be lost in any of them." Carlitos clutches his stomach. "So what do we do now?"

"They'll wait for our call while they're out searching." Mrs. Gallegos cups Carlitos's face in her palm. "And in the meantime, we'll wait too."

Each of the Gallegoses squeezes Carlitos's shoulder or pats him on the back on their way into the desert. Mr. Gallegos's footsteps cut a line through the tall grass, the sun a burning line at his back. Then he whistles and out of the brush I see the slender shapes of deer, the tall ears of a family of jackrabbits, a few wild hogs. In the midst of their snorting, a coyote yips.

"We thought he might need to call in some backup," Mrs. Gallegos says.

We stand on our toes, watching the Gallegoses and their animal companions disappear into the horizon, those brass compasses glinting in the sun and leading the way. Canción hovers next to me, just as curious. The second they vanish, she lets out a big yawn. I yawn too, my body suddenly so heavy I can barely hold myself up.

Carlitos and I slump, back-to-back, sipping our warm cups of maté while we wait for the bats to appear and Mrs. Gallegos to complete her ritual.

"The bats warned of a shape-shifter." Mrs. Gallegos rubs a sprig of rosemary between her fingers.

"El Cucuy," I say.

She nods, her face darkened.

"Can you tell us more about him?" I ask.

"According to legend, El Cucuy can take on many forms. He's walked among humans as the unsuspecting milkman, the old woman waiting at the bus stop, the stranger sitting alone at your local diner.

"But those are just the faces he wears when he wants to hide.

"At night, that's when he slips into his true skin. Smoke and sludge. Sharp claws and teeth behind a crooked smile carved into the flesh of a rotting gourd. Something foul that's been ripped up by the roots.

"The muck is where he makes his bed after wandering from town to town, searching for the scent of sadness. He feeds on it."

"This feeling..." Carlitos grimaces. "This is what he wants? For me to feel sad and scared and angry and—" His shoulders heave, tears coming again. "He's not even here to feed on it. To show his face. What a waste!"

"You're right," I say. "Why didn't he come back to feed?"

"El Cucuy lets nothing go to waste," Mrs. Gallegos says. "But the mouth that fashioned itself into a friendly grin over Chale's bed isn't the same mouth that returns to feed on the sadness left behind in his absence."

My stomach clenches. "Because he's a shape-shifter."

I remember the police lights, the sirens, the sound of those boots crunching across gravel.

I turn to Carlitos and at the same time we say, "The sheriff."

I clutch my cup of maté. "The disappearances started the same day he showed up."

"And posing as a cop means he gets to talk to every parent of every child who's gone missing," Carlitos adds.

"They let him into their homes." I clench my fists. "They cry on his shoulder."

"While he savors every second of it," Carlitos growls. He turns to Mrs. Gallegos. "How do we stop him?"

She sighs. "That's my concern. Because he's not just passing through like he normally does, taking a child, feeding on the parent's grief, and then making his way to the next town. He's lingering for some reason. Taking child after child. Feeding day and night." She meets my eyes. "Gathering strength."

Carlitos digs the music box out of his bag. "Before…it seemed like this thing might be the key. That it could put him to sleep somehow. Maybe long enough for us to banish him. But then it broke. I didn't mean to—"

"It's all right, mijito." Mrs. Gallegos takes the music box, turning it over and examining the metal parts. "Mr. Gallegos loves to tinker. He'll get it working again."

"We still need the words to the lullaby," I say.

"Even then, I'm not sure if it'll be strong enough," Mrs. Gallegos says. "Not anymore."

Carlitos shudders. "Then how do we save Chale?"

Mrs. Gallegos turns toward the sky, smeared indigo as the sun continues to rise. I hear the flap of wings, sharp and fast like rain falling on a tin roof. The bats are just a shadow at first. A storm cloud trying to outrun the light. Then they start to fall, swooping down toward the mouth of the cave. Like the meteor shower Mrs. Gallegos once predicted that painted the night sky gold.

I remember how excited everyone was, the entire town

213

of Noche Buena staying up late to see the lights. Our whole family sat watching the spectacle from the front porch, Abuelo pointing out every bright spark so I wouldn't miss it.

"That's how we got here, you know."

My eyes widened. "We rode here on a rock?"

"And collided with another rock." He laughed. "We were born up there in those stars and then we fell, as stars sometimes do, and were planted here."

I held out my hands, searching for a sprinkle of stardust, for the faint neon glow of the northern lights that we learned about in science class.

"What do you see?" Abuelo asked.

I looked harder but all I saw was brown skin and birthmarks like chocolate chips and faint white scars that seemed to have no magical origins at all.

So I frowned and said, "Nothing."

He smiled. "You want to know what I see?" Then he winked at me. "The whole universe."

I step out of the memory and back into the real world where Mrs. Gallegos is staring at a universe of her own, the bats falling like stars before disappearing into darkness. Canción leaps up, wings flapping as she watches them in awe.

Some hover before twisting into a cyclone, weaving in and out of one another like the tapestries sold at la pulga. Telling a story that only Mrs. Gallegos can understand. Her eyes scan back and forth, widening when the bats scatter. It's like an explosion. Like fireworks. Their dark wings beating as they paint the sky in shapes I can't quite make out. Until they form a giant star. Just like the one on the sheriff's chest. And then they fan out, spreading long and wide into…a pair of wings.

My heart stops.

I turn to Mrs. Gallegos.

And then I ask her the same question Abuelo asked me. "What do you see?"

She stands silent, waiting for the last bat to flutter its way into the mouth of the cave.

Then she turns to me, stares at me as hard as I did the night I was searching for stardust. Her eyes light up like she's found it as she says, "You. I saw you."

Mrs. Gallegos lays out a thick sheepskin rug and a mountain of blankets. Carlitos and I wrap ourselves up in them, squirming and stretching and trying to get comfortable while Canción builds herself a little nest at our feet. But I can still hear the adults' faint whispers outside. I can still see Luna's face when she heard Mrs. Gallegos's prediction. I can still feel the flutter in my own chest when she said it was me who would face him in the end.

And then Luna stepped between us.

She said we needed to rest.

She asked if there was somewhere we could sleep.

She told Mrs. Gallegos they'd finish talking in private and her eyes said not to say another word in front of me.

"She's wrong, Omega."

I startle at the sound of Carlitos's voice.

"The Gallegoses are never wrong," I say.

He sits up on his elbow, shakes his head. "They're wrong because there's no way I'm letting you face him alone."

I feel a lump in my throat, wanting to believe him. That we'd stick together like we always have. But then I think about Mrs. Gallegos's vision. Those wings. *My* wings. And I can't help but wonder if Carlitos is wrong.

"What if we don't have a choice?" I ask him.

Before he can answer, I hear the screen door squeal. The whispers finally die out and in the quiet we close our eyes, pretending to sleep.

I hear the shuffle of Luna's feet as she makes her way to the couch. I can tell she isn't sleeping. I can't doze off either. But it only takes a few minutes before Carlitos is breathing hard and drooling into his pillow.

After a few more minutes, I dare to peek with one eye to see Luna looking right at me.

"You need to sleep, Omega."

"What did Mrs. Gallegos say about me?"

Luna's face hardens. Then she crouches next to me and says, "I'm not going to let anything happen to you. Do you understand?"

I nod, afraid of what's behind her eyes. But not too afraid to ask, "How did you know Carlitos and I were being chased by the fog monster?"

"I didn't know you were in danger." She leans back, looks deep into my eyes. "But I did know you were dreaming."

I sit up, hugging my knees, as I remember the wind on my face.

"You were flying." It's not a question.

"How—?"

"Because I used to have those dreams too."

Carlitos snores and I jump. Luna holds a finger to her lips.

"It didn't feel like just a dream," I whisper.

Her eyes soften. "That's because sometimes...they're not just dreams."

"That's why you came looking for me?"

She nods.

I hug my knees tighter. "But if they're not dreams, then what are they?"

Luna's quiet for a long time and then she says, "I didn't just come back for me, Omega."

I go cold, thinking about the moonlight washing over my

skin, the strange lines that look like feathers. "The night of the storm you told Abuela that the transformation was already happening. Is this what you meant?"

"All empaths run the risk of transforming if they absorb too many negative emotions. Grief, rage, fear. They trigger something in us. But there are others...like me...like you...who live on that knife's edge from the second we're born. Who feel the moon's call from an early age."

"What does it want?"

"That's just it," Luna says. "It doesn't *want*. It waits. For the moment when that urge to be something new, when that yearning to take flight is just too strong. We're the ones with the deep desire."

"The deep desire for what?"

"To be free."

"So I should give in..."

"Not before you're ready," Luna warns. "Or else you'll end up trapped just like I was. But eventually...someday... you'll be able to control it."

I replay that night yet again—Luna in the rain while Abuela yelled about me being nothing like her. As if being like Luna meant being a monster.

"Abuela doesn't understand," I say, "does she?"

"She's trying to. But she was also raised to believe that

Lechuzas are dangerous. That our wings are shackles. A form of punishment."

"They didn't feel like shackles," I say, remembering how weightless I'd felt. "Does this mean they can't know?"

"It means, they might not be ready to know." She reaches for my hand. "But I'm right here, Omega. To help you through this. To teach you everything I know." She squeezes. "And I'm not going anywhere." She lets go before lifting the blanket so I can crawl back underneath it. "Now get some sleep. We'll have a lot more to talk about when you wake up."

I hesitate. "But what if I…?"

She brushes my hair back. "Those dreams are in a language spoken only by the moon." She glances toward the window. "But the sun's out now. You don't have to worry."

"Okay." I lie back, relieved. "Good night, Luna."

She winks. "I think you mean good morning."

As Luna tiptoes back outside, I roll over, watching Canción's small body rise and fall with each breath, her tiny paws twitching as she dreams. I close my eyes, finally drifting off to sleep, but instead of darkness, I see…light.

The meteor shower from my memories.

Abuelo on the front porch, waving me over.

"Abuelo…?" I say, lowering myself down next to him.

"You made it," he says.

"Am I dreaming?"

He smiles at me. "Does it feel like you're dreaming?"

I feel the cool night air against my skin. I smell the wisteria wrapped around the porch columns. But instead of just a handful of falling stars, there are hundreds. Like Abuelo and I aren't in Noche Buena at all but in a snow globe of this moment. Perfect and magical and even more real than the night it actually happened.

"It feels better than a dream," I say.

He laughs. "That's because it is." He lifts a finger, signaling for me to listen carefully. Then he says, "Dreams are where we go when we want to feel safe, Omega. Dreams are where we go when we want to remember."

CHAPTER 15

I WAKE TO MORE WHISPERING, THE SUN SHINING through the window and sticking the blankets to me. I peel myself from them, rubbing my eyes, before realizing the voices belong to Mr. and Mrs. Gallegos.

"So there was no message?"

"Not about the boy." Mrs. Gallegos hesitates. "Because this is bigger than him."

"Bigger how?"

"I'm not sure yet. But I don't think El Cucuy is the only monster in Noche Buena."

My heart stops. *More monsters?*

I wrack my brain for memories of tracks, of sounds that weren't actual animals. Of any sign that El Cucuy and his fog monster minions aren't working alone.

But then it hits me.

My skin feels hot and I bury myself under the blankets again. Staring at the ceiling fan as it turns in slow circles before my eyes track down to my skin. To the shapes that are hidden but that I know are still there. I stare, trying to sense the darkness in me. Because maybe Abuela is right. Maybe Mrs. Gallegos is too.

Maybe...the other monster in Noche Buena...*is me*.

It would explain this strange connection I have to supernatural beings; how overwhelmed I am when evil is near. What if it means I'm evil too? Despite what Luna says about freedom and power and learning to control it. What if I'm not like her? What if I *can't* control it? And what if that makes me dangerous just like Abuela thinks I am?

"Omega?" Carlitos stretches under the blankets. "Did they find him?"

I rub my eyes, pretending like I'm just now waking up too. "It sounds like they're still looking."

Carlitos's face falls. "I was supposed to look after him."

"Carlitos..."

"I was supposed to protect him." He clenches his fists. "That's what big brothers do. What Mom told me to do. And now he's gone. Just like Goyo."

"And if you had been home when El Cucuy showed up he would have taken you too. It's not your fault, Carlitos."

"It is." He tosses the blankets aside, yanks on his shoes. "Which is why I'm going to find him."

Carlitos bursts through the screen door, marching outside as I chase after him. Canción wriggles free of the blankets before running after us too.

"Where are you going?" I call out.

Mrs. Gallegos is crouched in her gardening hat, plucking the needles out of a cactus paddle before cutting it clean from the stem and adding it to her basket.

"They're sleeping." She doesn't even look up.

Carlitos bends over, panting. "You knew what I was going to ask."

"Sometimes I sense things. Right now, I sense your desperation."

He paces. "Is there a way to wake them?"

"And this is why desperation can be dangerous." She finally looks up, shielding her eyes from the sun. "We must respect the cycles of nature. If we don't, it stops speaking to us altogether."

"But if they could tell us where Chale is—"

"Not until twilight and in the meantime all we can do is pray for the answers you seek."

Carlitos's brow furrows. "You mean ask nicely and wait. Except that didn't work last time."

She gets up, grabbing her basket with one hand and patting Carlitos's shoulder with the other. "So we try again."

"We don't have that kind of time to waste."

She heads inside without another word, the slamming screen door like a punch in the gut. Carlitos stares at his footprints in the dirt, a warm breeze blowing between us.

Then he says, "No," and starts walking.

I chase after him. "No? What does that mean?"

"It means I'm not waiting. I'm looking for Chale *now*."

"But El Cucuy is still out there. He could be patrolling the streets with Deputy Medina this very second."

"Then we'll stay off the streets."

"And go where? We don't even know where to look."

Carlitos climbs onto a boulder, pointing to the tall rock formation up ahead. "*We* don't. But *they* do."

The cave is unusually cold, the breeze whistling between the rocks sending a chill down my spine. Every step we take echoes off the walls and I sidestep veins of trickling water, the sunlight peeking in through the cracks the only thing keeping me from falling.

"Carlitos, I don't think this is safe." My knees quake and I try to steady my steps.

Canción perches on my shoulder, a low rumbling in her throat like she's waiting for danger.

"I think it opens up over here...," Carlitos says.

His voice sounds far away and I realize I'm slowing down, my stomach tightening as my intuition tells me not to go any farther.

"Carlitos!" I hiss. "Maybe we should go back for Luna. She'll help us."

"By telling us to wait too? No."

A rock tumbles and my heart stops.

"Carlitos, I have a bad feeling about this."

He doesn't answer.

"Carlitos?"

I hold on to the walls, blinking and begging for my eyes to adjust.

"Carlitos, where—?"

"I'm right here." He reaches back for my hand, pulling me along. "I think it's this way."

Suddenly, the path narrows and Carlitos's steps finally slow.

"What is it?" I ask.

"Do you hear that?"

I go still, listening. In the quiet, I hear something sharp and high-pitched. A steady chirping. Like a swarm of locusts or maybe a den of wild mice. Canción's ears stick straight up, her hackles slowly rising.

"Omega..." Carlitos scrunches his nose.

"What?"

"Oh my God, Omega, did you just—?"

"Did I just what?"

He gags before pinching his nose. "What did you eat?"

That's when I smell it too—something musty and sour and making me choke.

"Ugh! It's like the stuff Abuela uses to clean the oven." Carlitos shuffles forward. "Stay back!"

"It's not me!" I shove him, a little too hard, and he trips over something beneath his feet.

He lands with a yelp and suddenly there's a deep rumble. Beside me, Canción growls, fire on her breath again like she's ready to attack. The sound ripples closer like a wave as dust falls from the cave walls above our heads.

There's a sharp crack, a jagged line racing down the side of the cave wall before a giant chunk comes tumbling down. Canción leaps up, wings snapping open as she snatches Carlitos by the shirt and drags him out of the way. The rock wedges itself between us, the sound of the impact echoing down the corridor.

This time the rumble is everywhere, pinging from all directions until I'm dizzy. Suddenly, my vision fills with a flurry of black dots and I think I might have hit my head. Until I blink, scrubbing the dirt from my face, and I see their wings.

The bats are in a frenzy, circling the small cavern until they've whipped themselves into a mini cyclone. I try to push the rock out of the way, reaching for Carlitos with one hand while he tries to crawl back through the gap. But it's too tight.

One of the bats dives too close and I swat it away. Their cries grow louder, the sound like fingernails down a chalkboard. Canción snaps at them too, spitting fireballs when they get too close.

Carlitos holds his ears, his eyes wide as he stares at the cave walls, filling with more cracks. "It's going to collapse!" he yells.

He's right. The bats are in such a panic they don't even realize the danger they're in, the danger we're all in if they don't stop. *Stop. Please. Stop.*

They're the same words I used to chant to myself when I was feeling overwhelmed and afraid. That's all the bats are, really—afraid. But not only do I know what it feels like to be stuck in fear, I also know what it feels like to face it.

"We have to reach them," I call out.

Carlitos stares back, confused.

"If we concentrate, maybe we can calm them down."

He nods, finally understanding, and then he looks up. We both do. Staring into a vortex of flapping wings. Then I reach out a hand, Canción placing a paw on my shoulder like she's trying to keep my feet on the ground. She floods me with calm and I breathe deep, trying to channel that feeling, to pull it through my body, guiding it straight to the tips of my fingers.

But the bats are too fast, each one slipping from my grasp. Carlitos is just as empty-handed, the rock pinning him out of reach.

There's a crash, part of the cave collapsing and sending a cloud of dust straight for us. Carlitos buries his face in his shirt, both of us coughing and struggling to see.

"We're running out of time!" he yells.

The sound of his voice ricochets. Just like it did when he fell. Just like the bats, their screeching sending a flood of vibrations up and down the cave walls. Vibrations I can *feel*...from the balls of my feet to the tip of my scalp. That's when I realize how I might actually be able to reach them. Not with my touch. But with my voice.

I take a deep breath, let it go, and then, even though we still don't know the words to El Cucuy's lullaby, I sing it anyway, humming the melody that has already saved us so many times before. I send up the notes, not caring how it sounds, or whether or not it's perfect. It doesn't have to be. It just has to reach them.

I see the moment it does, the tornado slowly growing still. Their cries dying out. The bats flutter toward the ceiling, huddling together like giant bushels of leaves. And then one by one, their wings curl in, their eyes fall closed, and they drift off to sleep.

Except for one.

It flutters down, landing on the rock wedged between me and Carlitos, and then it just stares with these big brown eyes that seem to *know*. That we came here for a reason. That we need its help.

I lower my voice to a near whisper. "We're looking for someone."

It chirps, understanding, and then it flies back toward the mouth of the cave, toward the sun it's never supposed to see, before hovering like a nightmarish hummingbird, waiting for us to follow.

"What did I say about respecting the cycles of nature?" Mrs. Gallegos is as red as a beet as she drags us from the mouth of the cave.

"We're sorry, Mrs. Gallegos." I wince against the bright light of the sun. "We really are."

Luna checks Carlitos's torn shirt, the scrape on his left elbow. "Do you understand how dangerous that was? If Canción hadn't alerted us you were trapped, who knows what could have happened." There's a sharp squeak, Luna whirling around to look. "What was that?"

The bat that followed us out of the cave flutters in slow circles.

I grimace. "Um…our GPS?"

"What is that supposed to mean?" Luna asks.

"It means it worked." Carlitos grins. "It's going to lead us to Chale."

"How do you know that?" Mrs. Gallegos asks, suspicious.

"Because…we asked it to…?" I say.

The bat comes closer and Canción immediately leaps up, hovering a few inches from its small wolflike face. She sniffs the air around it, curious. The bat lets out another squeak and Canción's eyes widen.

"It's okay," I tell her. "It's a friend."

Suddenly, the bat zips toward the road.

Just as Carlitos and I try to follow, Luna throws out a hand. "Stop! *I'm* going to follow it." She looks at each of us. "Alone."

"What?" Carlitos huffs. "But that's not fair."

Luna shakes her head. "It's too dangerous, especially if it's leading us where you think it is. Right to El Cucuy's lair. Right into enemy territory. But it could also be leading us somewhere else. Somewhere worse." She exhales. "Let me do this, Carlitos. For you. For Chale. While you two stay with the Gallegoses where it's safe."

Carlitos looks down, face red with frustration. I feel it too. Bubbling up inside me like hot lava.

Luna turns back toward the bat, approaching it with slow, careful steps. But instead of fluttering off in a new direction, it just hovers, panting under the hot sun.

"I'm ready," Luna says, motioning for the bat to make a move. "Where to next?"

It just blinks at her.

That's when Carlitos takes a step, then another. The bat squeaks before continuing its zigzag pattern down the road.

Luna looks back and says, "Wait."

Carlitos stops walking. The bat lands on a nearby tree.

"Looks like it's not going without us," Carlitos says.

Luna rubs her temple, thinking.

Mrs. Gallegos looks to Luna. "For nature to interrupt its cycle just to help them, it must be important."

Luna sighs, shaking her head in disbelief.

Then Carlitos yells, "Shotgun!"

CHAPTER 16

Mrs. Gallegos leaves us with a speech to rival Mami's—about listening to Luna and not wandering off and the danger we're in if we do. We smile and nod and make promises I'm not certain we'll keep. Not with Chale still out there somewhere. I can see in Carlitos's eyes that he'll do anything to save him. Even if that means breaking the rules.

She only grows quiet once she sees the bat, flying in circles in front of the windshield of Luna's car. A sign to all of us that this plan just might work.

Luna starts the engine and the bat takes off, zigging and zagging as we try to keep it in our sights. Behind us, Mr. Gallegos leads a caravan of trucks and dirt bikes, the family members who searched the desert all night still fighting sleep as they follow us into the afternoon sun.

Carlitos sits up straight, eyeing every turn. The worry pulses from him like the bass from a giant speaker. Low and crackling like he's about to pop.

"We're almost there," I tell him.

He looks back at me, hugging the music box that Mr. Gallegos fixed. "What if, without the lyrics, it's not enough?"

"The Gallegoses are powerful but if it's too dangerous we'll turn back," Luna says.

"What do you mean?" Carlitos shoots back. "I thought we were going to save Chale."

"And we will. But not at the expense of your safety. First, we'll find out where El Cucuy's taken them. Then, if we need to, we'll go back for reinforcements."

"But what if we don't have time?"

"Haven't you learned by now that this family is stronger together?"

Carlitos falls back in his seat because Luna's right. I may have been the one to finally reach her, to finally help her transform back into her human form, but that's only because of the love and strength I was able to draw from everyone else.

Maybe that means Carlitos was right about Mrs. Gallegos's vision being wrong and I won't have to face El Cucuy alone.

We slow to a stop, the road ahead forking east and west.

I look out the window and see the sign we were standing under last night. The one marking the county line.

"This is where Clau vanished," I breathe.

Carlitos finds my eyes in the side mirror. "We'll get her back too."

But then I remember what Tío Arthur and Bisabuela Ynez said about her disappearance. That she wasn't taken. She was called. That someone must have made her an ofrenda. Someone who cares about her. Maybe even more than I do. Which means...what if she doesn't actually want to be found?

"We'll bring her home," Luna says, sensing my sadness.

Unless we aren't really her home, I think.

The bat suddenly flies east and we follow.

"Why would El Cucuy take them out of Noche Buena?" Carlitos asks.

"And how?" I add. "In my vision of Matteo, they were traveling on foot."

"Doors," Luna says. "If they went through el Otro Lado, they could have ended up anywhere."

Anywhere. My heart clenches at the word.

We drive for another hour, the sun through the window landing against my face and tugging my eyes closed. Carlitos and I must have both drifted off because by the time I open my eyes again, we're turning off the main road, the tires kicking up so much dust I can barely see where we're going.

Until the sunlight glints off the gold steeple and a cloud of dust parts to reveal the peach clay walls of a church. It looks old. Like someone patched it together with the same dirt they built it on. With nothing but their bare hands and hope.

Carlitos unclicks his seat belt. "Of course El Cucuy's hideout is some creepy old church."

"Hold on a minute...." Luna puts an arm out in front of him, her eyes steely as she stares at the dirty windows. Like she's waiting for something to look back.

"What is it?" I ask.

Luna turns off the engine. She steps out of the car.

That's when I notice the words, cracking and faded over the arched doorway.

CASA ESPERANZA

I get out of the car, Canción hugging my shoulder tight as I follow Luna to the entrance. She looks back once to give Mr. Gallegos and the others a signal. *Wait.*

"What is this place?" Carlitos asks, still rubbing the sleep from his eyes.

Luna turns to us. "It's an orphanage."

Carlitos's face falls and I feel the panic rising from him like the hot steam from Abuela's teakettle.

"Chale!" Carlitos pushes open the giant wooden door. "Chale!"

I follow him down the nearest corridor, just as panicked. A nun in a light gray habit rushes out to meet Luna, both of them calling after us, but we don't stop.

"Chale!" Carlitos opens the door to a storage closet. "Chale!" He leans into an empty bathroom. "Chale, where are you?"

Suddenly the hallway opens up, sunlight cutting soft lines across a mural of fluffy white clouds. Beneath them is a row of cribs, children sleeping as nuns shuffle between them, smoothing their blankets and rubbing their backs. The soft cooing is its own lullaby, filling me with a buttery-soft tenderness. Like I'm cared for. Like I'm safe.

Carlitos scans the room, lip quivering like he can barely speak Chale's name anymore. But he does, his voice practically a whisper.

"Chale…Chale, where are you?"

"Carlitos?"

My heart leaps into my throat.

Clau.

She slides up behind the bars of one of the cribs. And she's…*beaming.* Brighter than I've ever seen her. As bright as the sun.

She flits over to us. "Omega! Omega, they found her. I

mean, I found her. I mean...more like she found me. Some-one made an ofrenda and put my stuffed bunny on it. They must have grabbed it from the car, thinking it was Candela's!"

Behind Clau, a small girl in a striped purple onesie clutches the bars of her crib. Her almond-shaped eyes are just like Clau's. She blinks at me, babbling to herself, and suddenly I understand why Clau's glowing. The love flow-ing between them like a river.

Against the wall is the altar—photos and trinkets and pieces of clothing scattered across a lace tablecloth. I graze the bunny's soft fur and I'm swallowed into the past. I see broken glass and flashing lights. The bright white walls of a hospital room. Candela being placed in this very crib. And then the nuns sifting through bags and boxes until they find the bunny. I see the moment they place it on the altar. The moment Clau disappears.

I finally let go, grounded in reality again but still confused.

So is Carlitos. But I can tell by the look on his face that he's not just confused. He's angry.

"You..." Carlitos clenches his fists. "We came here look-ing for Chale. Where is he?"

Clau shakes her head. "Chale? What are you talking about?"

"El Cucuy took him," I say.

Her eyes widen, her light dimming. "What? How—?"

She shakes her head. "And you thought he brought him here?"

Carlitos ignores her, turning his anger on me. "It's all your fault."

"What?"

"The bats connected with you. They *listened* to you. And instead of asking them to find Chale, you asked them to find Clau. That's why we're here. Because some ghost matters to you more than your own family!"

He storms out of the room and down the hall, before bursting back through the church doors. The sound of them slamming closed knocks the wind from my lungs. I clutch myself, breathless.

No, no, no. What did I do? How could *I?*

Clau reaches for me. "Omega...?"

I stare into her eyes, searching for even an ounce of the fear I've felt since she disappeared. But there's nothing. Only relief at finally finding Candela. Joy at the thought of being with her family. Her own flesh and blood.

That's when I can't stand to look at her anymore.

Because she's *fine.*

No monsters. No danger.

She's *happy.*

And without even realizing it, I wasted my magic on

finding someone who doesn't even want to be found. While Chale's still out there. Probably wondering where we are. Why we haven't come to rescue him.

Tears sting the back of my throat. When one of the nuns rushes over to me, asking me who I am and what I'm doing in here, I can barely speak.

"Are you all right?" the woman asks.

Suddenly, the sunlight pouring through the windows disappears. Snuffed out by a darkness that turns my stomach. Black and gray with swirls of green. Plumes of it beating against the windows like giant fists.

The nuns huddle in the center of the room.

"What's happening?"

"Is that thunder?"

"Should we get to the storm shelter?"

Before I can tell them that they're wrong, that there is no shelter safe enough to protect them from what's coming, there's a crack in the glass, sharp lines splintering out like a spiderweb. There's another bang and then it shatters, the fog slithering in through the open window.

Babies kick and cry in their cribs, some of them clutching the bars with their tiny hands. The nuns begin to cough before gently swaying back and forth. The drowsiness already starting to set in.

"Omega!" Luna calls from down the hall. She strides toward us and then she slows. She leans against the wall, eyes fluttering closed.

"Luna!" I yell.

But it's too late. As the nuns begin to snore, so does she.

I backpedal, bumping into Clau as I search for the exit.

The fog thickens, almost black. *Almost.*

Except there's something else moving within the haze. A tall cloaked figure with long limbs like tree branches. Sharp claws and a jagged smile.

"Tell me, Omega." His voice booms, rattling the walls. "Would you like to play a game?"

He swims closer, red eyes burning, and then he finally breaks free from the fog. As if he'd peeled himself from the pages of that book. The instruction manual detailing the same slumped, rotting pumpkin head partially hidden behind a ragged cloak and the same mangled grin full of sharp black teeth.

When he says my name—*Omega*—says it like he *knows* me, says it like he's been looking for me, that's when I realize how quiet it is.

The nuns have slumped to the floor. I scan the cribs on the far side of the room.

They're empty.

Someone cries out. The fog crawls closer, swallowing the sound. Another child snatched into the darkness.

"Candela!" Clau hurries to the farthest crib where Candela is gripping the bars, lip trembling like she's about to scream. "Omega, help!" Clau cries.

Her voice jolts me and I race to the crib, pulling Candela out. She latches onto me, sniffling and confused.

"It's okay," I tell her. "You're okay."

Clau circles us both. "There's no way out."

"The game isn't over yet." El Cucuy's voice is so loud it makes my teeth rattle.

The fog engulfs another crib. Another child disappears.

"Stay away from us!" Clau screams.

I hear the low rumble of his breath as he moves closer.

And then out of the fog reaches a hand, long sharp claws scraping at the air.

But before he can grab ahold of one of us, Canción darts between us, spitting fire. The bigger the flames get, the bigger she does too, her wings growing to the size of a sailboat and her paws leaving giant grooves in the floor. Until the three of us are pressed between her soft fur and the wall while she roars with all her might.

I stare up at her in awe as she drives back the fog, her thudding steps making the entire room shake. The darkness slowly retreats and with it, a trail of wicked laughter from El Cucuy.

That's when Clau and I lock eyes.

"Run!" she yells.

I hold Candela as tight as I can as we race back down the hallway. When we reach Luna, she blinks open her eyes and staggers to her feet, the drowsiness wearing off now that the fog's been driven back.

"Omega?"

"We have to go!" I say. "Now!"

Luna looks from me to Candela, confused.

"He took the others." I try to catch my breath. "The babies."

Her eyes widen with terror.

Suddenly, a sharp crack cuts across the ceiling, paintings and crucifixes falling off the walls.

When we reach the doors to the church, there's banging,

Carlitos's voice muffled on the other side. Luna, Clau, and I heave the door open, Carlitos's eyes wide as he spots Canción, her giant jaws snapping as she chases away the fog.

"What the—?" he breathes.

"To the car!" Luna yells.

Outside, lightning strikes. The fog still churning and angry even though it's keeping its distance. I can tell by the sharp flashes of light that it doesn't plan to stay away for long.

We pile into the car, Candela wailing in my ear. Luna cranks the engine as Mr. Gallegos and some of the other drivers from the caravan surround the church.

"Buckle up!"

Luna presses on the gas and Candela and I slam into the back seat. As soon as I click my seat belt closed, lightning strikes inches from the car. Luna swerves. We scream.

"What about the Gallegoses?" I ask.

"They've split up. Some will track El Cucuy from the church. The others will follow us back to Noche Buena."

I glance back and spot a row of headlights. They shouldn't be shining this bright this early in the afternoon. But the fog has spread, hanging like a curtain over the sun.

"They're not our only escort," Clau says, hanging out the open window.

I roll mine down, peering out too. The car is completely

covered by Canción's shadow. She flies overhead, blowing smoke rings from both nostrils.

"Real discreet," Carlitos huffs. "El Cucuy will find us in a heartbeat."

"You're right." I pinch my lip, whistling the way Papi taught me.

Canción's ears perk up.

I yell her name over the wind. "In here!"

She grunts and then with a wag of her tail she pops back into her smaller body before wriggling through the open window and tumbling into the seat next to me.

"You know, that trick would have come in real handy the first time that thing tried to eat us," Carlitos says.

Canción rests her head on her paws, panting. That's when I notice one of her baby teeth is missing, a sharp canine coming through, and I wonder how else she might be changing, what other *tricks* she has up her sleeve.

"Thank you for saving us," I whisper and she gives me her signature boop before licking my face. "Good girl."

When lightning strikes a second time, she hops up onto my shoulder, growling at the dark clouds swelling behind us.

"It's coming closer!" Clau yells.

Luna grits her teeth and then she says, "Hold on!"

She presses down on the gas, gripping the wheel so hard her knuckles are white. The car groans and then we zoom forward, the dial on the dashboard climbing higher and higher.

Carlitos's eyes widen as he registers one hundred miles per hour on the speedometer. "Are you sure this thing is supposed to go this fast?"

"She's outrun a few monsters in her time."

"There are *more?*" Carlitos shouts over the sound of the screaming engine. "That's it! As soon as we get back to Noche Buena I want an encyclopedia on every monster that has ever existed. You all are teaching us how to slay vampires and how to banish banshees and how to fight zombies." He wags his finger. "I want swords. I want crossbows. I want the spells Abuela says are off-limits because we're too young."

"You want to know how to fight?" Luna yanks the wheel, taking a tight turn. "Here's your first lesson." She taps her forehead. "You fight with this." Then she presses a fist to her heart. "And this."

"Okay, hands on the wheel!" Clau pleads.

Luna ignores her, still glancing over at Carlitos, her eyes hard. "What are they telling you now?"

Carlitos looks from the window back to Luna.

Behind us, I hear the sharp twisting of metal, one of the trucks getting caught in the fog and tumbling off the road.

"It's gaining on us," I say.

Carlitos bends over, rummaging in the floorboard, before

holding up the music box that Mr. Gallegos fixed. He rolls the passenger window down, his hair whipping around his face. Then he turns the crank.

"I can barely hear it," I shout over the sound of the wind.

He slumps back in his seat. "It's not working."

Another pair of headlights behind us disappears into the mist.

Clau wraps her arms around Candela. "We're not going to make it."

Next to my ear, I hear Canción's low purring, the vibrations tickling my skin. And I remember standing in the middle of all of those flapping wings, the sound reverberating off the walls of the cave. I used those same vibrations to reach the bats with my voice. If I could somehow amplify the sound of the music box the same way, maybe I could cut through the noise.

"Give it to me," I say.

Carlitos's brow furrows, still not quite ready to trust me. But he does as I ask, handing me the music box.

I roll down the window, my heart pounding as I stare back at the fog tumbling toward us like a giant wave. Then I turn the crank on the music box. At first, the sound is just as faint as it had been before. But then I close my eyes, concentrating. *Remembering.* Focusing on that feeling of forcing the sound up and out. Slowly, I sense the vibrations getting stronger, the sound piercing through the wind.

We hit a speed bump, Luna jerking the wheel, and I lose it.

"You can do this," Clau says.

I take a deep breath. Thinking about those babies as they were snatched from their cribs.

Chale.

I picture his face, cheeks covered in tears.

And then I exhale, thrusting out the sound until I feel the notes rattling in my own chest.

Clau and Carlitos hold their ears.

Canción whines.

And as the car and the caravan behind us continue to race forward, the fog begins to slow. Cresting. Like it's hit a wall.

"The county line!" Carlitos says. "We're almost there!"

We pass the sign, Luna finally easing off the gas. Then I see the words WELCOME TO NOCHE BUENA. Suddenly, the tires slip into the ditch, the car jostling forward as we slow down even more.

Luna's hands fall off the wheel.

Her eyes drift closed.

"Luna, are you okay?" Carlitos shakes her shoulder.

But she's dazed, head swaying from side to side.

The car barely rolls forward.

I reach for her next. "Luna?"

"Did we run out of gas?" Clau asks.

Luna tries to speak but a long yawn comes out instead.

"Luna, can you hear me?" I plead.

Her eyelashes flutter. Like she's fighting.

A truck bumps us from behind and the seat belt cuts into my collarbone. When I look back, the driver is slumped over the wheel. The car behind him is stopped too, headlights almost blinding me as I try to see how many more are stalled and piling up on the side of the road.

"Luna!" Carlitos shakes her again.

But she doesn't open her eyes. She doesn't answer us at all. Not until she slumps forward, letting out a small snore. Just like Tía Tita.

"But we outran it," Clau says. "The fog monster is miles in the other direction."

I wrench myself out of my tangled seat belt and then I finally step out of the car. When I look up, there's a strange green haze floating above the entire town.

"I don't understand," Carlitos says, looking up. "Why isn't the sleep paralysis working on us too?"

Then I remember El Cucuy's words. The question he asked me in the church and then his warning just before he vanished.

I turn to Carlitos. "Because the game's not over yet."

CHAPTER 17

"THIS CAN'T BE HAPPENING." CARLITOS JOGS TO the next car, banging on the window. When no one answers, he tries the next one. "Hello?" He wrenches one of the driver's side doors open. "Wake up! Can you hear me?"

"They're under some kind of spell," I call out as Clau and I try to squeeze Candela into the backpack we'd been lugging Goyo around in.

She grabs my face, giggling as I zip up the seams, leaving just enough room for her to poke her head out.

"Yeah, obviously," Carlitos says.

Then he stops, staring at the Gallegoses' oldest son, his arm slumped over the open window of his truck. Carlitos reaches for the brass compass around his neck and pulls the chain until it snaps.

I rush over to him. "What are you doing?"

He grips the compass and then he says, "I'm going to find Chale."

"Of course we are. Why do you think—?"

"No." He closes the compass in his fist, glares at me. "*I'm* going to find him. *Me.*"

"What are you talking about?"

"You heard me." Then he starts walking.

"Wait!" I reach for him and he shrugs me off. "Carlitos, I'm sorry, okay? I didn't mean to lead us to Clau. I didn't know...I didn't..."

"But you did and it's been hours and who knows how far away they could be by now? You heard Mrs. Gallegos. They might not even be on this plane. In this same world."

"So let me help you."

"No," he spits. "You've done enough."

The whoop of a police siren pulls my gaze, a cruiser winding its way between the trucks and cars stalled along the road. On the side of the car, painted in faint silver letters, I see the word SHERIFF.

"Oh no." Carlitos shudders.

I quickly slip on the backpack, clicking my teeth for Canción to climb inside too. Candela giggles before sinking deeper into the bag as if Canción is a warm snuggly blanket.

The sheriff steps out of the cruiser, his giant black cowboy

hat blocking his face. Until he takes it off, tipping it toward us in greeting. With that single motion, the glamour used to hide his true face begins to slip away, revealing the monster underneath. His pumpkin head is covered in warts, eyeholes slumping under black mold and rot. And there are worms… squirming from hole to hole. Just like the ones we found in the pan de muerto.

Fog twists around the sheriff's arms and legs, thickening until his uniform is replaced by a ragged cloak.

"The others have chosen much better hiding spots." He gives us a shark-toothed grin. "But they also had a head start."

"Others?" Clau places herself between Candela and El Cucuy.

"Why are you doing this?" I yell. "Why are you *here*?"

"You..." He drifts closer, the smell making me gag. Then he lifts a hand to his mouth before blowing straight up, the force parting the fog and the green haze. Just for a moment. Just long enough to reveal the rising moon on the other side. For the glow to pour over me like honey. The tiniest feathers sprouting along my arms.

"Omega...?" Carlitos's voice shakes.

The moon vanishes behind the haze again, the feathers disappearing. But it's too late. He and Clau saw the truth. El Cucuy did too.

"I heard there was a monster here." El Cucuy sneers. "A monster that could destroy all the others." He tilts his head, eyeing me curiously. "I'm here...," he growls, "to *destroy* you first."

The truth fills me like a bitter poison. Because he said it. What I feared all this time. What I knew deep down.

Monster.

I'm a monster.

I bite down hard on my bottom lip, using every ounce of strength I have left to hide my tears. I can't let him see them. I can't let him see that even though I'm a monster, I'm also just a girl. A girl who's barely able to control her magic. Who's lost without her family. Who's not strong enough to destroy a thing.

Because if he does. If he sees *that* truth, he wouldn't be

wasting time with these games, taking child after child to build up his strength. He would end me on the spot. Maybe Carlitos too. And then who would save our family? Without them, who would put this town back together?

So even though I'm not as powerful as he thinks…maybe I don't have to be. Maybe I just have to keep playing the game.

"You're right," I finally say, clenching my fists. "I *am* a monster."

Clau hisses by my ear. "Omega, what are you doing?"

"And this is my home." I glare, gritting my teeth. "You are not welcome here."

"This might be your home now," he says. "But it won't be…" His eyes seem to soften. Just for a second before they're burning into me again. "…When they find out what you are. They'll run you out of town." He snarls. "Trust me, I would know."

Suddenly, there's a pop, El Cucuy staggering slightly. An apple rolls on the ground next to him. Then another comes flying, hitting him in the chest. Then the shoulder. One knocking his hood right off his head.

"Omega, run!"

I whirl around at the sound of my name and spot Aiden and some of the other kids from school standing on the deck of the water tower. He has a bright red apple loaded into his slingshot.

"Run to the place where we saw the stars!" he calls down. "Go!" And then he slings another apple at El Cucuy.

Except this time, El Cucuy catches it with one of his giant claws. With a roar, he crushes it in his hand, head hanging back like he's howling at the moon that's hidden behind the fog again. Suddenly the fog begins to swirl into a vortex, more powerful this time, the fabric of his cloak billowing like he has wings.

"You heard him!" Carlitos says, already taking off running. "Let's go!"

We race for the trees, my heart hammering as I wonder if it's only our footsteps pounding against the hard earth. Behind us, I hear the grinding of metal and when I glance back I see El Cucuy climbing across the rows of stalled cars. Angry and animallike.

"This way!" An oak tree up ahead points one of its branches north.

A pecan tree shakes its leaves. "We'll make a path for you."

The trees ahead twist and bend, branches snapping closed behind us.

We zigzag through the forest until we finally reach Aiden's tree house. Carlitos tugs down the rope ladder before climbing up first. I grab the ladder with both hands and then I freeze at the sound of snapping twigs.

Leaves rustle, something breaking through them. I wait,

watching as a shadow moves in the dark. Suddenly, I can barely breathe. Until a breeze blows by, shifting the branches overhead, and I see Aiden.

"You made it." He hugs me and I feel the sweat sticking to the back of his neck. Relief washing like a wave over us both.

Candela reaches out and grabs a strand of his hair, yanking hard.

He laughs. "Who's this?"

"Uh...um..."

"Our cousin." Carlitos peers down over the platform.

"Right." I nod. "Our cousin Candela."

He grabs her hand, gives it a little shake. "Glad you're all safe."

"Thanks for saving us," I say.

He gives me a crooked smile. "You would have done it for me." Then he waves everyone else over. "Come on. We can regroup up here."

Once everyone is inside the tree house, Aiden loosens some old sheets in front of all the windows before searching in the dark for a fresh pack of batteries.

"She purrs any louder and she's going to blow her cover," Carlitos whispers, motioning to the bag.

I lay a hand on it, feeling Canción's warm body snug at the bottom. *Quiet*, I tell her and she listens.

Carlitos eyes the others, also whispering to one another

in the dark. "They're probably going to want an explanation for the monster that's trying to kidnap them but maybe we don't tell them everything just yet."

"Good idea," I agree, glad he's actually speaking to me. Like we're still on the same team.

There's a click as a small lantern lights up in the center of the floor. Within the faint glow I can finally make out the faces of the others. There's Abby's frenemies Naomi Davis and Joon Lee. Captain of the swim team Marcus Johnson. And Marisol and her little sister, Nena.

And for a second I wonder if this is all that's left, every other kid from school trapped in El Cucuy's secret lair somewhere. My stomach knots, thinking about where they might be, if they're scared, if they think no one will ever find them.

I turn to Marisol. "Where's Yesenia?"

Marisol's face darkens. She pulls Nena into her lap, stroking her hair, more gentle with her than I've ever seen her. Then she says, "It...took her." She grimaces, holding back tears.

"And Abby..." Aiden bites his lip.

Marcus speaks up next. "My little brother."

"Mine too," Carlitos says.

"Do we have any idea where they are?" I ask.

Aiden shakes his head. "The adults were gathering a search

party and then all of a sudden the sky turned a strange shade of green and they all started falling asleep. Right where they stood."

"My mom slumped over at the kitchen table," Marcus says.

"My dad was out knocking on doors." Aiden clenches his jaw, remembering. "He froze right there, in Mr. Peters's doorway."

"My mom was on the phone," Marisol adds. "Trying to call the police to tell them Yesenia was missing. It rang and rang but no one ever picked up."

"I wonder if that means he's using sleep paralysis on Deputy Medina too," Carlitos says. "And everyone else at the station."

Aiden raises an eyebrow. "Sleep paralysis?"

I nod. "The monster...we call him El Cucuy. He uses the fog to trap the adults in a deep sleep before taking their children from their beds."

"El Cucuy." Marisol shudders. "You mean the boogeyman? That's who's after us?"

"In Korea we call him Kotgahm." Joon Lee shakes his head, confused. "But it's *just* a story."

My throat tightens because this is it. Without Soona and her magic potions to erase my classmates' memories, whatever I tell them will stick. Changing the way they see my family...the way they see *the world*...forever.

I think back on the moment I realized La Lechuza was real, how it felt to see in real life the monster I'd been told only existed in my nightmares. Somehow, the lies only made things harder; they only made her scarier. And it was the most helpless feeling. Worrying and wondering and wishing I had the answers.

I see that same worry on Aiden's face. The same desperate hope for answers on everyone else's. And I could give it to them. Even if it changes everything. I could tell the truth. I could give them the answers they need to feel brave. The answers we need to make it out of this alive.

"It's *not* just a story," I say gently.

Carlitos pulls out the instruction manual from his backpack, plopping it down in the center of our circle. "He's real," he says, "and there's only one way to stop him."

Aiden leans over the book, flipping through the pages in awe. "Where did you get this?"

Carlitos gives me a look and then I say, "The library," deciding to follow his lead of doling out these hard truths one at a time.

"They have books like this at the library?" Naomi says, slack-jawed.

"If I had known that I might have actually checked one out," Joon adds.

"Here…" Aiden traces a finger down the torn page. "What's missing?"

"The words to a lullaby."

Carlitos holds up the music box. "We have the melody. It might be enough to put him to sleep."

"But not enough to banish him completely," I say.

"Well, how do we find it?" Aiden asks.

I shrug. "We don't know."

"That's easy," Naomi cuts in. "Whenever I get a report card I don't want my parents to see I just sneak out to the mailbox when they aren't looking and then hide the envelope underneath my mattress."

We all stare at her, not quite understanding where she's going with this.

She sighs, annoyed. "So if El Cucuy is the one who has something to lose if we get our hands on that song then he's probably the one who hid it in the first place."

"So you're saying we find El Cucuy? That would mean forfeiting this evil game of hide-and-seek," Carlitos says.

"Not El Cucuy himself," Naomi corrects him. "His hiding place."

"The train tracks." Nena sits up on her knees.

Marisol squeezes her hand. "What did you say?"

"That's where he wanted to play hide-and-seek."

"What are you talking about?" Marisol asks.

Nena sways back and forth, remembering. "At the parade. He grabbed me. Told me to play a game with him."

Marisol's breath catches and suddenly I remember too. Climbing down from the roof of the radio station. Nena slamming into me.

"Nena, what happened next?" I ask.

"I spun around and growled at him. Like Mami told me to do to strangers. Then he ran away. I went off to hide too. I thought maybe we were all playing."

"Whoa, whoa, whoa…El Cucuy was scared of a child?" Carlitos says. "But that's impossible. He *literally* collects them."

Nena finds a twig on the floor and scratches the outline of a flower into the wood. While she's distracted, face turned down, I notice a bit of face paint still stuck to her forehead from the day of the parade.

"He wasn't afraid of her," I finally say. "He's afraid of calaveras."

"The face paint…" Aiden searches through a trunk beneath one of the windows. "I think I might have one of those kid's paint sets up here somewhere…"

"Watercolors won't stick." Naomi stares at the purse hanging across Marisol's chest. "I know you've at least got something for touch-ups in there."

Marisol hugs the purse closer. "Just some lip balm. Sunscreen. The essentials."

Naomi's gaze narrows. "You're lying."

Marisol pouts.

"You want to get eaten by that thing?" Naomi says.

"Kidnapped. Not eaten," Carlitos corrects her.

I shrug. "He technically eats sadness."

"Whoa," Marcus says. "That's dark."

"Fine." Naomi sighs. "Do you want to get kidnapped by that thing or do you want to survive the night and possibly get your sister back?"

Marisol bites her bottom lip and then she dumps out her purse, random tubes and brushes and compacts spilling onto the floor. "Just be careful, okay? This is one whole paycheck from my parents' restaurant."

Naomi twists open a tube of lipstick and says, "Well, who's first?"

We each take turns, Naomi using a plum-colored lipstick to draw the stitching across our mouths before Marisol uses black glitter eyeshadow to fill in our eye sockets. Instead of covering ourselves in flowers and beautiful flourishes, we try to make ourselves look as ghoulish as possible. Eyeliner spiderwebs. Bruises made from various shades of blush.

I work on shading in Nena's eyelids and she laughs as the brush tickles her skin.

Marisol looks over. "Sit still, Nena."

She wriggles. "But I'm hungry, Mari."

Marisol sighs, digging through her purse one more time before coming up empty-handed.

"I'm sorry, Nena...I don't have anything for you to eat."

Carlitos nudges me. "Right inside pocket."

I dig in the backpack, giving Canción a scratch on the nose before I pull out a package of Reese's Peanut Butter Cups. Candela tries to snatch the shiny wrapper and Clau blows a cool breeze into her face until she's distracted, giggling again.

"When did you have time to snag this?" I ask.

"None of your business," he shoots back, still a tinge of anger in his voice.

I ignore him, turning back to Nena. "Do you like chocolate?"

She smiles wide, reaching for the candy.

"Wait." Aiden slowly crawls over to us. "The Reese's test."

"What's the Reese's test?" Marisol asks.

Carlitos and I exchange a look. Another secret. Another clue as to *what* our family really is.

Naomi crosses her arms. "Look, we know y'all are into all that supernatural stuff. So if this Reese's test can somehow help us defeat this evil boogeyman, you need to stop wasting time and tell us how it works."

Carlitos nods. "Okay. It's a way of receiving messages from the Universe. Messages about the future. About any danger we might be in. But it's not always accurate."

"Yeah," Aiden adds, "like that dog that showed up in my Reese's cup on Halloween. I thought I might wake up the next day with a new puppy but my dad still won't budge about us getting a pet."

"So you're saying there might be some kind of coded message in the peanut butter that could lead us to the lyrics of that lullaby?" Naomi asks.

"We can try," Carlitos offers. Then he turns to Nena. "And I promise, you can still eat them after we're done."

"Well…?" Naomi waves a hand.

Carlitos exhales. "Okay, here goes nothing."

He peels back the wrapper from the first peanut butter cup. I know with El Cucuy around it's not going to come out clean but what I was not expecting was for almost the entire bottom layer of chocolate to stick to the wrapper, revealing nothing but the peanut butter underneath.

Aiden looks closer, squints. "What is it?"

Everyone else gathers around too.

Carlitos shakes his head. "I don't think it worked."

"Unless…" I hold up the wax paper, examining it more closely. "There are small indentions," I say. Then my throat tightens. "Like craters."

"The moon?" Carlitos wrinkles his nose. "With all that green fog out there we can't even see the moon."

"Maybe El Cucuy's afraid of the moon too," Marcus offers.

I shake my head. "He mostly hunts at night."

"Maybe it's like a timer or something," Aiden says. "Like we only have until morning to banish him."

"That doesn't make sense either…," I say.

"Yeah, especially since he's been patrolling the streets in the morning with your dad," Carlitos shoots back.

Aiden blushes. "I…"

"It's not your fault," I tell him. Even though part of me wishes he'd do something about it. That he'd try. Maybe that's unfair of me to want. To put that kind of pressure on him. Maybe he's as much of a victim of his father's bullying as we are.

"Maybe it's a mouth," Nena says. "Maybe he's hungry too." She eyes the peanut butter cup, still waiting to take a bite.

Carlitos flicks the wax paper with his pointer finger. "Or maybe that's not the moon and this one was actually a dud."

"Try the other one," Naomi says.

Carlitos hands me the peanut butter cup this time. "Maybe you'll have better luck."

I'm not sure if *luck* is the right word. But with one shot left at getting a sign from the Universe I can't help but hope that my unique connection with the supernatural will work in our favor.

"Want us to count you down?" Carlitos asks.

I nod.

"Three," everyone says in unison.

I pinch a corner of the wrapper.

"Two."

I tug it free.

"One."

Then I pull, peeling back the wax paper and taking a chunk of chocolate with it.

"Are those stripes?" Joon asks.

"Please don't tell me there are tigers out there too," Marcus adds.

I place the wax paper on the floor, turning it in one direction, then the other. Trying to make out the body of an animal or a specific row of trees.

"Maybe they were both duds," Carlitos says, handing the peanut butter cups to Nena.

She stuffs the first one in her mouth before glancing at Candela. Silently, she holds out the peanut butter cup, letting Candela have the other one. Candela squeals, kicking as she sucks on the chocolate.

"Maybe we can hit up Allsup's on our way to the train tracks and get some more," Aiden offers.

"Yeah, maybe…" I shrug, still confused as to why, on a night teeming with so much supernatural activity, the Reese's test wouldn't be able to detect any of it.

"You finished with that eyeliner?" Marisol asks, nodding to the tube by my knee.

"Yeah." I roll it over to her, waiting for the others to finish with their calavera masks.

"How do I look?" Joon puckers his lips while Naomi snaps a photo.

"We're not getting ready for some kind of party," Aiden says.

Carlitos swats at the air. "And turn off your flash!"

"Okay, okay." Joon puts his phone away. "Sorry."

"Wait…" I look from the music box to Joon's cell phone. "Who else has a phone?"

Marisol raises her hand. So do Joon and Marcus.

"It doesn't matter," Marisol says. "It's not like we can call any of the adults for help. I even tried calling my Tía Rosa who lives in San Antonio but it didn't even ring. That green fog must be messing with the cell towers or something."

"We don't need them to make phone calls." I reach for

the music box. "This thing has already broken once. But if we can capture the recording on all these different cell phones, we don't have to worry about what happens to the real thing."

"And it means we can split up," Aiden says. "Cover more ground."

"Joon, Aiden, and I can search the western tracks," Naomi says.

Carlitos clears his throat. "Marcus and I can go east."

My heart clenches as I realize that I was wrong about thinking Carlitos and I were still on the same team. I stare at him, waiting for him to look back. When he doesn't, I feel those tears bubbling up again.

Marisol nudges me. "What about us?"

"Uh...we'll..."

I wrack my brain, trying to think of where else we might look now that the east and west tracks are taken.

East and west.

East...

That's when I realize the tracks running east head straight for...

I reach for the Reese's wrapper again, turning it until the stripes are running vertically and then I realize they're not stripes. They're bars.

"What is it?" Aiden asks, a look of concern on his face.

"The police station." I slide the wax paper over to him. "These are bars just like the ones on a jail cell."

Aiden's eyes widen. "The Reese's test worked?"

"But El Cucuy could be there," Carlitos says.

I want to snap back, *Why do you care?* But instead, I take a deep breath, trying not to make a scene, to hint that I wish he was going with me.

"He could be anywhere," I finally say. "Hence the face paint and each of us having our own recording of the lullaby. But the police station is one place we're at least certain he's been, which means it's worth checking to see if he's stashed the lyrics there. Not to mention the fact that, if all of the adults are trapped in a deep sleep there's still one person we'll be able to talk to. One person who might be able to help us."

"Who?" Carlitos asks.

"Abuelo."

CHAPTER 18

WHEN WE FIRST FOUND THE WORMS IN the pan de muerto, one of the scariest things about it was the fact that Abuelo's prophetic dreams hadn't seen it coming. But that doesn't mean he hasn't seen what might happen next.

This morning when I dreamed of Abuelo and me gazing up at that meteor shower it had felt so real. *Dreams are where we go when we want to feel safe, Omega. Dreams are where we go when we want to remember.* It was like he had summoned me there on purpose. In a way, it feels like he's summoning me now. I just wish I wasn't going without Carlitos.

I glance over at where he and Marcus are testing out Aiden's walkie-talkies and pretending like they're G.I. Joe.

"Just put some fresh batteries in these." Aiden hands me a

walkie-talkie too. "Hold down the green button to talk. The volume's here."

"Thanks."

"Maybe we should come up with some kind of code word," Marcus says as he and Carlitos make their way back to the group.

"Good idea," Aiden says. "That way we can signal if he's nearby."

"But it has to be a word we wouldn't normally say while doing something as dangerous as monster-hunting," Joon adds. "That way we don't accidentally say it and give the wrong signal."

That's when everyone starts talking at once.

"*Chowder!*"

"Are you serious right now?"

"*Long johns!*"

"Who?"

"*Gooseberries!*"

"What?"

"*Paper clip!*"

"No!"

Nena hops up on her tiptoes. "*Ketchup!*"

Joon snorts and then everyone starts cracking up too.

"Looks like we have a winner," Aiden says. "*Ketchup* when you see El Cucuy."

"And *mustard*," I add, "to signal that you're safe."

"Got it," Naomi says, clutching her group's walkie-talkie.

Marcus holds up his too.

"We ready to do this?" Aiden asks.

A hush falls over the group, the night air suddenly thick with dew. A reminder of the haze covering Noche Buena. The fact that we're trapped.

"Keep your thumb by the play button on your cell phones," I remind everyone.

"And check in often," Aiden adds.

Everyone nods, agreeing.

"Okay then…" I exhale. "Let's go."

The farther we get from the warm glow of lantern light still peeking out from between the slats of Aiden's tree house, the heavier my steps feel. Like one false move, one snapped twig might summon El Cucuy to this very spot.

"How will your abuelo be able to help us if he's sleeping like the others?" Marisol asks.

"If I can somehow get into his cell, close enough to touch him, I might be able to communicate with him."

Her eyes widen, seeing me in a new light just like I knew she would. "You can do that?"

I hesitate, not knowing if that light paints me as something good or something just as evil as El Cucuy. If she's starting to see the monster in me like he did.

"Wait!" Clau chirps up. "You dream walked? When?"

I ignore her, still trying to keep her a secret.

"I knew there was something up with you and your family." Marisol shakes her head and my stomach drops, waiting for her to attack me with accusations the way Mr. Montgomery and Matteo's mother did when they showed up at our house yesterday. Instead, under her breath she says, "That's so cool."

Clau gives me a look, still waiting for an explanation.

I lower my voice. "I didn't dream with him for long. I don't even know if I'll be able to do it again. But I have to try."

Ahead of us, Nena swings Marisol's arm like we're on a walk in the park. As oblivious to the danger as Matteo was when El Cucuy first took him.

Candela seems oblivious too, Clau playing peekaboo with her until she's cackling.

Suddenly, Marisol holds up a hand. "Shh…"

The rest of us freeze.

"Did you hear that?" she whispers.

I hold my breath, listening. And then I hear it. Beneath the breeze whistling between the trees and the random warble of invisible birds I hear the thick pad of footsteps. Something sniffing at the air.

"What is that?" Marisol shivers, pulling Nena closer.

At the bottom of my backpack, I hear Canción let out a small growl.

I slowly reach for the branch in front of us, pushing it out of the way.

A few yards ahead, there's a shadow moving within the trees. Tall with long limbs. I trace the shape until I see where it stands, hidden behind leaves and brush. Suddenly, the creature shifts and I see the shape of its long snout.

Nena takes a step and accidentally sends a rock skittering across the ground.

The beast growls, lips peeling back in a snarl, and then it bounds for us on all fours.

Marisol throws herself on top of Nena. I scramble for higher ground to get Candela out of harm's way.

And then I hear a roar. The same roar that forced El Cucuy and the fog monster to retreat. Canción wriggles out of the backpack before swelling up like a balloon and leaping onto her hind legs.

The beast skids to a stop, hackles up. Its fur is thick and matted like a bear's but its face is like a wolf's, its canine teeth snapping as it catches sight of us. Then, slowly, it rises onto its hind legs, standing as straight as a man.

"No." My mouth falls open.

"¿El lobizón?" Marisol breathes.

"Werewolf . . . ," Clau whispers.

Canción lets out another growl and the werewolf tosses its head back, letting out a wild howl, before it staggers back into the trees.

I reach for the walkie-talkie, my hands shaking. "Uh, guys?"

Aiden answers first. "*Mustard* or *ketchup?*"

"*Mustard,*" I exhale. "For now. But we've got a problem."

"What is it?" Carlitos asks, his voice crackly.

Then I say, "Lobizones."

"I knew it!" Carlitos snaps. "I knew there were more monsters they hadn't told us about!"

"What do you mean *more* monsters?" Joon's voice comes in next, sounding panicked.

My mind races, thinking back on every fairy tale, on every myth, on every bedtime story that was never a bedtime story at all. How many more of them are out there? And why?

"If El Cucuy is real, if the lobizones are too, there might be others. Everyone keep an eye out."

"*Mayo*," Aiden says. "It's the code word for any monsters that aren't El Cucuy."

"*Mayo*. Got it."

"Omega?" His voice softens. "Be careful, okay?"

"We will…"

I clip the walkie-talkie to my jeans and when I turn around, I see Marisol and Nena, still on the ground, cowering in front of Canción.

"Oh, shoot." I kneel in front of them. "Are y'all okay?"

"And that?" Marisol trembles, pointing to Canción who's still as big as a house. "Is that a monster too?"

"The glamour…" I attempt a smile but it's more of a grimace. "She was supposed to be hidden by magic but I guess it wore off."

"Sh-she?" Marisol stammers.

I rest a hand on Canción's paw to signal that she's friendly. "She, as in, Canción. She's my…pet alebrije."

Marisol goes pale. "You mean those are real too?"

Nena squeals. "She's so pretty!"

Marisol yanks Nena back by the collar of her shirt.

"It's okay," I say. "She won't hurt her."

Nena reaches up to pet Canción's snout. Canción purrs in response.

Clau floats higher, searching the trees. "How many more of those things do you think are out there?"

"I don't know and I don't want to find out."

Marisol eyes me. "Who are you talking to?"

I look from Clau back to Marisol.

"Just tell her," Clau says. "Then you can stop ignoring me and I might actually be able to help."

"You're right." I turn to Marisol. "Give me your hand?"

She hesitates before finally reaching for me.

"Marisol, this is my friend Clau. Clau, this is Marisol."

Marisol's eyes widen, taking in Clau's sparkly outline.

"She's a ghost," I clarify.

"And also Candela's sister," Clau adds.

Marisol's face flushes. "I think I'm going to faint."

I let go of her hand and start fanning her face instead. "I know it's a lot but I promise she's friendly and she's going to help us and you and Nena are perfectly safe."

Marisol motions to the swaying trees. "Not here we're not."

"Good point."

"How do we even know we're going to make it out of this forest alive?"

"Uh-oh," Clau says. "She's going into full-on panic mode."

That's when I reach for Marisol again, concentrating on the worry like a swarm of cicadas in her stomach.

I swat them away, searching for a memory that feels like sunshine.

I find one—the morning of her quince, she Yesenia and Nena all in fluffy dresses and sitting at the kitchen table eating blueberry pancakes. When their mother wasn't looking Nena snuck the can of whipped cream out of the fridge and drew silly shapes on each stack. A heart for Yesenia and a star for Marisol.

Marisol lets out a long breath, the worry loosening its grip on her. "How did you do that?" she asks.

I don't want to overwhelm her again so all I say is, "Magic." She smiles.

"Marisol's right about the forest not being the best place to travel on foot," Clau says, examining Canción. She rubs her chin, thinking. "Maybe you four don't have to."

"What do you mean?" I ask.

Clau circles her, arms out wide. "I *mean* what if instead of walking to the police station...we flew?"

I look from Canción to Marisol and Nena. "Either of you afraid of heights?"

Marisol approaches Canción, staring at her giant wings. "If it means avoiding running into any more creepy-crawlies? I'm in."

"Speaking from experience," Clau says. "We would get there faster."

I exhale. "Okay…but only if Canción gives us permission." I turn to her, looking her right in one of her amethyst-colored eyes. "Would you mind giving us a ride?"

As if she understands, Canción lowers down to her belly, nudging me with her snout. She boops me, almost knocking me off my feet, but just before I hit the ground, she snatches me up by the shirt and places me gently on her back. Candela claps, enjoying the ride.

I laugh, scratching behind Canción's ear. "Thank you."

After the others climb aboard, each of us holding to her fur like reins, Canción sniffs the ground, searching for a break in the trees. Once we reach a clearing, she leaps, my stomach dropping as we soar up and up.

"I can't look." Marisol pinches her eyes shut. "I can't look."

"It's okay." I reach for her hand. "She's not going to let us fall."

We fly over the forest and the broken cornstalks and the field of cows. Over the Allsup's and the old radio station and the town square. Down below, the adults are frozen mid-motion, just like Aiden said they were.

I see Belén, hand raised in a wave at Señora Delarosa who is carrying a bag of groceries. There's Señor Rivas shaking hands with Mr. Huerta, and Señora Salas sitting on the edge of the empty fountain.

All of them with their eyes closed. Perfectly still.

A moment later, Canción lands on the pavement with a thud and we take turns quickly climbing down her back legs before running for the glass doors of the police station. I glance back and whistle, Canción shrinking back to her normal size before following us inside.

"Getting you a pet is the best decision your mom has ever made," Clau says.

"I wish I'd asked for an alebrije for my quince," Marisol adds.

Canción drapes herself around my neck as if bashful at the praise.

I nuzzle her. "Thank you."

I lift the walkie to my mouth. "We made it to the police station. Everyone else safe?"

A chorus of *mustard*s comes through the speaker.

"Let us know if you need backup," Aiden says.

"Got it."

"Omega…?" Carlitos says softly.

"Yeah?"

"If my dad's there…"

"I'll let you know."

I clip the walkie to my jeans again. Then I realize how eerily quiet it is in here. Mrs. Bernal is slumped over in her chair and drooling all over herself. We check the bathrooms, adults' shoes visible beneath the stalls. There's even a maintenance man in the hallway, asleep at the top of his ladder as if he dozed off just before he was about to change a bad light bulb.

We wander down the hallway, searching every door for the way to the jail. Finally, we reach a metal door with a small glass window. On the other side I see the bars.

"This is it." I snap my fingers and Canción gets to work on the lock.

A siren sounds when we push it open but we don't stop, knowing no one's coming. The first cell is full of people in T-shirts with Matteo's face on them, including Father Torres. In the cell across from them is Matteo's mother. Matteo's mother who accused my family of having something to do with Matteo's disappearance. Matteo's mother who trusted the police and Mr. Montgomery only for them to lock her up in here too.

"Can you get these locks?" I tell Canción, motioning to every cell we pass.

When we turn the corner, it's Mami I see first. She and Luisa are slumped back to back, Luisa's mouth hanging open. Abuela is next to them, curled on her side on the bare cot.

I grip the bars. "That means Luisa never found Soona."

"Maybe she was still in the library after all," Clau says.

"No. She would have sensed us there too. She would have come to help."

Canción finally gets the lock undone and I slide open the cell door. I reach for Mami's hand. It's warm. Warm like a roaring fire. Like roasting marshmallows under the stars.

"I smell hot cocoa," I say. "I hear laughter." I look back at Clau. "She's not afraid."

"At least we know she's not stuck in a nightmare," Clau says. "Sounds more like a party."

"Or one of our family camping trips," I say.

Canción yips, letting me know she's unlocked the next cell. Inside, Papi's slumped over in a chair, his hat crooked on his head. I straighten it, sitting him up against the wall for support before walkie-ing to Carlitos that Tío Juan is safe here too. Then I make my way over to where Abuelo lies on a cot.

"Do you really think this will work?" Clau asks.

"I don't know…," I say.

Until I take Abuelo's hand and I feel the warmth of that same roaring fire. I smell marshmallows and melted chocolate. Then, in the quiet of my mind, I scream his name and with my eyes pinched shut, with my heart wide open, I wait for an answer.

CHAPTER 19

THE FIRST THING I NOTICE IS THE quiet. Silence so deep it feels like I'm at the bottom of the ocean. As I blink myself into the dream, it looks like the bottom of the ocean too. Cold and pitch-black.

My heart starts to race and I wonder if I ended up in the wrong place. If I made a mistake.

Until I blink and see a prick of light.

A single star.

Winking at me like a friend.

Beckoning me closer.

I take one step and then another but it feels more like swimming. Or maybe dancing. A strange joy spreading across my limbs and carrying me toward the light.

The brighter it gets, the more the darkness peels away, revealing a dirt path lined with cacti. One I've traveled down before. It bends and suddenly I hear voices. The laughter I heard when I touched Mami's hand. Loud and boisterous. *Papi's* laughter.

I smell mesquite and fried tripas.

I hear the sound of an accordion coming through a crackling speaker.

I feel the warmth of the flames. Of Abuela's favorite sarape. Of Mami's hugs.

And as the sky above begins to fill with stars, the moon being born right before my eyes, I finally see them up ahead. Standing around the campfire. Smiles on their faces.

Because they're okay.

My family is okay.

Mami spots me over her shoulder and I wait for her to yell or cry or run to me.

Instead, it's my eyes that water, my heart that pounds, my legs trying to force me into a run.

But then she says, "Omega, dinner's almost ready. Come grab a plate."

And it hits me that...she doesn't realize where she is.

She doesn't *know* she's *dreaming*.

So I don't run to her. I don't make a scene at all. And when she offers me a plate of food, I take it without saying a word about how much I've missed her, about how scared I've been. Instead, I choke back my tears and stuff it all down.

That's when Abuelo comes up behind me, resting his hands on my shoulders as he says, "You found us."

I turn to him, almost dropping the plate of food.

He winks at me. "I've been keeping them distracted. Your mother was running herself ragged trying to claw her way out of here. But I told her you'd come." He squeezes my shoulder. "I knew you would."

"Is that why you came to me? To show me that I could?" I set down the plate of food. "How long have you known?"

He smiles. "Since the day you were born." Then he presses a finger to his lips. "Let's wake them first, shall we?"

Then Abuelo snaps a finger and the expression on Mami's face changes from peaceful to panicked. She looks around, then at her legs, her hands. She turns to Abuela, who's just as dazed.

"Why are we still here?" Mami looks square at Abuelo. "How long…?"

Then she sees me, the sight stealing her breath.

She throws herself at me, almost taking us both to the ground. And then she's rocking me, squeezing so hard I can barely breathe.

"Mami, I'm okay. I'm okay."

She kisses me on the forehead, repeating Abuelo's words. "You found us."

Abuela grabs me next. "What's happening? Where's Carlitos? And Chale?"

"Carlitos is fine." I try to speak. To tell them what happened. But suddenly it's like I'm back in Chale's bedroom, staring at his rumpled blankets, at the curtains fluttering in the wind. Feeling the sting of that moment all over again.

"Omega…what's wrong?" Mami asks.

"It's Chale." The tears come, so hard I'm practically choking on the words. "He took him. He's gone."

Tía Tita gasps, shaking uncontrollably while Tío Juan holds her in his arms.

"He's not the only one. The entire town is under some kind of spell. All of the adults are frozen with sleep paralysis. The kids he hasn't found yet are trapped in a sick game of hide-and-seek. But he's not the only monster out there hunting. We saw…"

"You saw what?" Luisa asks.

"El lobizón."

Mami looks at me, more serious than I've ever seen her. "Omega, I need you to tell us everything that's happened since we were arrested. Step by step."

I nod, starting with the fog monster that chased us to the school and then the instruction manual we found in el Otro Lado. I tell them about the music box and Luna taking us to the Gallegoses and the bat that led us to Candela and Clau. I tell them everything.

Everything except…the dream I had of flying. El Cucuy calling me a monster. Maybe I should have. Maybe they would have told me he was wrong. Or maybe it would only confirm what they've always suspected. Maybe they would end up fearing me too.

When I finally run out of breath, Luisa presses a finger to her temple, thinking. "When the fog monster that was guarding the music box chased you back to the library, did you close the door behind you?"

I remember racing back to the bog and then clawing our way under the bed before running as fast as we could through the stacks, through the empty hallways of the school, across the clearing, and back through the trees all the way to Carlitos's house.

"Omega," she says, louder this time, "did you *close* the door?"

A wave of nausea rolls over me.

My knees buckle, Mami leading me to a chair by the fire.

Because all I remember is running.

Running until my legs were aching.

Running without looking back.

I finally meet Luisa's eyes. "No. We didn't close the door behind us."

Her face falls.

Mami starts to pace.

Abuela clasps her hands like she's praying.

"What do we do?" Tía Tita's still frantic, tears streaming down her face.

Abuelo steps to the fire, staring into the flames, and then he says, "We wake up."

He waves me over, and I follow, confused. "I don't understand."

He takes my hands and then he holds them, palms down, over the campfire. "Do you feel that?" he says.

I concentrate, feeling the heat against my skin. At first it feels as real as everything else. The smoke sticks to the back of my throat. The crackling mesquite popping like tiny fireworks. I close my eyes until the hum of the radio grows louder, a song I've heard before trying to tug me back to the past. And it's in that moment, between the memory and the present, that I sense something else churning within the flames.

A different kind of heat.

Power.

"What is it?" I breathe.

"The spell," Abuelo says. "The source of it."

"You want me to snuff it out," I say, finally understanding.

Then he says, "You're the only one who can."

I feel my family circling around the fire too but I still don't open my eyes to look. Instead, I hold on to the in-between, to this energy that feels like the sun. My hands move, dancing in the smoke, and I sense that I have a choice. To stoke the flames, making the spell stronger, or to dampen them, releasing its bind.

Abuelo places a hand on my shoulder again, like he can sense that I'm in some kind of tug-of-war.

That's when I take a deep breath and then I imagine the flames in my mind's eye. Burning bright. And then shrinking. Going dark. I think about raindrops and ocean waves and long winter days.

I fill my body with the sensations and then I thrust them out, feeling the heat receding as the campfire dims. I open my eyes and see the embers, burning red, and then gone, nothing left behind but smoke. And as that smoke floats between us, wrapping around Mami and then Papi and the others, I watch them go dim too. Flickering like fireflies before disappearing completely.

When I'm finally standing there alone, I close my eyes again, reaching for the real world with all my might. Then I hear my name, far away at first, like someone's shouting at me from the end of a tunnel.

"Omega? Omega, can you hear us?"

I hear Mami's voice. I feel Papi's hands.

I blink open my eyes, and in their arms, I'm home.

"Thank goodness you're all right." Mami hugs me again. "I was so worried."

"We're fine. I promise."

At the mention of *we* Mami turns to look at Marisol who has Candela hiked up on her hip while Nena holds her other hand. Clau hovers nearby and I see the moment Mami registers their resemblance.

"She looks just like you," she says to Clau.

Clau beams.

Abuela takes Candela in her arms as her eyes well up with tears. "All this time." She shakes her head. "She was out there all this time."

"Omega?" A strange high-pitched sound escapes the walkie-talkie.

I unclip it from my jeans. "I'm here."

"Omega...wasn't...moo."

"Carlitos?" I climb onto the cot, trying to get a better signal. "You're cutting out."

"Upstairs," Papi says. "We might be too far underground."

We race back down the corridor before bounding up the basement steps.

Once we reach the first floor of the precinct, I try again. "Carlitos?"

"Omega, it wasn't the moon!"

"What?"

"The Reese's test. It wasn't the moon we saw. It was a tunnel."

My heart stops. "The train tunnel." I turn to Mami and the others. "That's where El Cucuy's keeping them."

"We're almost there," Aiden says, his voice cutting through static.

That's when Mami takes the walkie from me. "Aiden, do not go into that tunnel."

"Mrs. Morales?"

"Omega broke the spell for us. The men are coming to you now. Do not move until you see Tomás. Do you understand me?"

Abuelo, Papi, and Tío Juan push through the glass doors of the police station before breaking into a run through the fog.

"Yes, ma'am."

And then, Aiden's thumb still on the green button, I hear a strange noise in the background. Loud and long. At first, I think it might be a siren or even a train horn as it barrels down the tracks. But then it comes again and Mami loses her breath.

"Aiden?" she says. "Aiden, what was that?"

For a long time we just listen to him breathe. Like he's too afraid to speak. Then he whispers, "I don't know. But it's getting closer."

That's when I hear branches breaking, heavy footsteps thudding across the ground. Followed by a wild howl that stops my heart.

"Aiden?" Mami yells his name. "Aiden!"

The sound cuts out. The silence floods in. And I remember the mysterious shape of a dog stamped in Aiden's peanut butter cup on Halloween. The long sharp canines. Its head thrown back in a howl.

"Mami?" I tug on her arm. "Mami, is Aiden going to be all right?"

She looks at me, remembering something too. The promise she and Abuela made to never lie to us again. Which is why she doesn't tell me he's going to be fine. That we'll save him.

She doesn't say anything at all.

When we exit the police station and enter the square, Mami almost stumbles, taking in the sight of all the people frozen mid-step, mid-laugh, mid-conversation. Completely unaware of the fact that they're in danger.

"We can't have all of these people helpless like this with so many monsters on the loose," Abuela says.

Tía Tita nods. "We have to find a way to lift the spell."

Abuela stops, examining some of the people more closely. "I'm not sure it's just a spell."

Mami moves her hands through the green fog the same way I gathered the smoke from the campfire. "It feels more like a curse."

Abuela sighs. "And the only way to break a curse is to break the one who created it."

"You said Carlitos has the music box?" Mami asks.

"Yeah"—I nod—"but Marisol has a recording of it on her cell phone."

Marisol holds out her phone, letting Mami see.

"How loud does that thing go?" Abuela asks.

Marisol turns the volume all the way up.

Mami shakes her head. "If we want to confront him from a distance, we need something louder."

I think back to the sound of that campfire radio, the way it had swelled inside my head. I step around the square, not just noticing the still people but the stalled cars too.

"Clau."

She pops to attention.

"How much strength do you think it would take to turn all of these cars on at once?"

She taps her chin. "It depends on how angry I can get."

Abuela waves her hands. "Wait a minute. Anger isn't the only power source."

"What else is there?" Clau says.

Abuela squeezes Candela tighter, looking between her and Clau. Then she says, "Love."

Clau takes Candela's hand and gives it a soft squeeze. "What do you say, Candela? Will you be my little battery?"

Candela squeals, kicking her feet.

Clau laughs. "I think…" She turns back to me. "I could get maybe five. Six tops."

"If the lullaby was blaring from six car speakers, do you think that would be enough?" I ask Mami.

"Maybe…," she says, thinking. "But how are we going to connect Marisol's phone to six different cars?"

I face the parade route, the road we drove down just yesterday as we headed to the cemetery. Then I point. "The old radio station."

"We'd have to lure him here," Abuela says. "To this very spot."

"He'll come," I say.

"How do you know that?" Mami asks.

"Because of me." I meet her eyes. "Because he's looking for me."

CHAPTER 20

Tía Tita takes Marisol, Nena, and Candela to the old radio station for safekeeping while they await Clau's signal that it's time to press play.

"Are you sure about this?" Mami asks.

"I'm the one connected to supernatural beings. El Cucuy sensed it too. If he thinks I'm alone, that I'm vulnerable, it might draw him out."

"I don't like the idea of using you as bait." Abuela shakes her head. "It's too dangerous."

"It is dangerous," Mami says. "But so is standing in this fog while monsters roam free through the town. While the children are still out there." Mami takes one of Abuela's hands before reaching for one of mine too. "Which is why we'll be *right* here."

"Once the song weakens him"—Abuela raises an eyebrow—"you let us do the rest, do you understand?"

I nod.

"Okay, then." Mami kisses me on the forehead.

Abuela marks me with the sign of the cross, whispering a brief prayer.

Then they walk away, Mami hiding behind a police car while Abuela's concealed behind a vine-covered trellis.

And then I wait, staring out into the fog as it churns like a vortex to another world. Every inhale feels thick like I'm swimming in a bowl of soup. But beneath that sticky wet feeling…there's also a strange warmth. That's when I remember what Abuelo said about the campfire. That it was the source of the spell. The battery keeping it going.

I sway from side to side, dancing my hands through the fog, and I feel that same power. The source of the curse. *El Cucuy.*

"*I'm here,*" I shout into the void.

There's a long moment of silence and then suddenly, I hear a wretched laugh that makes my knees quake. The sound swells, tumbling toward me like a wave, until I'm on the ground, gripping the pavement just to keep from being blown off my feet.

And then the sound disappears, the force that held me down gone too.

I stand, catching my breath, and then there he is.

Something *ripped up by the roots* just like Mrs. Gallegos said. A part of the earth we're never meant to see.

He smiles at me, sharp teeth glinting, and I gag at the smell of rot.

"The moon's not here to save you."

I look up, the sky beyond the fog still hidden completely, and I realize that he's snuffed out my power source just like I snuffed out that campfire. As if the moon isn't my enemy but my ally.

"And you?" I say, my voice fierce. "Who's here to save you?"

He snarls, charging straight for me.

I call to Clau. "Now!"

And then one by one, headlights burst to life like small moons, engines rumbling. Clau flexes her fingers, teeth gritted as she works the radio signals, flipping through channels of chatter and static until she lands on the lullaby.

The melody pours through the speakers as she cranks up the sound.

But it's not enough. El Cucuy swings his arms, swatting at the noise. But he's still standing. He's still strong.

One pair of headlights flickers out, the engine cutting. Then another.

"Omega!" Clau strains, groaning as she fights to hold on to the sound. "I'm losing it!"

El Cucuy straightens and then he screams, letting out a bloodcurdling sound that has me holding my ears. A second later, the ground begins to tremble and then I see a procession of fog monsters breaking through the trees. They bound toward us, rumbling with thunder and lightning.

"Omega!" Mami abandons her hiding spot, running toward me.

El Cucuy lifts a hand, thrusting a cloud of fog in her direction.

She darts behind the fountain in the center of the square.

I see the fog monsters getting closer. I brace for the impact. And then I hear a loud whoosh. Something swooping down overhead.

I look up and see Canción rushing the fog monsters, toppling them like bowling pins. But the harder they fall, the angrier they get, the rage puffing them up like balloons until they double in size.

Canción circles them like she's herding cattle while they hurl lightning strikes like spears. One nicks her paw and she yelps.

"Canción!" I scream, the sound of my voice suddenly reminding El Cucuy that I'm still standing.

He lunges for me and I scramble out of reach. But not far enough to escape the fog. He gathers it like a rope and then he slings it around my ankles. As soon as it touches my skin,

I feel my legs start to go numb with the same sleep paralysis he used on the adults.

I hear Mami screaming.

Clau groaning as she tries to increase the volume.

Abuela's incantations.

But beneath it all there's something else. Faint. Familiar. A high-pitched cry.

Like a bark.

I twist my body to get a better look and then I see Goyo sprinting down the road. But he's not alone. Behind him is a sparkling avalanche. Every ghost that was summoned to an altar in Noche Buena. There's Ana and Tío Arthur and Bisabuela Ynez. Ghosts I remember seeing at the cemetery yesterday morning and dozens of others I don't recognize.

Tío Arthur slams into El Cucuy, still using the trick Clau taught him to become corporeal. El Cucuy tumbles, in shock at the sight of them.

"How can we help?" Ana yells.

"...car radios." Clau fights to speak. "Loud!"

The ghosts spread out, raising their hands and igniting a cacophony of static and clashing instruments. Until slowly, the lullaby starts to cut through.

El Cucuy registers it too, the sound making him grimace. Like it hurts. But there's something else behind his eyes, the pain not just physical. It's emotional too, the sound tugging on whatever heartstrings he has left.

Dreams are where we go when we want to feel safe, Omega. Dreams are where we go when we want to remember.

That's the look on his face. He's not just listening. He's *remembering*.

"¡Ahora!" Abuela yells and then she and Mami are running straight for him.

El Cucuy clutches himself, trying to stay on his feet. But the melody's hold on him is too strong.

Mami and Abuela lay their hands on him, chanting. While Canción wrestles one of the fog monsters to the ground. While the ghosts wrench the volume to a fever pitch. Everyone locked in battle.

But it's still not working.

It's still not enough.

Not without the words.

Words that might just be locked in the same memory that holds the melody. The same memory playing behind El Cucuy's eyes right this moment.

So even though I'm supposed to stay back, to let Mami and Abuela fight this battle, I know, deep down in that part of me that summons the supernatural in the first place, that calls to it like a siren song, that I might be the only one who can reach him.

I step between them, laying a hand on El Cucuy, and it's like being sucked through a vortex. I feel the real world rip apart at the seams and suddenly I'm standing in the middle of a pumpkin patch under a full moon.

It's eerily quiet and much colder than it is in Noche Buena in the fall. Which must mean I'm not in Noche Buena.

I jump at the sound of a warbling bird and spot a scarecrow in grubby overalls and a straw hat. The hat hangs limp over a jack-o'-lantern face and my heartbeat ticks up, waiting for a pair of eyes to appear, staring back.

But they don't, no one in this pumpkin patch but me.

Instead of staying put, I start walking and rubbing my arms to try to keep warm. Eventually, I hear voices, the wind carrying them up the hill. Yelling. Laughing. A moment later I see a small boy running and glancing over his shoulder. A group of older kids, much bigger than him, are calling out, whooping and hollering like they're on the hunt. Their faces are covered, each of them dressed in a different ghoulish costume.

"Come back!"

"It was just a game."

"We're not going to hurt you!"

The small boy glances back once more and then he trips, caught on one of the vines slithering out from the soil. He tugs on it, trying to free himself. Just as he leaps to his feet again, one of the older boys snatches him by the shirt collar. This close, I can finally see the mask he's wearing. It looks old, made of wood or maybe papier-mâché. Painted the color of bone. *A skull.*

He's not the only one; every kid is dressed as the dead. That must be why El Cucuy was so afraid of Nena's calavera face paint. That must mean the boy...the one they're all chasing...*is* El Cucuy.

"Didn't you hear me?" The older boy tosses El Cucuy in the dirt. "The game's not over yet."

The game's not over yet.

My stomach clenches, remembering El Cucuy's voice as he spoke the same words.

"Okay, I think you've made your point." A girl lifts her calavera mask, taking a step between the older boy and El Cucuy. The dress she's wearing looks strange. *Old.* With a high collar and sharp pleats.

"Come on, Soona," the older boy says, "we're just having a little fun."

The air is knocked from my lungs. *Soona?*

Suddenly, two boys grab El Cucuy, heaving him up by the arms. He kicks his legs, trying to escape, but he's too small.

Soona chases after them. "It's not funny anymore. Let's just go."

But they don't stop. They drag El Cucuy toward the

scarecrow before taking it apart, putting the dusty overalls on him instead. They grab the lopsided pumpkin next, forcing it down over his head.

Then they lift him up, hanging him back on the frame. The older kids stand there, marveling at their handiwork. Except Soona. She crosses her arms, staring at the ground.

Do something. I shout the words in my mind.

"She can't hear you."

I spin at the sound of the voice. Soona—the version I know, the one that's been missing for almost two days—places her hand on my shoulder. She squeezes, holding me close as we both look on.

"Now for the final touch." One of the other boys approaches, slamming the straw hat down on El Cucuy's head.

And then without another glance, they turn and walk away. While the younger version of Soona follows.

They leave El Cucuy in the dark. In the cold.

"How could you?" I pull away from Soona, barely recognizing her.

"I was young."

"You were cruel. Being young is no excuse. Isn't that what you've always taught me? To be kind? To be good?"

"You're right. It's not an excuse. That's why I came back here. To fix things."

"This is where you've been all this time?"

She kneels, brushing the vines at her feet. "Moments like these, they play on a loop for a reason. Because they're powerful. Because they change us. I thought if I found my way back to this shared memory, I could rewrite it for both of us. But all I've been able to do is watch. Over and over and over again." She pinches her eyes shut. "How I was scared. How we hurt him."

"So what now?" I shake my head. "Are you saying there's no hope?"

She stands again, taking both of my hands. And then she says, "The hope...is you."

I remember Mrs. Gallegos's vision, what she saw hidden within all those flapping wings. *You... I saw you.*

"But how?" I breathe.

"By going somewhere the rest of us can't." She presses a fist to her heart. "The same way you did with Luna."

I turn back to El Cucuy. In the silence I hear him sniffle, crying softly. Like he's still trying to make himself small. Like it's the only way to keep himself safe. And even from here, I feel his loneliness like an endless stretch of beach. Like a black hole.

I watch him fall into it. Deeper and deeper.

A flower blooming in reverse. Withering while all I can do is watch.

Except I'm not here to just watch.

I take a step closer. Then another.

"Memories are delicate things," Soona warns. "Every second made of glass. Push too hard and you might just shatter the whole thing."

"What if he can't hear me?" I ask.

"Then you'll have to reach him another way."

I step directly in front of El Cucuy, watching his eyes shift behind his pumpkin mask, and then I reach for him, finding his hand in the dark until I'm falling into the same black hole.

Except it's not as empty as I thought. There are voices. Laughter. Taunts that echo, swarming around us like gnats.

Coward.

Rat.

Crybaby.

The voices become a storm, telling him that he doesn't belong. I can't help but get swept up in it too, the pain striking me in the same spot that Carlitos's rejection did. Like the moment I betrayed him, the moment he decided we weren't a team anymore, has left behind a bruise.

But bruises heal. Maybe Carlitos can't forgive me today. Maybe I don't deserve his forgiveness yet. But that doesn't mean I've lost him forever.

The loneliness El Cucuy feels is not just a bruise. It's an open wound—a gaping hole he's been trying to fill his whole life.

"I'm here," I try to tell him. "You're not alone anymore."

But at the sound of my voice, the ground suddenly begins to groan, rumbling beneath my feet. Leaves tremble in the dark as the vines begin to slither toward El Cucuy. I jump out of the way just as they reach the base of the wooden frame, climbing the post before coiling around El Cucuy's legs like snakes.

"No!" I lunge for the vines, trying to rip them down.

Soona tries too, chanting a spell beneath her breath, but they're too strong.

El Cucuy twitches as the vines tighten around his arms and legs until he's so tangled in them that I can't tell where they end and the boy begins. But as they stretch into long limbs, my breath catches, and I realize that might be the point.

"This is how it happened," I say.

"Not again," Soona breathes.

But before she can try another spell, El Cucuy is ripping himself from the wooden frame, standing tall on his own two feet. Half-man, half-nature. He lifts his hands, for a long time just staring at them. Marveling at his new form.

Then he looks up and in that same gruff voice I've come to fear, he says, "You."

I shudder, unable to form words.

But then I realize that he's not looking at me. He's looking at Soona.

She stares back, taking in the monster she helped create. And then she says, "I'm *so* sorry."

Her lip quivers and I reach for her hand the same way I reached for El Cucuy's, squeezing hard so she knows she's not alone. In the quiet, we both brace for El Cucuy to attack. But he doesn't.

"You're family," he says, looking between us.

Soona nods.

"You know, that's all I ever wanted." He hangs his head. "To belong somewhere. To *someone*."

"We should have let you in." Soona shakes her head. "We should have—"

"I had a choice." He cuts her off, lifting his vine-covered hand again. "I could have fought back. But the truth is, it was a relief. To become a part of something bigger."

"But you didn't stop there," I say. "What about Chale? What about Matteo and the others? You took them. Why?"

"You're right," he says. "Those choices were mine too." He reaches for the gourd atop his head, squeezing like the weight is almost too much. "In the beginning, everything was so simple. All I wanted was a friend. One day I found one. He looked just like me. Like maybe in another life we could have been brothers." He stares off, wistful. "We were playing hide-and-seek and it was my turn to hide. As the sun began to set, I worried he wouldn't find me. Then I heard footsteps, voices calling out his name." He hisses between his teeth. "It was the boy's parents. They were frantic. That was the first time I ever tasted fear."

The hairs on my arms stand up, remembering La Lechuza recounting a similar story. How she thought she'd been chasing one thing and then it turned into an appetite for something so much worse.

"So I stopped hiding and I started seeking."

"You found the boy first," Soona says, stepping in front of me.

He nods. "And then I hid him and what I tasted next was so much more satisfying than fear."

"Grief," I say, my voice small.

"I couldn't get enough of it."

"You said it was a choice." Soona meets his eyes. "Why not make a different one now?"

He sighs. "I wish I could."

"You can," I tell him. "Please. You have to."

He's quiet and I think maybe he's considering. But then he turns to me and says, "He won't let you stop him."

"Who?" I say.

He looks up at the sky. Then back at me. "The monster I became."

Lightning strikes, storm clouds tumbling in like giant plumes of smoke.

"That's why he came to your town in the first place. It was all a game of hide-and-seek. From the very beginning. And now that he's found you, he's not going to let you win."

Another lightning strike. This one closer.

"Then help me," I plead. "You can make a different choice. We can stop him together."

At the word *together*, he goes still, and I remember what he said about wanting to be a part of something bigger. So I reach out my hand, giving him the chance.

He doesn't take it at first, still unsure.

I hear Soona's voice in my head. *Reach him another way.*

I take a deep breath, and then I hum that familiar melody. Quietly at first. My voice shaking. But El Cucuy doesn't leave me to fill the silence alone. Suddenly, he starts humming too.

Slowly, the sound grows, and then he opens his mouth and begins to sing.

Rest little rabbit
the day is done
close your eyes
nowhere else to run
Sleep little rabbit
Mommy's right here
to keep the wolves at bay

no need to fear
Dream little rabbit
of a new day's dawn
of sunshine in the meadow
the foxes all gone

He finally grips my hand and I see the memory playing behind his eyes, what he's been trying to recreate all this time. *His mother.* Holding him *so* tight. I feel that sense of belonging he's been searching for. As she rocks him, singing softly in his ear, I feel the love he's so desperately needed.

And even though I don't see the moment it all ends, I sense her death lurking in the shadows of El Cucuy's memory like its own boogeyman. One he couldn't escape from no matter how hard he tried.

I see him trying now, singing with his whole heart. But as our voices grow louder, the ground beneath our feet begins to rumble again, jagged lines tearing through the dirt. The cracks spread up and out, light spilling through like we're in a broken snow globe.

"He knows we're here," Soona says, pointing straight up.

A jack-o'-lantern smile tears across the sky, lightning striking against dark green clouds. But he's too late. Because I already got what I needed.

Soona and I reach for each other just as the memory rips itself to shreds, sending us tumbling back into the present. I blink my eyes open to see my hands still clutching El Cucuy's cloak, Mami and Abuela still chanting in my ear.

"He remembers," I say. "He remembers the words."

At that, El Cucuy howls, knocking us back. I roll against the fountain, the air knocked from my lungs.

"Omega!"

I blink, scrubbing the dirt from my eyes, and then I see Clau heading straight for me. "Omega, are you okay?"

"I'm okay."

She pulls me to my feet. "So, what's the plan?"

"The plan is...we sing."

She raises an eyebrow, confused.

I squeeze her hand but instead of letting her read my emotions, I let her read my mind.

Her eyes light up as the lullaby plays in her head too. I take a deep breath. She does the same. And then we open our mouths to sing.

El Cucuy growls, the sound of our voices stoking something in him. But just like with the car radios, the two of us alone aren't powerful enough to stop him.

Then Clau says, "I have an idea."

She swirls around a woman who's frozen to the edge of

the fountain, gathering strength, and then she aims for her heart, flying straight into her chest.

"Clau!"

The woman blinks and I think Clau's somehow broken the spell. Until I realize that the only thing moving is her mouth as she joins in our song.

Clau wriggles free from the woman's body. "It worked!" And then she's off, possessing every person who's frozen in the town square.

The swell of our voices grows louder, Mami and Abuela singing at the top of their lungs as the ghosts join in too.

El Cucuy stumbles back, the lullaby forcing him to his knees. But as I watch him wrestle with the sound, with the weight of his own memories, I realize that we were wrong about the words being the key.

The lullaby makes him vulnerable but it doesn't make him whole.

It doesn't make him human again.

I stagger to my feet, body still aching from the fall, and then I run. While Mami and Abuela yell for me to stop. While Clau begs for me to come back. I run and then I throw myself on top of El Cucuy, wrapping my arms around him in a fierce hug as I reach deep inside for the boy he used to be.

The boy who was bullied and alone. The boy he buried under so much anger. I claw through the muck of his memories, through darkness and despair, and I find him. Waiting in the middle of that moonlit pumpkin patch. For me.

And just like I did with Luna, I take his hand, and lead him into the past. Into a memory as sweet as candied apples, warm like a roaring fire. Of him in his mother's arms, the lullaby just a soft hum in her chest before finding its way to her lips.

> *Sleep little rabbit*
> *Mommy's right here*
> *to keep the wolves at bay*
> *no need to fear*

The memory swaddles us both, safe in a cocoon of so much love. And then it spreads, chasing away the darkness in him. Except it doesn't just vanish. The grief he consumed from so many suffering families. The loneliness that's chased him from town to town for centuries. It doesn't disappear.

It sticks to me.

It slithers inside like poison and buries itself deep in my heart. While Abuela's warnings sound in my head. While Luna screams in my memory, her wings spread wide.

I look down at my arms and see my own, sprouting like

thorns. Feathers spring up along my chest and neck, spreading to my back, all the way down my spine. Until I'm covered in them. Then I feel my skin stretch, my nose being hooked into the shape of a beak.

I stumble back, losing my hold on El Cucuy and suddenly I'm back in the town square, the fog gone as the moon shines bright overhead.

"Omega!" Mami screams, taking in the sight of me.

But she doesn't come any closer. She just stares, the terror behind her eyes filling mine with tears.

"Mami…" I breathe and she grimaces at the sound of my voice.

But then I look at Abuela and in her eyes I don't just see terror. I don't just see her worst fears coming true. I see confusion. I see disgust.

My new wings spread wide in both directions, waiting to take flight. Like they know that I'm not welcome here. And maybe because I can't stand to see them look at me like that for another second or maybe because I'm just as scared, I leap, climbing up and up until the moon is all I see.

CHAPTER 21

IT'S EVEN BETTER THAN IT WAS IN my dream. Wings out-stretched. Night breeze ruffling my feathers. I feel weight-less. I feel home.

Or maybe that's the moon talking. Maybe home is what I left behind. Mami. Abuela. I scan the houses below, the warm glow in every window. I imagine them on a night that isn't cursed. Full of laughter. Full of love.

That's why Luna came back after all. Because it was lonely out there. But she also came back for me. Because she knew this would happen. Because she knew Abuela might react this way.

El Cucuy did too. *This might be your home now. But it won't be… Not when they find out what you are.*

I slow, unsure of where to go. Down below, the houses

grow sparse, replaced by miles and miles of trees. Noche Buena becoming smaller behind me while the shadow of my wings only grows, the moon a blinding spotlight at my back. I stare at their outline against the trees and they look like the sails of a ship. Like I'm the captain steering myself across an endless sea.

The thought makes me feel even lonelier. Like I'm not steering myself at all but drifting. Farther and farther from the things that matter most.

Suddenly, down below, I notice a flash, another dark shadow moving in the trees. I hover close to the canopy until I hear twigs snapping, heavy footfalls in the dirt. Something bounding through the forest at breakneck speed. I follow, gaining on it, my flapping wings parting the leaves until I finally see the slope of its back, its spine jutting up through matted fur.

El lobizón.

The werewolf.

It tears forward like it's on the hunt.

I climb higher, trying to get a better look at what it's chasing. That's when I realize what's in its sights. Not an animal or someone who's just woken from El Cucuy's curse. But the mouth of the train tunnel.

The children.

Except they're not the only ones who el lobizón might

try to make a meal out of. Papi, Abuelo, and Tío Juan were headed for the train tunnel too. Unless…they never actually made it there. Unless el lobizón got to them first.

I gather the wind beneath me, forcing myself forward as fast as I can. My shadow passes over el lobizón and it glances up before letting out a howl that makes me go cold.

When I reach the mouth of the train tunnel, I barrel into the pitch black, not bothering to test my landing skills. There's no time for that. But when I finally do hit the ground, there are no tracks. Only tilled soil and damp vines. Just like in El Cucuy's dream.

I blink, my eyes adjusting, and then I remember what Abuela said about doors. That they're everywhere. The mouth to the train tunnel must be another one, this door leading me back to this moment that keeps playing in El Cucuy's mind on a loop.

Except this time he's not hanging off a stake, dressed like a scarecrow. And there's more than just gourds growing in the vines. The children are tangled in them too, slowly yawning themselves awake, bleary-eyed and mumbling.

"Chale…" I breathe.

He's rubbing the sleep from his eyes. When he sees me, he lets out a small gasp. But he's not the only one.

Tío Juan drops his pocketknife where he was cutting Chale free.

Abuelo helps Abby to her feet before they both see me and freeze.

And Carlitos…

He stares at me, stunned. "No." The word is like a stone. He hurls it again and again. "No, no, no, no…"

"Omega?"

I turn my head and see Papi. His eyes are wide, his mouth ajar. And he's looking at me like I'm a stranger. Like *whatever* I am…I'm not his little girl anymore.

"Papi," I plead.

But before I can say another word, there's something else coming through the portal. Something wild.

El lobizón leaps and I don't think. I spread my wings wide and it crashes into me, sending us both tumbling. I feel a sharp burn, one of its claws scraping my skin. It opens its jaws wide, yellow eyes pouring into mine. But just before it bites down, it yelps. And then it wobbles on weak legs before slowly slumping to the ground.

I look up and see Mrs. Gallegos, her family free from El Cucuy's spell and standing behind her. She's holding a long river cane to her lips. That's when I see the dart in the werewolf's shoulder. Mrs. Gallegos comes to my side, rolling the beast over until it's snoring.

A moment later, the rest of my family steps through the portal. Soona and Luisa rush to help the others release the children from their binds. Tía Tita scoops Chale up in her arms. Mami embraces Papi. Abuela keeps her distance. All of them watching. *Waiting.*

Except Clau. She floats forward, taking me in. "Omega...?"

I try to smile but I know she can't see it. "It's me."

Abuela finally takes a step closer. Then another. She peers up at me and then she reaches out a hand, grazing my feathers. Her eyes glisten with tears and as she cups my face I feel her sorrow like an anchor drifting to the bottom of the ocean. She searches my eyes for the girl she knows and it fills me with a bitter cold. Like even though she's right here, I'm more alone than I've ever been.

"We'll fix this," she whispers. "Together."

"Renata..." Luna steps through the portal, her gaze shifting between me and Abuela. She looks scared.

That's when I feel it. Heat sparking from Abuela's fingertips, her hand on my face warming until I can't take it anymore and I jump back. At the twitch of my wings, everyone else jumps back too. Just as scared as Luna. Except it's not *me* that Luna fears.

"Renata," she pleads, "I know you're frightened but there's no reason to be. It's still Omega. It's *her*. Your granddaughter."

"You're right," Abuela says. "My granddaughter who used

her powers to save you from the same fate. Now it's our turn to save her."

She thrusts out her palm, a beam of light almost striking me in the chest. I dodge it, letting out a screech that has everyone holding their ears. I turn toward the portal opening, wings ready to take flight. But just before I leap, something sharp pierces me in the wing.

I look down, my vision suddenly blurry. Like I've been spinning on a merry-go-round, the whole world shrinking down to a single prick of light. And just before it blinks out, I see Carlitos, the river cane at his feet.

I wake up in my bed. No more beak. No more feathers. No more wings.

And I've never felt more trapped.

I wrench myself out of the blankets, needing air and the sky and the moon and—

"Omega, what's wrong?" La Virgen shouts, trying to get my attention. "Omega, you're scaring me!"

"Just breathe," Selena offers. "In and out. That's it."

I try to do as she says but my body feels strange. Like I'm not really in it. One moment it's a loose-fitting costume I can slip on and off and the next it's a straitjacket getting tighter and tighter until I'm suffocating.

"Are you sick again?" La Virgen asks.

"Can't you see?" the lamp interjects. "The girl's not sick." It croaks out a mischievous laugh. "She's something much worse."

My heart stops, remembering all the reasons I should be afraid, but the truth is, nothing scares me more in this moment than Abuela's words—*We'll fix this. Together.*

As if I needed to be saved.

That's what Carlitos thought he was doing when he shot

me. Or maybe…he did it because he still hates me. Maybe my heart choosing Clau over Chale was all the proof he needed that I was a monster before I actually became one.

But is that even what I still believe? It's what I feared. When I absorbed El Cucuy's darkness, I feared turning into a monster too. Except all it did was give me wings.

And I have to get them back.

I step to my closed bedroom door, listening to the voices on the other side.

"Candela's finally down. Clau hasn't left her side," Luisa says.

"Good. Better to keep Clau close." This time it's Soona who speaks. "Luna suspected she was special but I doubt she could have imagined this."

"Have you ever heard of a ghost being able to possess an entire crowd like that?" Mami asks, concerned.

Soona lowers her voice. "I have. But…it wasn't a ghost."

"What do you mean it wasn't a ghost?" Luisa asks.

Soona's silent for a beat and then she says, "It was a god."

I listen to them shifting around the kitchen, someone pacing, Mami letting out a deep sigh. But it doesn't make any sense. How could Clau be an immortal *and* a ghost? Part of the living *and* the dead?

"This stays between us," Abuela finally says. "Do you understand?"

"Understood," Carlitos says, a small quiver in his voice.

"And all the more reason to keep a close eye on Candela too," Luisa adds.

"What about the nuns at the orphanage?" Abuela asks.

"On their way," Soona says. "We'll discuss guardianship with them once they arrive."

The screen door squeals, followed by the sound of Tía Tita's voice as she steps inside. "Still no news."

I hear Papi next. "Jack's going to turn this town upside down."

"If it was Carlitos out there, I would too," Tío Juan says.

I crack the door, peering out. Hoping if I can catch a glimpse of their faces I might be able to figure out who they're talking about. But then I remember seeing Abby with the other kids, dazed as the adults cut them from the vines that had them trapped. And then I know.

Aiden.

"Do you think she saw anything?" Mami asks, tossing her voice down the hallway to my bedroom.

I ease back, trying to stay out of sight. All while my heart pounds in my chest. *Aiden's still out there?*

"We can ask her when she wakes up," Abuela says. "But for now she needs to rest. The spell on those darts probably hasn't worn off yet."

I go to ease the door closed again but just before it shuts, Carlitos looks in my direction. He sees me through the crack, his eyes widening.

I shut the door, rushing to the window. *I have to find Aiden.*

Suddenly the phone rings, distracting the adults. While the chatter grows louder, I hear footsteps nearing my bedroom door. Then it opens, Carlitos slipping inside.

For a long moment he doesn't say anything. Until he realizes that my hand is on the glass. That I'm about to escape.

"You can't be serious," he hisses.

"You heard them. Aiden's still out there somewhere."

"And you have to be the one to find him?" Carlitos crosses his arms. "Why? Because you suddenly have wings?"

"Had," I say through gritted teeth. "Until you shot me."

"I didn't know what else to do!"

"I wasn't going to hurt anyone."

"I know you weren't. But you were going to run away before Abuela could help you. Just like you're doing now."

"Because I didn't ask for her help."

His brow furrows. "What is that supposed to mean?"

I straighten, trying to make myself tall. "It means that I didn't need saving. I still don't." Then I look from my closed bedroom door, imagining the voices on the other side, before I turn back to the window. To the moon that still calls to me. Then I look right at Carlitos and say, "But Aiden does."

And I know that what I'm about to do will break Abuela's heart.

That she might disown me like she did Luna.

That leaving might mean saying goodbye before I'm ready.

But as I peel back the curtains and step into the moonlight, the shadow of my feathers rising to the surface, it doesn't feel like the end of anything. It feels like the beginning.

"I…I won't let you." Carlitos steps in front of me. Sweat trickles down his forehead, his fear like a fever boiling him from the inside.

I lower my voice. "Move."

He doesn't. He *won't*.

Dreams are where we go when we want to remember. Dreams are where we go when we want to feel safe.

I close my eyes and remember the feeling of taking flight. The night air. The stars. My body remembers too, feathers suddenly sprouting along my skin. I open my eyes just as my wings snap open and then Carlitos has no choice. He falls back and I break through the glass, soaring higher and higher until it finally feels like I'm home.

EPILOGUE

I'M ALMOST TO THE SIGN MARKING THE county line when the forest beneath me opens into a clearing. I see the eastern train tracks, a few abandoned boxcars, and then in their shadow, curled up on the ground, a body.

Aiden.

I swoop straight down, landing in the grass a few feet away. A twig snaps beneath my feet and the sound makes him stir. He rolls onto his side, groaning like he's in pain.

"Aiden?" I whisper his name.

He blinks and then he scrambles back, in shock.

"Aiden, it's me. Omega."

He exhales, taking me in. "Is it really you? H-how…?"

"It's…a long story."

He nods. But still…he doesn't run. Instead, he asks, "Are you okay?"

The words get caught in my throat. Because he's not scared. He's concerned.

"I'm okay," I say. "Are you all right? What happened?"

He looks down at his leg, his jeans ripped over a small red stain.

"I think I…" He presses a hand to his forehead. "I think I fell."

"We should get you to a doctor," I say, letting him use my wings to get to his feet.

He stumbles, still dazed. But eventually he manages to take a step. As soon as he does, he grits his teeth, fists clenched.

"What's wrong?"

He falls back down, writhing on the ground.

"Aiden?"

I force back his pant leg, staring at the wound. Two deep puncture holes.

Bite marks.

I stare up at the moon, full and shining down like a spotlight on us both.

Aiden claws his way onto his hands and knees. His

muscles swell beneath his clothes, his body contorting. He gnashes his teeth as they grow long and sharp.

He looks at me. "Omega, run!"

And then he throws his head back, howling a lullaby of his own.

Acknowledgments

I'd first like to thank the other middle-grade authors who have joined me in reserving space in their upcoming books to honor the victims of the tragic school shooting at Robb Elementary that took twenty-one lives. Most of the victims were the very children we write stories for, and now it's our responsibility to ensure *their* stories live on—who they were and who they could have been had they not been taken from the world so soon. But most importantly, all admiration goes to the families of the victims who continue to fight tirelessly to hold our state and federal officials accountable to make schools safer for all children and educators. They are heroes worthy of a thousand stories. You can find ways to support them @LivesRobbed.

I'd also like to thank my incredibly generous editor, Sam Gentry, for allowing me to continue Omega's journey. In addition to expertly helping me excavate the heart of each story, I am eternally grateful for your advocacy behind the scenes. Thank you for helping me build a body of work at LBYR that I am so immensely proud of. And to my agent, Andrea Morrison, thank you for being an incredible sounding board and business partner. But most importantly, thank you for helping me slowly carve out the career of my dreams. I'm so grateful to be able to do this work full-time and to be able to bring these stories into the world that mean so much, not only to me but also to my community. And finally, thank you, once again, to the entire LBYR team for shepherding my stories into the world with such care. I'm so happy to be a part of the family.